SHE'S GONE

EVERY MOTHER'S WORST FEAR

SUSAN WILKINS

For Sue Kenyon, who makes it all possible.

PROLOGUE

He throws her into the back of the van like a sack of rubbish. Her shoulder slams into the metal wheel arch. She hears the bone crack as she rolls away from it and across the hard floor. She ends up on her back. The pain is excruciating. Her lungs are still screaming for air after being held in his throttling grip. She's dizzy from lack of oxygen. Now she feels sick.

Her stomach clenches with fear. If she loses consciousness now, then it'll all be over. She must focus and fight back. But her head is swimming with random thoughts. She's spiralling downwards. The pain is fading. A bad sign. She remembers her mother's smile.

Is this how it ends? Slipping away. What do you think of in your last moments? Is it easier to let go, accept the inevitable?

1

Friday 7.15am

For the first week after Phoebe left for university, Marcia Lennox couldn't pass her daughter's bedroom door without opening it, taking a peek at the unnaturally tidy interior and thinking: she's gone. But as the days pass, the sense of loss is becoming more muted. Getting on with things is the solution, obviously. Moments of desolation still hit her; the smell of coffee in the morning. She always took Phoebe a cup to encourage her out of bed. Teenagers need their sleep. She read it somewhere. Quite natural.

Now it's just the two of them. But that's fine.

It's all as it should be. She's done the job she set out to do. She keeps telling herself that.

She wrinkles her nose as she flips the sizzling bacon with a steel spatula. The enticing aroma floods the large, airy kitchen. But it doesn't entice Marcia. To a vegan, it's disgusting. She turns on the extractor fan. It reminds her of what?

The shrieks of pigs being dragged to slaughter. Is that a genuine memory or some TV documentary she once saw?

Hard to tell.

She forces her mind back to the now. To her easy-wipe induction hob and her task: making breakfast for her husband.

A grey dawn filters through the full-length windows. The screen of shrubs covering the garden wall is heavy and dank. London in October.

Dull and depressing. Summer's gone. The worst time of the year because there's nothing to look forward to.

Rain patters on the skylights. It'll be a miserable journey to work.

Marcia wears a navy and white apron reaching from her neck to her calves. The name of a French Michelin-starred chef is embroidered in the top corner. A Christmas present from her daughter. As she turns to the granite-topped kitchen island, where a sourdough loaf sits waiting on the breadboard, her husband heaves a sigh.

Harry Lennox is perched on a stool, elbows resting on the breakfast bar. He peers through his glasses at the laptop open in front of him. Picking up his mug of coffee, he takes a sip and huffs again.

Marcia scans him. She doesn't speak. She cuts two slices of sourdough and transfers them to a plate.

Harry glances up. 'Can I have butter?' he says.

'No,' says Marcia.

'Ketchup?' He has the pleading look of a small boy.

'No.'

'Tomato's a vegetable.'

'It's loaded with sugar.'

Marcia transfers the cooked bacon to a square of kitchen paper to drain.

'At least leave some fat on it,' says Harry.

'It's the fat that's the problem. For heaven's sake, Harry, I'm trying to take care of you.'

'Maybe just a little mayo then?' He tilts his head and gives her his trademark cheeky grin.

That grin. How many women have fallen for that? How many are still falling for it?

'Rocket and some sliced tomato,' she says, returning his smile.

'Okay,' he says. 'You win.'

Harry is fifty-seven, over six foot, loose-limbed and rangy. Even though his cholesterol is way too high, he'll never look fat. He has a full head of hair with a floppy grey-blond fringe, the rom-com good looks of a breakfast TV host.

He returns to his laptop and continues to scroll. Endless columns of figures. Dow Jones, FTSE, Nasdaq, Nikkei, Hang Seng. Marcia is familiar with the main stock market indices, but she doesn't know what he's looking at, only that every morning he checks the markets. Harry is the number two at a major equity hedge fund in the City. He could be number one if he wasn't so lazy.

One wall of the kitchen is covered with floor to ceiling cabinets. Marcia's fingers slip into the carefully engineered side groove, and she pulls open the fridge.

The hand-built kitchen is one of the delights of her life. It operates like a machine. Never lets her down or surprises her. She opens the salad drawer at the bottom, takes out a tomato and a packet of rocket.

Harry puffs out his cheeks. 'Bloody ridiculous,' he says. 'We've just taken a huge position in Chinese telecoms and now the US is having another pop at the Chinese. I warned Tom it was too risky. The price'll tank.'

Marcia washes and slices the tomato, assembles the bacon

sandwich, cuts it in half diagonally, and places it next to the laptop. He seizes it in his right hand and takes a large bite.

The stink of roasted flesh pervades the room. She turns the extractor to full blast.

'That's unfortunate,' she says.

'Damn sight more than unfortunate,' he replies with another sigh. He demolishes half the sandwich in three more bites, wipes his mouth with his fingers and says, 'It's not that bad with tomato.'

She takes off her apron. 'Glad you like it.'

She's wearing the silk pyjamas he bought her on his recent trip to Dubai. Oyster grey. A colour she likes. Not that he knows that. She can imagine him diving into the airport shop and grabbing the first thing that looked expensive enough.

But he's not looking at her. She wants him to look. But she won't beg. Never, *never* beg. His eyes are back on the screen as he devours the other half of his sandwich.

Eventually he turns and says, 'What're you up to today?'

Marcia is Head of Account Management at an awarding winning advertising agency in Notting Hill. But Harry has the knack of making her feel as though this is just an interesting hobby.

'Oh, you know,' she says. 'Whatever's in the diary.'

'Bit wet out there. Is that why you're not running this morning?' He finishes his sandwich. He's making conversation. Ticking the communicate-with-the-wife box. Ask a question and pretend you care about the answer.

Harry smiles. Now he's waiting. Caring about the answer.

She smiles back.

Marcia is forty-three but as lithe as when she was twenty; she runs through nearby Richmond Park three times a week to keep it that way. Her hair, cut in a neat bob, is without a trace of grey. She has a manicure, pedicure and facial once a week.

'It's Friday,' she says. 'I've got my personal trainer at lunchtime.' Why does he always forget?

'Oh, yeah. I always forget.' He nods. He's preparing to leave. His thoughts are already up and off.

She feels a surge of panic. Such an old reflex.

'I was thinking,' she says briskly. 'On Sunday we could drive up to Cambridge and take Phoebe out to lunch.'

He shakes his head and sighs. 'Darling, leave the poor girl alone. It's her first term at university. She's only been there two weeks.'

'Three, this weekend.'

'Whatever. She needs time to settle. And she'll have so much to do. People to meet, parties to go to. She's eighteen. You remember what it was like. Let her enjoy it.'

Marcia remembers the damp basement flat she lived in and the two jobs she had to work to pay the rent. And the scabby landlord who tried to… but she's put all that behind her.

'I thought she might be homesick. Or a bit lonely.'

'I doubt it. Not very Phoebe, is it? She'll be in the thick of it.'

'But—'

'Take my advice,' he says, 'and wait to be invited.' He closes his laptop and looks at his watch.

Marcia has a stabbing pain in her chest; acid reflux from the anxiety twisting in her gut. She should eat. She thinks about her daughter, her beautiful golden child. Since she left, the house is like a mausoleum. No awful music with a thudding bass-line vibrating the floorboards, no laundry all over the bedroom floor, no coming down in the morning to find strange young people asleep on the sofa.

The large Edwardian villa on the edge of Richmond Green has six bedrooms and a sizeable extension at the back. When they moved in fifteen years ago, she knew it was the perfect family home. Harry's sons from his first marriage visited every other weekend. Lively and full of laughter, it was the hub of all their lives, that's how Marcia remembers it. Back then they knew the neighbours. They even had a dog, a scrappy terrier that barked at everyone.

'I know you miss her,' says Harry. 'It's only natural.' He tucks the laptop under his arm and smiles.

She can hear the but, although he doesn't say it. He must think she's stupid. Their daughter is eighteen — *only eighteen!* — officially an adult. Marcia wants her to have a wonderful life. And freedom. Especially that. And not to waste her opportunities. And to watch out for men trying to spike her drinks. And to look both ways when she crosses the road. And... and... She sounds awful and preachy, even in the confines of her own head.

It's easy for him; child-rearing's done. Pack up your feelings — the fears, the regrets, losing that bouncy little person, who always adored you — and get on with the next thing. What is the next thing?

'Will you be home for dinner tonight?' she says.

He frowns. His gaze slithers away and he sighs. 'Not really sure. Tom's got a new client he wants me to meet. Just drinks, but you know how these things drag on. Don't go to any trouble.'

'Fine,' she says.

'I'll text you.' He's still avoiding eye contact.

'Okay.'

He smiles, gives her a peck on the cheek and disappears through the kitchen door. World's worst liar.

Does he not realise how transparent he is? Perhaps he doesn't care.

Marcia is left standing alone at the centre of her beautiful kitchen. She strokes the cold granite with her fingertips. Her thoughts are blank. She feels at a loss. Why doesn't he look anymore?

The tears prickle.

This is no good. She gives herself a stern reprimand. The kitchen she'll leave for the cleaners. They come in at ten.

She goes upstairs to shower and dress for work. It's a blip. All relationships have them. She'll soon turn this around. She always has. And she will see Phoebe. She'll text her.

2

Friday 10.15am

Carol Cook stands on the concourse at Waterloo Station. Her stomach tightens. She looks around at the sea of faces. Too many faces. Coming at you. Dodging round you. She feels giddy. She has to remember to breathe.

The journey from Guildford took about forty minutes. In order to stay calm, she stared out of the window most of the way. Trees, fields, a kaleidoscope of buildings flashing by. No one bothered her. She waited for the other passengers to get off the train so that once she stepped onto the platform, the crowds had dispersed. But now she must face the next part of her journey — the underground.

During her time on the resettlement programme, they'd done one practice train journey: a day out to Windsor. That's all the help they gave you. She's read the pamphlets, watched the videos, listened to the advice and instructions. But is she ready for this?

Remember: no one knows you. No one's looking at you. No one cares who you are.

Breathe.

The holdall she's carrying is standard issue: cheap black polyester with a detachable shoulder strap. It's only half full. They gave her a new pair of denim jeans, a plain shirt and a choice of jacket. The advice was *don't pick a hoodie.* She chose a grey windbreaker. It's best to be anonymous.

She tries to think back to the last time she was in London. Probably when mum was alive. They came for a day out, went to the Tower of London and had their photo taken with a Beefeater. But that must be thirty years ago.

She has her instructions written on a piece of paper in her pocket, although she's memorised the route. The tube to Liverpool Street — Northern line to Tottenham Court Road, change to the Central line — and back on the overground train to Norfolk. Her ticket is valid all the way. She can see the entrance to the underground.

An escalator carries you down. People in front and behind. What if someone pushes you? That's the scary bit. But she has plenty of time. She has the whole day to make the journey. Her off-peak ticket from Liverpool Street is valid until four o'clock.

Why not stop and buy a coffee? Or go to the bookshop and check out the magazines? Who would know?

Now she can do what she wants. Even go to the Tower of London?

She notices a man staring at her. Scrawny, rough, feral eyes from too much smack.

'You looking for a place to stay, love.' A whispery voice as he sidles up. 'I could maybe help you out.'

She turns to face him and instinct kicks in. Is this what she looks like? A victim? A lost soul to be preyed upon?

She fixes him with a steely gaze. 'Get lost! Unless you want your balls shoved down your throat and pulled out the other end.'

He blinks at her, mumbles and scurries away. A young woman passing gives her a curious glance. She notices two police officers wandering along and chatting. Her heart is thumping. Make a decision!

The coffee shop is long and narrow, with tables both inside and out. Walking in feels good. She had a work placement at a coffee shop in Guildford. They were nice to her. The boss was Turkish. He didn't ask awkward questions or single her out. He treated all the staff the same. All he expected was that you were polite to the customers, even the arseholes, and did your job.

As she waits her turn to be served, she reads the menu board, which calms her down. A different franchise, but they all serve the same stuff.

'Can I help you?' The barista smiles. She looks young and confident. And friendly.

'Um, yeah, I'll have a Honeycomb Latte Macchiato.'

'Good choice!' The barista sounds excited for her. 'Regular milk?'

'Better make it semi-skimmed.'

A smile to hide her nervousness. Her first proper encounter on the outside as a free woman. Not technically free, they made that clear. She's on a life licence, still serving her sentence. A life sentence means you're always subject to recall. But she can pretend she's free. No one knows you. No one cares who you are.

'Any cakes or muffins?'

Carol is tempted, but she reins herself in.

'No, I'm fine.'

She was forty-one last birthday, and she's tubby, some

might say fat. Inside, she never cared about her appearance. What was the point? And not thinking about clothes or hair-cuts or nails or make-up was a relief. Ever since she can remember, her body has been a burden. Tits too big, developed too young. Which always made it her fault. Men found her provocative. From the age of thirteen, she had to fight them off.

Stay invisible, that's best.

Inside, some girls were obsessed with the gym. They thought it would make them tough. Carol learned early on that the key to survival was attitude. Don't back down. Don't defer. Even if you get hurt. Don't believe the screws will help you; they won't. Anyone who thinks women are less violent than men hasn't been inside a women's jail.

Carol collects her drink and chooses a table with her back to the wall. She's tempted to sit outside and watch people passing by. But she's not used to crowds of strangers; running for trains, diving past each other, checking their phones. It's dizzying to watch. She must pace herself. Too many difficult things at once could tip her over the edge.

Are you ready? Do you want this? Her offender manager had made it clear that if she was going to succeed with the Parole Board, she needed a convincing answer to these questions.

She told them what they wanted to hear.

Seventeen years, nine months and thirteen days behind bars is a long time. Her original tariff was sixteen years. But when she was in HMP Bronzefield, she got into a bad fight with a skanky bitch who'd abused kids and helped run a paedophile ring and boasted about it. She was pure evil. Carol saw red, and she'd used a shiv she stole from the workshop. She slashed that bitch. No regrets, it was the right thing to do. She had time added on and they shipped her out to the prison in Surrey, where she served the rest of her sentence.

That's where she got into gardening. They had land to grow things on, and Carol found something she could enjoy. As a kid, she was always happier outdoors. Fields of barley and hedgerows remind her of innocent times, back when Mum was alive. Once the screws noticed she had a knack for it, they gave her more to do. Hard graft had never been a problem. Hands in the dirt, digging, weeding, planting; she was happy with all of it. It brought a calm rhythm to her days. When they asked her what sort of job she wanted on release, she said anything outside on the land.

She knows that the next few days will be crucial. Get through the first week and she'll probably be all right. One day at a time.

She sips the Macchiato and enjoys the sugar hit. If it makes her fat, so what!

No one knows you. No one cares who you are or what you did.

Stay safe. Stay invisible.

3

Friday, 4.10pm

TFMK has been named as one of Campaign Magazine's top creative agencies two years in a row. But it remains a boutique operation. Marcia Lennox is not one of the founding partners — two brothers — but she's worked there from the start. She has a seat on the Board and parcel of shares because the brothers know she's a rainmaker. In the industry, she's known as a tough competitor who goes the extra mile to win new business.

But as she sits at her glass desk in her large corner office, staring at her phone, she doesn't feel that tough. She's been waiting all morning for Phoebe to reply to her slew of texts. How long does it take to write a stupid text? Ten seconds? It's made her hot and irritated. Or perhaps that's her hormones? Could she be menopausal already? That's an awful thought. She should get her oestrogen levels checked.

The morning has been a parade of annoyances. An intern put dairy instead of soya in her cappuccino — she got shouted at. A junior account manager admitted to a major client that there was an issue with the artwork. He got a bollocking. Her PA was being peevish because his boyfriend had dumped him. This she simply ignored. And to cap it all, her personal trainer cancelled because her toddler had fallen over at nursery and cut his head open.

Without her scheduled forty-five-minute workout between 1.15 and 2pm, Marcia is squirrelly and quarrelsome. When she heard about the last minute cancellation, she lambasted Phoebe in a long text and was greeted with a resounding silence. Over three hours later, she got a curt reply:

Ma, go for a jog.

She jabs her third version of a response into her phone — and then deletes that, too.

She gets up and walks round the office. What the hell is wrong with her today? Get a grip. Is this what happens when your child leaves home for university? You sink into some miserable menopausal swamp?

She flops down in her chair, picks up her handbag and roots in it. At the bottom she finds what she's looking for: a blister pack of Xanax. She considers it for a moment. She's been rationing herself and in the last week has done well. But this is an emergency. Just to help her get back on track. She pops one out, swallows it and washes it down with Evian from the glass carafe on her desk.

She opens her laptop, going straight to Phoebe's Instagram, but there's little to see. The photo of her daughter at a sherry party hosted by the Master of her new college is several days old. She's wearing her gown, grinning and holding the phone up to capture a selfie with two other girls. The other girls appear self-conscious and bookish. Phoebe, in contrast, with her mane of golden hair, looks like a star in the making. Marcia smiles. Okay, she's biased.

She flips the laptop shut and sighs. Stalking your own child on social media is desperate and pathetic. She stands up. She must get out of the office, move her body, go for a walk. Picking up her bag and her jacket, she heads out.

As she passes the desk of Lawrence, her PA, she hesitates.

He glances up from his keyboard.

'Lawrence, if anyone needs me—'

'Yeah, I know. You've got a meeting in Soho.'

She smiles at him; he smiles back.

'Treat yourself,' he says. 'Nails, massage, you do you, babe.' He raises his eyebrows.

She gives him a proper smile and heads for the door. She thinks about Harry, his self-absorption, his emotional blind spots. Men.

The afternoon is gloomy; the light is already fading. She walks round the corner into Kensington Park Road. The shop windows are glittering with light and bursting with colour. She strolls and browses, so many lovely things to catch the shopper's fickle gaze. Everything is reassuringly expensive.

She pauses outside a new boutique that's recently opened. A hot young designer. A simple tailored jacket hangs on the mannequin in the window. Brown velvet, very sixties retro, which would look perfect on Phoebe. Marcia could get it for her. Then if they went up to Cambridge on Sunday, she wouldn't go empty-handed.

But she hesitates. What if Phoebe reacts? They always used to go clothes shopping together, and Phoebe loved all the amazing things her mother picked out for her. Then about two years ago she became really awkward. Everything Marcia liked, she hated. It was a teenage thing, Marcia understood that. It also coincided with Harry giving Phoebe her own credit card and a rather generous clothes allowance.

Money gives you choices. Marcia, of all people, appreciates that. She wants her daughter to make her own choices, of course she does.

Marcia lets her eye run over the jacket. It's beautifully made, and versatile; it would look great with jeans or a skirt. But she should probably leave it. The gesture would be misinterpreted. Phoebe would think Marcia was trying to control her. She doesn't understand. How could she? It's never been about control.

Phoebe's happiness is what matters. Always has been.

She walks away. She could pretend she bought it for herself then, if Phoebe likes it, give it to her. But that's manipulative and her daughter's smart, she'll see through it.

Marcia continues down the street, stopping at a window full of cookery books. She considers buying one; her favourite vegan chef has his latest offering displayed in the window. But when is she going to try out a load of new recipes? Harry'll just complain and sneak out for fried chicken. He's always been a sneaker.

She's frustrated. It's starting to rain, a fine drizzle. There's a hollowness in the pit of her stomach.

She turns on her heel and walks back to the boutique. She goes in and buys the brown velvet jacket. She can work out later how to give it to Phoebe.

4

Lacey is safe in the barn. She's created the perfect nest for herself, hidden away between the bales of straw. It's warm and sheltered. The stalks can be sharp where they've been cut, and the tangy smell makes her nostrils twitch. But she's well away from the house. Her mother will shout her from the back door, but she can pretend not to hear. This is her secret place. She has the two things she needs: her phone and her dog. Daisy's a border collie, a proper sheepdog; although her dad doesn't keep sheep anymore. No money in it.

Daisy's great, but she is just a dog. The phone is her lifeline. The broadband signal is good since the rural upgrade, and she has no problem getting on social media. Whenever she can escape from the house, this is what she does. She connects and chats to her mates. They understand her. It's the only time she's happy.

But tonight is different. Special. Tonight everything will change.

Lacey's been waiting ages for this day. Now it will all be different and the horrible spell of this place will be broken.

That old bastard sits there in his armchair, staring like an evil toad. And he stinks of piss and shit and fags. Her parents dance around him, serving him like he's some lord. They think they're being good Christian people by taking care of him. Her dad won't hear a word against him, refuses to see how it really is. But Dad's just a weak old twat who hasn't got the balls to stand his ground. Much less stand up to his brother. Never has according to Steve. He hides behind the religious spiel.

Offline, her brother Steve is the only person she can really talk to. School's okay. But she doesn't let her guard down. Ever. You can't let them see who you really are. The girls are mostly two-faced bitches and the boys are childish and just after a picture of your tits.

Everything she's learned that really matters has been on the net. In school it's X plus Y equals Z, or some crap like that. What's the point? What does it even mean? Beijing became the capital of China in 1421 — whatever! Some dead King got fed up with his wife and killed her. Quelle surprise!

What Lacey has learned on the net is that you can decide for yourself who you want to be. You're your own invention. Once you believe that and act accordingly, then the whole universe starts to help you. That's true science. Not some stinky experiment in the chemistry lab or cutting up a sheep's eyeball in biology.

Sometimes Steve takes her clubbing with him. She's fourteen but she can pass and if you've got a good fake ID most places don't care. Some of his friends are cool. They have cars and make money. But she has no intention of getting stuck with a disappearing bloke and a baby she doesn't want, like Mum did. She's got plans, places to go.

It's pitch black outside now. Just a faint orange glow from the lights on the main road. Steve has already texted her and told her it's on. It's happening. She's excited, although she'd never admit it. Okay, he's doing the legwork. But it was her idea. She made the connection. He can't claim credit for that.

But he wouldn't. As big brothers go, he's all right.

About a year ago, one of her really good mates online sent her some rune stones. Like little pebbles, they have ancient letters on them. Lacey uses them to read the future. She knows it's not magic; she doesn't believe in crap, she's not stupid. But it's more like a useful tool. Another way to look at stuff. They've helped her make important decisions or work out how to cope with stuff at home. They've guided her and pointed her in the right direction. When she came across those posts, it wasn't luck; it was meant to be. She knew that straight away. The rest was just time and patience. People think kids aren't patient, but she is.

Daisy pricks up her ears, way before Lacey hears Steve's pickup driving down the lane. The dog gives a little yelp and Lacey heaves herself out of the nest and jumps down between the bales to the floor of the barn. She brushes the straw off her top and runs her fingers through her hair. She wants to look her best and make a good impression. She's waited a long time for this. But it's happening at last. She's coming home.

5

Saturday, 2pm

Marcia sits at the kitchen table, laptop open, catching up on emails. She could use the study or the conservatory, but this is her favourite room. She has a small ceramic pot of green tea and a dish of walnuts; on fasting days this counts as lunch. She doesn't need to work on a Saturday, but it helps her keep any emotional niggles at bay. A busy mind can't brood.

After her morning run — two laps of Richmond Park clocking up an easy 20k — she realised Harry was right. She's let things get on top of her. Change management is part of her CV, and she's done it in business for years. Now Phoebe's departure means she needs to apply it in her own life. This sharp longing for her daughter's presence must be reined in. Separation is necessary and healthy. The issue is one of self-control; she'll be fine.

Harry wanders in, barefooted, in trackie bottoms and an old rugby shirt.

'Morning,' he says brightly. He adds a teasing smile. 'Except you're going to tell me it's afternoon, aren't you?'

She takes off her glasses and smiles at him. 'Wouldn't dream of it.'

Harry rolled in about five am. He took a shower in Phoebe's bathroom before creeping into the bedroom and slipping into bed beside Marcia. She pretended to be asleep.

Marcia knew when she married him that the only way she could stay in the driving seat in their relationship was to allow him a measure of latitude. Placing too many emotional demands on him would not work, nor would attempts to change him. His first wife had tried that, and it didn't end well.

'Can I make you something?' she says.

He flaps his hand. 'No, no, you're busy. I can manage.'

He opens the freezer and extracts a bag of Danish pastries.

She scans him. 'How was the new client?'

He's peering myopically at the instructions on the bag. 'Oh,' he says. 'Annoying. A real lads' night out, that's what they wanted. To tell you the truth, I've got a bit of a hangover.'

He doesn't look annoyed. Or hungover. A drunken lads' night out, he'd be whiny and wanting her to cook him a disgusting fry-up. But he looks perky and pleased with himself. The other thing, then.

She decides to let him struggle with the pastries. He dumps three in the microwave, considers the dial and gives it a cavalier spin.

He leans on the kitchen counter.

'I've been thinking,' he says. 'A girl in the office mentioned this amazing new Japanese restaurant. Top-notch chef and loads of vegan dishes. They've been getting rave

23

reviews. I thought I could take you there for Sunday lunch tomorrow. Instead of Cambridge.'

He beams. This is typical Harry, assuaging any guilt by giving her a treat.

Marcia looks at him. Whoever she was, she must've been a bloody good shag.

'Lovely,' she says and returns to her emails.

When Marcia and Harry started out, she was the other thing, the secret shag, his midlife crisis affair. She's fourteen years his junior and knows that what hooked him were her looks, her body and then her difference, in that order. A ballsy advertising exec, she was the opposite of her upper class, snooty and demanding predecessor.

Harry grew up spoilt; wealthy parents who were easy going. Plus, he had brains and good looks. The best schools, the best of everything. He was used to having his own way. She always assumed their affair would run its course, and he'd move on. When he popped the question, it stunned her. They married on a Caribbean island and she immediately set about constructing a life to meet both their needs. And mostly, she's succeeded.

In her peripheral vision, she can see him getting the pastries out of the microwave and burning his fingers. Crumbs everywhere, no cleaners at the weekend; this will be her mess to clean up.

He claims his evening was annoying, clearly a lie. She's the one ticking with annoyance now. She puts up with his casual infidelities, that's the deal. It's how the marriage stays afloat. But it's not reacting to them that saps her energy. She takes a deep breath.

He gets a plate from the cupboard, sits on a stool and eats.

He munches through the first Danish in silence.

Then he says, 'Phoebe's such a lucky girl to have a

mother like you. And she knows that. You just have to give her a bit of space, sweet pea. Y'know, let her find her feet.'

Sweet pea? That old nickname from their days of secret sex in hotel rooms. It feels like a kick in the gut. Sometimes kindness is harder than cruelty, if cruelty is what you expect.

'I know that.' She readjusts her glasses, so he doesn't see the tear in her eye. 'Really, it's not a problem. You're right. She needs time to settle and find her feet.'

The doorbell rings.

He frowns. 'We expecting anyone?'

'I'm not,' says Marcia.

Harry disappears into the hall to answer the front door.

Marcia gets up to make herself a fresh pot of tea. She can hear voices in the hall and immediately composes herself. An unexpected visitor? Game face on.

Simon Lennox wanders in, hands in the pockets of his baggy shorts. She relaxes.

'Hey, Ma,' he says. He gives her a sheepish grin. He has his father's looks and likeable manner but half the brains and zero motivation.

'Hello Simon,' says Marcia.

What is it this time? Money? Simon always needs money. Some exotic foreign trip that he can't miss? Or maybe he owes his coke dealer?

'I'm starving,' he says, picking up one of the pastries and taking a bite.

It was Simon's older brother, Eddie, who came up with the fun notion of calling her Ma. Harry thought it was a witty idea and would help his adolescent sons cope with a new, glamorous stepmother who set their hormones racing. Marcia hates it. But it's become her nickname and a family joke. She hated it even more when little Phoebe adopted it.

Harry is talking to someone else, and as he wanders back into the room, Marcia sees he has Jack Palmer in tow.

Now she is annoyed.

Jack and Simon went to the same expensive public school and have been best mates ever since. But whereas Simon has a certain lazy charm, Jack Palmer put Marcia's hackles up the first time she met him. Even as a boy, she sensed a watchfulness and an icy need for control in him that was all wrong.

'Hello, Ma,' he says, with a chilly smile.

'I prefer Marcia, if you don't mind,' she replies.

He dips his head. 'Sorry. Force of habit.' There's a touch of the Uriah Heep about Jack.

'Well,' says Harry, clapping his hands. 'What can we offer you boys? Beer? Glass of wine?'

So much for the hangover.

'Or coffee?' says Marcia.

'I'm fine, thank you,' says Jack.

'Listen, Dad,' says Simon. 'This is all a bit awkward. Jack's... well, he needs to explain. Might be nothing to worry about.' He shoots a look at his mate. 'I mean, it probably isn't, is it?'

Marcia's stomach lurches in anticipation. This is about Phoebe. They should never have let her go to Ibiza with the boys back in the summer. A luxury villa owned by the Palmer family and a cool, month long house party. Simon'll take care of her, that's what Harry had said. And she begged them to let her go. But she was only just eighteen, and the rest were a bunch in their late twenties. Marcia relented. She let her guard down. It was a mistake. Phoebe got swept up in a holiday romance with Jack Palmer. He preyed upon her.

The thought of him with his hands on her daughter...

'Let's hear it then,' says Harry.

Jack clears his throat. There's a crack in his usual smug confidence.

'I don't want you to take this the wrong way,' he says. 'But I know what it's like when you first go to uni. Wild times. I just wanted to keep an eye on Phoebe.'

Marcia erupts. No way she's listening to any of his bullshit. 'Keep an eye on her? It was a summer fling, Jack. And she made it very clear to you it was over. She's gone to Cambridge and wants to be free to make new friends of her own age.'

'And I respect that,' he says. 'I was always willing to give her the space to—'

'You don't need to give her the space!' Marcia realises she's shouting. 'She dumped you. Move on!'

'Okay,' says Harry. 'Calm down, darling—'

'It was never that cut and dried, Ma,' says Simon. 'You know what Phoebe's like. She loves to flirt. She knows Jack's a catch. She was always going to keep her options open.'

A catch? A shark's a catch, but you wouldn't take it home. Marcia is seething. The arrogance of it.

'I don't need you to tell me what my daughter is like!'

Her heart is pounding in her chest. The three men are standing in a circle around her, like a pack.

Harry has his hands on his hips. He sighs. 'Let's just listen to what Jack has to say, shall we?'

Marcia takes a breath and turns a steely gaze on Jack. It's easy to see what attracted Phoebe. On the surface, he's got it all. Tall, athletic, blond curls, a sports car. She's only eighteen and her head was turned.

Marcia folds her arms. 'Okay, I'm listening.'

Jack juts his chin. 'As I said, I was concerned. I wanted to make sure she was all right and stayed safe. So I put an app on her phone.'

'What sort of app?' says Harry.

'Just an app to keep an eye on her. You know, location, date, read her texts.' He makes it sound casual and normal.

'Read her texts?' exclaims Marcia. 'Spy on her? You mean you put a spy app on my daughter's phone? That's stalking.'

'Only as a precaution. And frankly, it's a good job I did.'

'What do you mean?' says Harry.

'The phone hasn't moved or been checked or used for twenty-one hours.' He makes it sound precise, like data from a spreadsheet.

'Well, she's probably in her room, working, sleeping, I don't know.' Marcia feels her head spinning as she tries to process this.

'But that's just not Phoebe,' says Simon. 'Think about it. She would not be off the grid for twenty-one hours. She'd be checking in, that's normal. And this is not normal. We think you should call the college, get someone to go round to her room and check. Make sure she's all right.'

Marcia seizes her phone and calls her daughter's number. It goes straight to voicemail.

She turns to her husband. She can feel the tears. She swallows hard to suppress them. Is this the fear she's had from the beginning, the fear every mother has, of a loss too terrible to bear, of the abyss opening up?

Harry has a stern look. 'Yes, okay,' he says. 'I think I'll do just that.'

6

Saturday, 5.45pm

Marcia drives. Harry was resistant at first, insisting he wasn't that hungover. But she was in no mood to accede to his wishes, and he backed off. The Mercedes hugs the fast lane of the M11 and eats up the miles. It's twilight as they reach the outskirts of Cambridge and begin the slow crawl into town. Saturday traffic, shoppers and crowds of tourists milling; there'll be the usual nightmare of finding somewhere to park. Marcia taps the steering wheel with her index finger, the only sign of her impatience.

Harry's call to Phoebe's college was put through to the Porter's Lodge, and after some shilly-shallying a member of the college staff went to check Phoebe's room. It was empty.

Marcia received the news calmly. She was already formulating a plan of action. Within fifteen minutes, she and Harry were in the car and off. Jack's offer to accompany them was curtly dismissed.

The first part of the journey passed largely in silence. In

the privacy of her own mind, Marcia examined and analysed every explanation she could think of for her daughter's supposed disappearance. She had no idea what her husband was thinking and didn't want to know.

He scrolled on his phone, fiddled with the satnav. And he kept calling their daughter. *Hey, Dad, here. Give us a bell, sweetheart.*

Harry Lennox's optimism is one thing Marcia has always liked about him. But it's easy to believe in platitudes like *you make your own luck,* when you're born with every advantage. However, in the years they've been together, he has softened her outlook on the world. She still suffers with anxiety but, with the help of medication, that's been reduced to a background hum. She's learnt how to keep her fears under control.

Harry sits, arms folded, in the passenger seat. 'You know what I reckon,' he says. 'Phoebe's a smart girl. Plus, she's really tech savvy. You only have to listen to her talk about her online stuff.'

'And your point is?' Marcia knows she sounds hostile, but today his breezy tone grates on her. Their daughter's missing, in trouble maybe, and only last night he was out on the prowl like a raddled old dog sniffing out any bitch on heat.

'Think about it,' he says. 'As you pointed out, she dumped Jack. Okay, somehow he secretly puts a spy app on her phone. What if she found it? Or knows about it?'

'How?'

'I don't know. But Marce, these kids understand this stuff far better than us. I reckon she got wise to Jack and has decided to flush him out and teach the silly sod a lesson.'

Marcia considers this. It's an appealing theory. Phoebe is whip smart and has always been brilliant with computers. She learned simple programming aged ten at primary school. She's always using some device; filming and editing footage on her phone, taking stills, posting. A week before she left for Cambridge she was boasting about the fact some hot new rap artist Marcia had never heard of, but who'd just won the Mercury prize, was following her and sharing her posts.

By the time they drive into the multi-storey car park near Lion Yard, Marcia is allowing Harry's optimism to seep into her. He's right. There will be a sensible explanation for all this. And now they're here, they'll be able to sort it out. Phoebe may even be in college waiting for them, a little contrite for having caused her parents so much worry. But if this is all about teaching the obnoxious Jack Palmer a well-deserved lesson, then Marcia's got no problem with that. The three of them can go out to dinner and laugh about it.

They walk through the side lanes and onto Trumpington Street. Phoebe's college is one of the oldest in Cambridge and right in the centre of the city. But its ancient stone buildings and enclosed courtyards have a quiet, cloistered feel.

Harry gives their name at the Porter's Lodge as Marcia watches her daughter's fellow students come and go. She can see that her panic has been unnecessary and blames Palmer for winding them up. He's a vicious snake. Marcia had encouraged Phoebe to give him his marching orders. He knows that and this is his spiteful revenge. The whole thing will shortly be resolved. Perhaps Phoebe accidentally dropped her phone down the toilet? That's the most likely explanation, and it wouldn't be the first time.

After a few minutes, a small woman appears. She introduces herself as Dr. Grayson, Phoebe's tutor. She has spiky hair, large tortoiseshell glasses and can't be much older than the undergraduates she teaches. Marcia remembers Phoebe saying how cool Dr G is and how well they get on.

She seems timid to Marcia as she invites them to accompany her.

'Where is Phoebe? Is she all right?' says Marcia.

'We have made a thorough search and I've spoken to the other students on her corridor.'

'What are you saying?'

Dr. Grayson pushes her glasses up her nose. Her obvious nervousness is making Marcia jumpy.

'According to the girl in the next room, Phoebe went out for a jog yesterday evening at around five o'clock. Apparently, she likes to—'

'Yes, yes, we know she jogs, usually in the late afternoon.'

Grayson stares up at Marcia. The look on her face says this is going to be bad.

'Well,' says the tutor, 'as far as we can discover, no one has seen her since then. We don't think she returned to college. It's over twenty-four hours. I've spoken with the senior tutor and he agrees with me that in the circumstances we should contact the police.'

7

Saturday, 7.30pm

Saturday evening is the least popular shift in the CID office, but Detective Sergeant Jo Boden volunteered for it. As a new member of the team, it's a ploy to win brownie points. But she's also new to the town, knows no one, and has nothing better to do on a Saturday night.

Boden sits at her desk, flipping her pen end-over-end between her fingers. She has one eye on her computer screen and the incident log; it's early yet. A few domestics that response can deal with, a brawl in a bar, a punch-up over a parking space.

She gets up and walks across the office to the coffee station. She's already eaten the healthy salad she brought in, plus an apple and a banana. Someone from the day shift has left an iced bun in a box. It's tempting, but she resists. She presses the button and pours herself a decaf. New job, promoted to Sergeant, finally! New town, healthy new habits.

She's raring to go. The only problem is, even on a Saturday night, there's not much kicking off.

She scans the empty office. This move to Cambridge is looking like a huge mistake. Has she steered her career up a blind alley?

Boden transferred from the Met a month ago. Her last birthday dumped her firmly on the wrong side of thirty. She passed the sergeant's exam fourth highest in her cohort. But she's also got a reputation and a shadow that's hard to shake. A court case. A lengthy internal investigation. She was tainted, nothing she could do. Her old boss made it clear that if she wanted promotion, she'd have to look elsewhere.

Leaving London has been hard. The university town of Cambridge and the flat Fenlands that surround it feel alien to Boden. The culture of a small regional force is different to the Met too. She misses the buzz of the capital, the adrenaline rush of kicking doors, the 24/7 lifestyle. But she needs to make this work.

One desk where the DCs sit is occupied, the other is empty.

She wanders over.

A nervous young DC looks up; she seems about twelve. She gives Boden a tentative smile. Boden's noticed her on the day shift, but they've never been introduced. The girl's eyes dart around like a frightened rabbit. She has a training manual open in front of her.

Boden hovers next to her desk. 'Hey,' she says, 'I'm Jo Boden. Don't think we've been properly introduced.'

'Yes, ma'am. I know,' the girl speaks in a whisper. 'I'm DC Chakravorty.'

Boden smiles. 'Just transferred out of uniform, eh?'

'Yes, ma'am. Two weeks ago.'

Chakravorty could have been picked for her brilliance,

but she's also small and Asian. Boden suspects that the bosses saw this as an opportunity to improve their stats. But she's all for positive discrimination. It's well overdue.

She gives the girl a warm smile. 'And you're shit scared, I'm guessing? Cause now you're a detective, but no one's explained anything.'

Chakravorty cracks a smile. Shy, but there's an underlying confidence. 'Scott's mentoring me. That's DC Mackie.'

Boden puts her hands on her hips and looks round at the deserted office.

'And where is DC Mackie?'

'Gone out to get a Chinese, that's what he said.'

Boden laughs. 'I hope he's getting us all some. Okay, what's your first name, Chakravorty?'

'Prisha.'

'Well, Prisha. You don't call me ma'am. Save that for the bosses, DI and above. You call me Jo. If you get really pissed off, you can call me Boden. Not skipper, never call a sergeant skipper. I hate that. We're both rookies here. So we'll be learning the ropes together. Fancy a coffee?'

The DC nods. She has a sunny smile which makes her look even younger.

'Actually,' she says, 'Scott left me with something to sort out, but I wasn't sure what to do.'

'Okay, what is it?'

'He said it was a PPP. I've been looking in the manual, but I can't find it. I didn't know what to do.'

Boden frowns, 'I'm not surprised. It's a new one on me. PPP? You sure?'

Chakravorty refers to her notes. 'Yes, he definitely said PPP. He talked to comms. Call came in from one of the colleges about a misper. First-year student. Went out for a jog yesterday. Hasn't been seen for twenty-four hours. They're worried.'

'Has uniform been round to the college to check this out?'

'Probably not. Scott said CID get the call if it's from one of the colleges and comms think it's sensitive.'

Boden huffs. Sensitive? Then why the hell has Mackie disappeared? She recognises the whiff of politics when she smells it. In a small city, dominated by a prestigious university, and with a large resident student population, it would be surprising if there weren't some delicate issues.

'Right,' she says. 'Have you got a number for Mackie? Call him.'

Chakravorty pulls out her phone, but as she does so Scott Mackie comes strolling through the swing doors. He's got a large pair of Bose headphones on and is swaying slightly to the music. He dumps his bag of takeaway on the desk.

Boden watches him, which is enough to wind her up.

'Take those bloody headphones off,' she shouts.

He stops in his tracks and stares at her. Only a few years her junior, he's big and squarely built like a rugby player with a shock of red curly hair. She's noticed him a couple of times, checking her out and grinning. Boden is tall with the kind of looks that get her noticed. This can be tedious at times.

Mackie removes his headphones. 'What's the problem, Skip?' he says with a teasing smile.

Boden knows the type. Every squad room she's worked in has at least a couple of young men like Mackie. Full of testosterone, confidence, and swagger. And he assumes that she'll welcome his admiration, that she's just sitting round the office, mentally filing her nails, waiting to flirt with him.

Red rag to a bull.

'What the bloody hell's going on?' she says. 'You get a

shout from comms and you just wander off without telling anyone? And what's a PPP when it's at home?'

'Posh parents panicking,' says Mackie with a shrug. 'And I told Prisha to follow up.'

'You're supposed to be mentoring her. How's she supposed to know?'

'Phone up the college and get more details. Get them to check it out. I should've thought it was obvious, skip.' His tone is bordering on the surly. He resents being challenged, which is what Boden has been waiting for.

She steps forward into his personal space; she's tall enough to face him eye to eye.

'Mackie,' she says softly. 'You need to understand a few things here. You do not call me skip. And you do not blame a colleague who's only been in the job two weeks, for your laziness and incompetence.'

Mackie reels. His chin juts, and Boden feels the anger zinging off him.

Inside, she's smiling. This is the most fun she's had in Cambridge since she arrived.

She stands stock still and lets her eyes bore right into him. She watches his anger turn to confusion.

His gaze dips, and he exhales. 'Sorry, Sarge,' he says. 'Misunderstanding.'

She doesn't move a muscle. Just waits until he's forced to take a step backwards.

Then she smiles and says, 'Now I've got your attention, let's start again. What's happened? And why didn't you tell me straight away?'

Clearing his throat, he seems disorientated. He's not used to this kind of challenge from a woman.

'Well,' he says, 'Comms called about a misper. First-year student. We get this all the time. Especially at the beginning of term. But mostly it's bullshit. Posh parents panicking, we call it. Their little darling has gone off on a jolly, or got wasted and crashed out somewhere, and they're worried and expect a full-scale police search. Helicopters, sniffer dogs. Last one we had, kid had gone to Paris for the weekend with her new boyfriend.'

'So why doesn't response check it out first? Why did comms call you direct?'

'Special initiative, Sarge. Daughter of some cabinet minister got raped last year. And we got slated in the media. So DCI Hepburn says we have to maintain a close working relationship with the colleges.'

Boden smiles. 'Well, we'd better follow his instructions, hadn't we? What's this girl called? Do we know?'

'Phoebe Lennox,' says Prisha. She's been watching saucer-eyed at the way Boden dealt with Mackie.

'While you eat your Chinese, DC Mackie,' says Boden. 'You can check with passport control. Find out if Phoebe Lennox has left the country. Gone to Paris or anywhere else. Also check the hospital A&E admissions lists and RTA's within a fifty miles radius. Text me your findings. ASAP. Meanwhile, DC Chakravorty and I will go to the college and speak to her posh parents.'

Scott Mackie nods.

Boden watches him glance at his takeaway. She suspects he's lost his appetite. Serves him right.

8

Saturday, 8.05pm

Marcia Lennox stands in the middle of her daughter's room. She feels at a complete loss. The hope that they'd arrive in Cambridge and find Phoebe waiting seems to have made things worse. Marcia blames Harry and his stupid *look on the bright side* philosophy. He has his hands in his pockets and a vacant look on his face, as he stares out of the window at the dark college gardens. He sighs and checks his watch.

Only three weeks ago she was here, helping Phoebe unpack. The string of fairy lights above the bed. She fixed them up with Blu-tack. The poster of the Dorothea Tanning exhibition at Tate Modern; they'd laughed as they struggled to get it straight.

Clothes are strewn across the unmade bed; Phoebe has always been untidy. The room even smells of her; a hint of Jo Malone Pomegranate Noir. Her wallet with her credit and debit cards is on the shelf, and next to it, her phone.

Marcia turns to Harry. She doesn't know what to say.

Inside, she's screaming. She just wants him to do something. Take charge.

His hapless expression flips her back to their last major row. A family wedding, the daughter of a cousin of Harry's. It was a lavish two-day affair in a castle. Harry wasn't even that drunk. He got caught having sex with a waitress in a bathroom. He tried to deny it, called it a drunken kiss, but everyone knew. Marcia had walked out; it was too embarrassing. Phoebe had left with her, which meant it was bad.

'Don't worry,' says Harry. 'The police will sort this out. They have the resources. And there will be a perfectly logical explanation.'

'Do you really believe that?'

He faces her. 'Yes, I do,' he says fiercely. He has tears in his eyes.

She wants to slap him.

There's a tap on the door and Dr. Grayson enters. She's accompanied by two women. A tall, almost elegant blonde with hair tied back in a messy ponytail and a small, neat Asian girl who's ridiculously young.

The blonde homes in on Marcia. She holds out some kind of badge, which must be a warrant card.

'Mrs. Lennox,' she says. 'I'm Detective Sergeant Boden and this is my colleague, DC Chakravorty. I'm so sorry if we've kept you waiting. Saturday evening is a busy time.'

Marcia paints on a smile. 'Thank you for coming.'

The girl can hardly be thirty. Her clothes are scruffy, as if she's trying to dress down. Why? That's obvious. She's far too good looking to be a police officer. They've sent the office juniors. What's needed is someone older and more experienced. An inspector, at least. That would feel like they were being taken seriously.

Harry steps forward, hand outstretched. He can't take his

eyes off her, which makes things worse. 'Harry Lennox,' he says gruffly. 'We appreciate your time, Sergeant. She's probably just gone off and done something silly.'

'Well,' says the sergeant. 'Let's hope we can resolve this quickly. Do you have any ideas or theories about where your daughter could be?'

'We wouldn't be here if we did,' says Marcia. Stupid question from a stupid young woman.

The police officer gives her a wry look, almost as if she's laughing. But then she says, 'Of course not. And I can see you're very worried. So, I suggest we approach this systematically.'

Patronising bitch.

'I don't mean to sound abrupt,' says Marcia with chilly civility. 'As my husband said, we appreciate you coming.'

'When did you last hear from your daughter?'

'She texted me,' says Marcia. 'On Friday.'

'And that was from the phone that I see there on the shelf?'

'Well, yes. That's her phone.'

The Asian DC is pulling on a pair of vinyl gloves. She's quiet and stealthy as a mouse.

'Do you mind if we take it and examine it?' says the sergeant. 'Obviously when Phoebe turns up, we'll return it at once.'

'If she didn't have it with her, how can… oh, God, take it. Take the bloody thing.'

Marcia reins herself in; being angry won't help.

The DC picks it up and puts it in a plastic bag.

'Is it usual for her to go jogging without her phone, Mrs Lennox? Doesn't she listen to music?'

'Yes, I suppose—'

Dr Grayson, who's standing in the corner behind the door,

pipes up. 'I believe there's a school of thought that prefers a complete electronic detox when running. A chance to tune into the rhythms of one's own body. I never take any device with me when I run.'

School of thought! Stupid academic-speak! Marcia glares at the tutor as her anger veers in that direction. It's her bloody fault that Phoebe went running after dark without a phone?

The sergeant turns round to face the spiky-haired little idiot. 'In your opinion, Dr Grayson, is Phoebe adjusting well to student life? Is she happy here?'

Grayson shrugs, 'Well, I think—'

'I don't think Dr Grayson is qualified to answer that question,' says Marcia. 'She's known my daughter less than three weeks. I'm her mother and I can tell you she was so excited to come here. She's a well-adjusted and sociable girl, clever but not some nerdy nit-wit who has trouble fitting in.'

Marcia realises everyone is staring at her.

The sergeant nods her head, 'Okay,' she says. 'Let's move on to family and close friends. Anyone she could've just gone to see, had a few drinks, stayed over?'

'She has two step-brothers. I've checked with them,' says Harry. 'My parents are in Scotland. I haven't been in touch, but I doubt…'

'Maybe call them?' says the sergeant. 'What about your side of the family, Mrs Lennox?'

'My parents are dead. There's no one else.' Marcia turns to Harry. 'I think we ought to tell the police about Jack, don't you?'

Harry shrugs.

'Jack?' says the sergeant.

'Jack Palmer is a good friend of my younger son,' says Harry. 'Back in the summer he and Phoebe were involved for a while. A summer fling. Nothing serious.'

'She finished with him and then he put a spy app on her phone,' says Marcia. 'That's why we're here.'

'What? Because he told you she was missing?' says the sergeant.

The DC is scribbling notes.

'Yes. He's a very controlling individual,' says Marcia.

'Come on, darling, that's a bit of an exaggeration,' says Harry.

Marcia looks at the two police officers. They need to take action. Now! This could be her one chance to convince them. No way she's holding back.

'I'm sorry, Harry. But I'm not going to lie because he's a friend of Simon. He's a vicious little shit. And he's obsessed with Phoebe. She wanted nothing more to do with him. She told him that. And we discover this afternoon that he's been stalking her. Stalking! You asked if we'd got any ideas or theories? I reckon he could have quite easily done something to her. Kidnapped her, I don't know.'

The sergeant is watching her.

Harry shakes his head and turns away. 'It's nonsense.' He turns back to face the sergeant. 'My wife is upset. But Jack is not the sort—'

'Oh, shut the fuck up, Harry!' screams Marcia. 'Phoebe's gone. She's missing. The police need all the relevant information to do their job.'

9

Saturday, 8.55pm

Boden and Chakravorty walk out of the back gate of the college and down the lane towards Emmanuel Street.

'What do you make of all that?' says Boden.

'Honestly? Not sure. I took lots of notes like you said.'

'That's what you do first. Listen and gather information. What's the first question?'

Chakravorty shrugs. 'Umm, well, is she missing?'

'Quite right,' says Boden. 'She's eighteen, and she's an adult. She's perfectly entitled to go off without telling anyone.'

'But it is weird. Goes for a jog, doesn't come back. No phone, no money. She could've had an accident.'

Boden checks her phone. 'Nothing from Mackie, so I'm assuming he hasn't come up with any leads. But that's still a possibility. Fell in the river? It may take several days for a body to turn up.'

'I'd say she is missing.'

'I agree,' says Boden. 'Next question: is she a vulnerable misper? The tutor says she's getting on fine at college. No obvious mental health issues. Doesn't sound like she's the sort of girl to just go off and not tell anyone. But then we have the dodgy boyfriend. Mum's pointing the finger at him.'

'If they broke up recently, he could've come hassling her and they had a row which turned nasty.'

They cross the road. 'Yep,' says Boden, 'a definite possibility. I'm going to call the DCI, see what he wants us to do. The alleged facts are: she goes out for a jog, doesn't come back. Medium risk misper, an allegation of stalking but no obvious crime. We'll need to check the CCTV and see if we can get a sighting.'

Chakravorty nods. The top of her head lines up with Boden's shoulder. 'I felt sorry for the dad,' she says. 'The mum was pretty full on.'

'She's upset. She's worried. You've got to look beyond that.'

'Strikes me she's a bit of a control freak too.'

Boden stops and smiles. 'Well spotted, Prisha. Now you're thinking like a detective. So what would you do if she was your mum?'

They walk round the corner into Parker Street.

Prisha chuckles. 'She is like my mum. Reckons she knows best about everything. Bossy. Doesn't see me as a grownup.'

Boden nods. 'And, of course, as a result, you tell her every little thing you get up to.'

Prisha laughs. 'No I don't. Certainly not.'

'Exactly. And I think our working assumption should be that Phoebe Lennox is like you. The key to this is cracking open the phone. We need to get it to the digital investigations unit, ask them to turn it around ASAP. Meanwhile, we look at CCTV to confirm the facts.'

'Do you think something bad has happened to her?'

'You mean do I have a hunch?' Boden looks at the DC; she seems rather innocent. What to say? Her own past is full of shadows. It's easy to assume the worst when that's what you've seen and experienced. But she's also aware of the dangers of an emotional reaction.

'We have to keep an open mind,' she says. 'Not jump one way or the other. Mackie didn't take it seriously enough. That was his hunch. He took the lazy option.'

Prisha gives her a sly sideways glance. 'I wish I was big enough to look him in the eye like you did.'

'I caught him off his guard, Prisha. And he seems like a decent bloke. But it doesn't always work. I tried a similar thing once with an Albanian gangster. Ended up with a broken nose.'

Boden is aware she's boasting. Playing the cool cop educating the rookie. But she's also enjoying herself. And why not? It's the first time since she started this new job. Okay, word will spread round the office that she's a head-banger. Mackie will make sure of that. Then DCI Hepburn will get wind. Boden's not sure how he'll react; he's young for a DCI and, she suspects, a player. It'll be interesting to find out.

Still, her mood is upbeat. She's got a busy weekend ahead, and she does have a hunch. And a secret hope that she can't admit. If Phoebe Lennox really has disappeared and it involves foul play, then this is her chance to shine. She'll show Hepburn that she doesn't need a DI to tell her what to do. It's possible this could turn into a big case, she's in on the ground floor and she intends to take full advantage of that.

10

Saturday, 10.30pm

Harry got them a room at the Hilton in the city centre. Clean and functional and a place to retreat to with minimum hassle. They've brought nothing with them. He offers to go out and shop for toothbrushes and toiletries.

Marcia can feel his tension and discomfort; they've spoken little since her outburst. He apologised to the police several times and to the little idiot tutor. Embarrassing emotional outbursts are not okay in Harry's book. He's been programmed over generations to behave like an English gentleman. Feelings are private, displaying them overtly is a sign of weakness. She can feel him retreating from her. He's itching to get away, that's obvious. Perhaps they could both do with some respite. The errand is an excuse. She sits on the end of the king-sized bed and watches the door close behind him. It's a relief to be alone. But her head is in a spin. What can she do? She must do something.

She gets up and wanders round the room. It's spacious

enough and reassuringly anonymous. She could be in any major city, looking at the same beige walls, abstract prints and inoffensive furniture. She opens the well-stocked mini-bar. All the snacks are fat and salt laden. She ignores the chocolate and settles for a ready-mixed gin and tonic in a can. It will be dire and loaded with aspartame, but it'll do. She goes down the corridor to the ice machine to fill the bucket.

She's ditched her shoes and her bare feet sink into the deep pile carpet. Why on earth did she wear such silly shoes? They left the house in a rush. No time to worry about appearances. But there's something rather common about high heels and denim jeans. Harry's first wife, Louisa, would sniff that out in a nanosecond. Loafers with jeans, obviously. Like Harry she was schooled in all the nuances of behaviour which reveal if you're *one of us*. Marcia knows she isn't. Doesn't matter how hard she tries. But Phoebe is. She belongs. For her, it's effortless. On her, heels and jeans would be cool, not a telltale sign of poor taste and inferiority.

As Marcia fills her ice bucket, a giggling couple disappears into an adjacent room. They seem young, maybe even students. But why are they in a hotel? A clandestine meeting? Secrets to keep? Does her daughter have secrets to keep? Why would she? It makes no sense.

For Phoebe's entire life, Marcia's tried to give her daughter everything she needs. Not indulged. Not spoilt. There's always been discipline and lessons in deferred gratification. Marcia read all the child-rearing books; from day one, she was determined to get it right. Phoebe was such a gift, and Marcia made her well-being the number one priority. But is there something she missed? Did she do something wrong? Is this all her fault? Is she being punished? It certainly feels like it.

As she returns to the room, her phone pings. She rushes

over to it. Finally! A text. Phoebe's texting her. She clicks on it to find a brief message from DS Boden. Does she know if Phoebe has more than one Instagram account? Could she use other names or nicknames on different platforms?

Marcia flings the phone on the bed in irritation. She sits down and bursts into tears. It's not her intention. She must stay in control and make a plan. She'd be a fool to rely on Harry. First order of business, make an appointment with the officer in charge. The search for Phoebe cannot be left to the likes of DS Boden, they must make that clear. Harry must be galvanised into action. He has plenty of contacts in Whitehall, he'll know who to call. For Chrissake, his ex-father-in-law was once Home Secretary.

She picks up the phone again. Take concrete action. Start a list.

As she's tapping away, the door of the room opens and Harry appears. She looks up.

'That was quick.'

He's grinning like a fool. 'Look who I bumped into in the foyer,' he says.

Simon and Jack Palmer follow him into the room.

For Marcia, this is the last straw. Her hand clenches the phone, but her fury remains contained. No more outbursts, no more hostages to fortune.

'That's useful,' she says in her iciest tone, 'Because I believe the police want to have a word with you, Jack.'

'Well,' says Harry. 'Obviously they'll want to talk to all Phoebe's friends.'

Jack meets Marcia's gaze. He chuckles, puts his hands in his trouser pockets and walks into the middle of the room. The arrogance grates on Marcia's nerves, but she manages to hold on to her temper.

'I know you hate me, Marcia,' he says. 'I don't think

there's any doubt about that. But if she's definitely missing, there are a few things we need to talk about. And tell the police.'

'What things?' Marcia glares at him. She won't be browbeaten.

'How much her social media following could've made her a target.'

'You mean all her friends on the net?'

'No, I mean her profile as an influencer. Phoebe has thousands of followers all over the world. She's become a media personality. I realise you may not be up to speed with how all this works.'

Up to speed. Another patronising shit.

'I work in advertising, Jack. We deal with influencers all the bloody time. But if Phoebe had developed some kind of platform, I would know about it.'

'No you wouldn't, Ma,' says Simon. 'Phoebe didn't tell you, because she wanted it to be something she did for herself.'

'That's ridiculous.' She turns to Harry. 'Did you know about this?'

The knot inside Marcia's stomach is so tight it's painful.

He shrugs. 'Well, no. But she wanted to stand on her own two feet. She probably felt you'd interfere.'

'I've never stopped her from standing on her own two feet. I've always encouraged her.'

Palmer is staring. A viper waiting to pounce. He's done something to Phoebe. She's convinced of it. If Harry was half a man he'd beat it out of him, instead of standing there, detached and bemused, like the fool he is.

'Listen, Ma,' says Simon. 'We're here because we want to help. Jack's not the villain here.'

Marcia focuses her gaze on Jack Palmer. This is a diversion. He's trying to be clever.

She holds out her phone to him. 'Okay. Show me then.'

He takes the phone. He's smirking. Which is fine. Let him think he's won.

11

Saturday, 10.45pm

Carol's limbs ache, but in a good way. She's done her first full day's work on the picking gang. They worked until after dark with lights rigged on the back of the trailer.

Today's job was pumpkins for Halloween. Great big orange monsters, like over-inflated, ribbed footballs; they were wiped, passed hand to hand down the line and stacked in crates. It was almost fun. Carol couldn't recall ever having pumpkins when she was a kid. Halloween wasn't a thing. But Mum sometimes made toffee apples for Bonfire Night and they lit sparklers in the yard, twizzling them around their heads until they were giddy.

She'd arrived in Norfolk the previous afternoon; a bloke in a van picked her up at Diss station. He spoke little English, but he was friendly enough.

There are twenty pickers in the gang which moves from farm to farm across the county, depending on the season and the crop. They live in static caravans on a small plot of land owned by the gangmaster, just outside the town. She shares with three other girls, much younger and all Romanian. One has a smattering of English.

They gave Carol a corner bunk with space underneath to put her things. Not unlike a prison cell in many ways, and Carol knew the drill. Keep to yourself, don't encroach. She watched them talking about her in their own language, speculating probably. But they all smiled a lot and didn't seem to want to give her any hassle.

In the yard there's a marquee where they all eat. Cooking is on a couple of old Calor gas stoves, but everyone seems to muck in. Bed and board are part of the deal.

The gangmaster's name is Vasile, a shaggy bear of a man with a tiny wife, Alina, who's just had a baby. She carries it everywhere with her in a sling. They live in a small bungalow, the only permanent structure on the property.

He greeted Carol when she first arrived.

'We work like a team,' he said. 'Meet deadlines, get produce to supermarket fast, then everyone get bonus. You work, money is good.'

'I'm not scared of hard work,' Carol replied.

He was looking her over, weighing her up. Carol wondered how the probation service persuaded him to take ex-cons, especially a lifer like her. Maybe she was his first? But as a Romanian gangmaster, if he didn't want problems with the authorities, it was wise to co-operate.

'Most Brits don't like this work,' he said.

Carol shrugged. 'Cause we still think we rule the world.'

Vasile laughed and nodded. He said something to his wife. She laughed too.

A few pumpkins from the crop were rejected as misshapen or damaged. One of her fellow pickers had been a chef back home, and he turned them into a steaming vat of pumpkin soup. Carol was handed a bowl with a hunk of bread and it tasted like the most amazing thing she'd ever eaten. She went back for seconds. A bottle of something fiery and alcoholic was passed round; she had a slug of that too.

Lying on her narrow bed, she's finally relaxing. This is the happiest she's felt since she got out. The place is okay and so is the work. Most of the gang speak no English. But she doesn't mind being the odd one out. In fact, it's a good thing. It makes her invisible, nameless, just *the English woman,* or more likely *the poor English bitch,* whatever that is in Romanian. She doesn't care because it helps her feel more secure.

No one knows she's here except her probation officer. No one would think to look for her in a place like this. She's safe.

12

Sunday, 6.45am

Jo Boden has been up all night. Her neck is stiff, and she has eye strain from staring at a screen for hours on end. Mackie finished his shift at five, but Prisha volunteered to stay. Boden seems to have found an ally.

Between them they've assembled all the CCTV footage from the city centre that can be accessed remotely and are trawling through it. The number of female joggers pounding the pavements between four and six pm on Friday surprised Boden. If only they'd had some facial recognition software, it would've been much easier.

The parents have provided several photos of Phoebe Lennox. She's quite a show-off and loves the camera; a beautiful girl on the cusp of a beautiful life. Boden has spent her Saturday night gazing into those sparkling blue eyes and wondering: are you dead already?

They've done a thorough check and drawn a blank in terms of hospital admissions and RTAs.

Boden is across the room getting fresh coffees when Prisha jumps up out of her seat.

'I think I've got her!'

On Prisha's screen there's a grainy shot of a girl, medium height, with a bouncing ponytail. A good half of the female joggers in town seem to favour baseball caps and ponytails. The girl turns and there's a brief glimpse of her face.

Prisha freezes the frame and rewinds. Boden comes and leans over her shoulder.

Prisha replays it. 'What do you reckon?'

'Again,' says Boden. She peers intently at the screen. It could be her.

Prisha repeats the process. The image plays again; it's rough and pixilated. Hardly conclusive.

'Okay,' says Boden. 'Let's suppose it is her and see if we can match what she's wearing with anything from anywhere else. And that may lead us to a better image.'

They play the clip a couple more times.

The baseball cap is dark, probably black, which isn't helpful but the running leggings appear to be a fuzzy khaki green with a matching dark green top.

'I think the leggings are some sort of camouflage print,' says Prisha. 'I nearly bought some like that.'

Boden glances at her; she seems an unlikely athlete. She's tiny.

'Do you run much?' she asks.

'A bit,' says Chakravorty. 'I've done a few marathons.'

Boden laughs, 'A few? How few?'

'London three times. And Boston once; I've got a cousin who lives over there.'

'I considered London once and bottled out. Come on, 'fess up. Fastest time?'

'My best was three hours, thirty-five.'

'Wow! And I was about to suggest we go for a jog together sometime. But you can forget that.'

Prisha smiles. Still shy, but the pride is obvious. It strikes Boden there's more to her than meets the eye.

They focus on the leggings and top. It takes another half hour to extract two more sightings of the same girl from the system.

Boden plots a potential route on the map. 'Problem is,' she says, 'if Phoebe Lennox came out of the back gate of the college, there was no camera in the vicinity to record her. The only CCTV is at the Porter's Lodge. But, let's say she did, and she ran down the lane and round the corner, here's where she could've hit the main drag, and, bingo, that's where we first see the khaki girl.'

Boden has been keeping the DCI updated by text. Her professional relationship with Alistair Hepburn is embryonic. When she first arrived on the squad, he was friendly but wary. And Boden understands why. He's ambitious, already marked out as a high-flyer. The last thing he wants is some reject from the Met trailing controversy in her wake. This case will be the first proper test of their relationship.

More trawling produces another sighting. Boden rubs her eyes, which are smarting. Then she almost misses it: on screen a girl in khaki leggings rounds a corner outside Sainsbury's in Sidney Street, bumps into a male figure in a hoodie and stops to talk to him. Greeting a fellow student? Giving a passer-by directions? Is the girl surprised or uncomfortable? Is it even her?

Boden scrolls through the clip several times, then asks Prisha to come and look.

As they pore over it, the swing doors open and the DCI walks in. Boden glances at her watch. It's a quarter to eight on a Sunday morning. This is a surprise. He's certainly on it, strolling through the deserted open plan office in a pink polo shirt, chinos and an expensive leather jacket.

'Morning, ladies. How's it going?'

Boden gets up from her desk and smiles. 'Morning, sir. We think we may have found her.'

'Good.' Hepburn is small and compact, hair receding at the temples. Nothing about him is threatening except the chilly, flint grey eyes. Boden towers over him, but he must be used to that.

'CCTV needs to be enhanced,' says Boden. 'But if this is her, then we've got her talking to someone outside Sainsbury's. At first glance, she appears to know him. At the very least a witness, but could be something more.'

'What are we saying? Is this a thing? Is she missing?'

'Yes, sir. She went jogging. Didn't come back. Everything, including her phone, was left in her room. No one's seen her.'

'Who goes jogging without a phone?'

'Electronic detox, apparently. However, the parents allege that an ex-boyfriend put a spy app on her phone, which is how they knew she was missing. Mother regards him as a stalker and bad news.'

Hepburn exhales. 'Well, the Assistant Chief phoned me at seven am. It seems the parents know people and are in a position to make waves. The fact you've spent all night trying to track her down is good news.'

'DC Mackie explained about *posh parents panicking*. But I wouldn't say it was that. No reported accidents that have come to light.'

'Okay, she's gone. Voluntarily or under duress? Running away or taken?' He sighs. 'And, of course, alive or dead? And are we moving towards suspecting a crime has taken place?'

'Can't answer any of that, sir. Yet. Although, I'd say, not a runaway. No apparent problems or mental health issues. We've also got the phone. Parents agreed. We're waiting on digital investigations to send us a download.'

'Good forward planning. Rich parents? Blackmail for ransom is a possibility. Depends how rich they are. You'd better ask if they've been approached.'

'Okay,' says Boden.

The DCI nods to himself. He's calculating his next move. Boden watches. He must've already figured that as Senior Investigating Officer, if this goes the course, it could be a biggie for him too.

'Right,' he says, 'we need to ramp this up. Move it up to a high-risk misper. Problem is, I've got one DI off sick and the other's on his honeymoon. I'll drum up some additional help myself. I'll give digital investigations a call and ask them to hurry up. Meanwhile, can you hold the fort, Jo?'

'Absolutely, sir. No problem at all.'

He nods, turns to Chakravorty and gives her a smile. 'In at the deep end, Prisha. Good experience.'

'Yes, sir,' says the DC.

As Hepburn walks away, Prisha turns to Boden and whispers, 'Does he think she's already dead?'

Maybe. What he knows is he's got the Assistant Chief on his back and he's hedging his bets. That's the politics of this.

But Boden shrugs and points at her screen. 'If she isn't, she could be with this guy in the hoodie. We need to track this through. Did they just speak for a moment or did she go off with him? That's the key.'

13

Sunday, 6.47am

Carol wakes at first light. The clocks have gone back an hour, reverting to GMT, which takes her by surprise. She steps outside the caravan into the chilly autumn air and watches a watery sun rise through skeletal trees edging the property. It's a moment of pure joy. Not something she's experienced much of in her life. She decides to go for a walk.

She's been zoned out on drugs enough times, but that's a different feeling. The rush of the high then blankness; nothing close to the serenity she feels on this quiet Sunday morning. The idea of going off on her own for a walk is scary at first. Should she tell someone where she's going? Ask permission? There's no work on a Sunday. She assumes most people are still in bed.

As she wanders up the muddy lane, she finds there are still a few blackberries in the hedgerow. Some are squidgy and stain her fingers when she picks them. They taste delicious. Being alone, noticing birdsong, seeing a small furry creature dart across the track ahead of her, these things throw her back to another time. To before. To when Mum was alive.

Over the years, she seems to have lost the capacity to recall her mother's face. She has no photos to remind her. Those terrible last few months keep coming back; they dominate her thoughts and she can't seem to stop them. She was old enough to recognise her mother's pain, but too young to know how to comfort her. Mostly she hid.

The problem is, it's hard to go back beyond that to a better time, to when they were a family and happy. Were they ever happy? Before Mum got cancer. She thinks they were. She remembers random things: on her tenth birthday, her parents bought her a flute and she started to have lessons. The teacher told her mother she had genuine talent. When did she last hear any flute music? Impossible to remember.

The landscape is flat. She climbs over a gate and finds herself near a river. It cuts through the farmland, deep and meandering. In several places, the river has broken its banks and flooded the fields. Carol navigates her way around small lakes. There are a couple of moorhens, swimming and bobbing for food and seagulls wheeling overhead, which this far inland seems strange. It takes her breath away, the beauty of it. And it makes her sad; this is what she's been missing for all these years.

She has no watch or phone and loses track of the time. It feels an indulgence to wander. But why not?

Hours have passed by the time Carol finds her way back to her new home.

Breakfast has been and gone. She helps herself to a bowl of cornflakes and douses them in milk. She searches but can't find any sugar. One of the girls from her caravan comes over.

'Sugar?' she says.

The girl says something in reply. It makes no sense. The

girl repeats it and gets frustrated. Carol smiles at her and shrugs. She hates cornflakes without sugar. But she's starving. The girl walks away.

A few of her fellow workers are hanging around, smoking, drinking coffee. Carol perches on the end of their table. They smile at her. One of the older blokes is telling an anecdote, he gestures with his hands, pulls a face — the punchline? — all the others laugh.

Carol finishes her cornflakes. She's still hungry. She goes in search of something else to eat.

Alina comes out of the bungalow and hurries towards her. She has the baby in its sling, it's dozing, but Alina looks hassled. Too many sleepless nights? Vasile speaks passable English, but Alina struggles.

She flaps her hands at Carol as she searches for the right word.

'People… come,' she says, 'want you speak…'

'People? You mean Rosa?'

Rosa is her probation officer, an upbeat young woman with a mop of black frizzy hair and glasses.

Carol tries to mime her hair. 'Curly, big hair? And glasses?' She circles her own eyes with her fingers.

Alina shakes her head. 'Is man, in truck.' She points at the Mitsubishi pickup belonging to Vasile.

'A man?' The word hits like a kick in the gut. A man? What man? She takes a gulp of air. A man looking for her, but how?

She was feeling so good, but with one word she hurtles back.

Every year for seventeen years, on the same day, that day, she's received a card. Something flowery and fancy. The words inside are always the same: *thinking of you still, Carol. You're never out of our thoughts.*

62

It was innocuous enough and never aroused the curiosity of the prison censor. But Carol knew what it meant.

A threat. And a promise. He was waiting. And he was making sure she knew that one day he'd have his revenge.

Alina is staring at her. 'You okay?'

Carol nods. But she's finding it hard to breathe. Panic is choking her. 'Yeah, I'm fine… When was he here?' She taps her wrist with her index finger, 'When?'

'Yeah, maybe since half hour. Two peoples in truck.'

'Two?' She glances around her wildly. They'll be back, that's for certain. But what should she do? What can she do? Two of them. Shit!

She backs away from Alina. Fear is flooding her body, but the adrenaline will help her run.

In prison, she was out of his reach. Though on a couple of occasions, she wondered.

Now he's on her trail. Still, after all these years. He hasn't given up.

And like the monster he is, he wants blood for blood.

14

Sunday, 10.35am

Marcia spent a sleepless night, wired and tense, peering at her phone in a darkened room like a demented teenager. Harry lay beside her in bed, snoring. How could he sleep? His mantra of *leave it to the police* was frustrating. She'd forced him to phone his ex-wife and explain the situation. Listening in to their conversation was maddening.

'Lou, I know,' he said, in that whiny, boyish tone of his. 'She's probably just gone off with friends. But Marcia is worried.'

He's passing the buck and blaming her. Why can't he just say *we're worried?*

'The local police are looking into it. They sent a young DS round. But Marcia thinks she's not up to scratch. Would you call your father? Oh, I know. That would be brilliant. Absolutely brilliant! Thank you. Sometimes they just need a kick up the backside.'

Harry had hung up and turned to her with a smug grin.

'She adores Phoebe,' he said. 'Thinks of her like a daughter. She's happy to do whatever she can. Don't worry, darling, we will sort this out. I promise.'

A call from Sir Edwin Muirhead, former Home Secretary, to the appropriate Whitehall mandarin and instructions passed down the line to the police. It was one thing to tick off her list. But begging a favour from Louisa Muirhead was a measure of her desperation.

Thinks of her like a daughter? Marcia has long resented her predecessor's attempts to co-opt Phoebe into her family circle. *Oh, she's such a lovely little girl.* She can still remember Louisa saying that in a tone of mild surprise. How on earth had that happened, that's what she meant, given that Phoebe was not of the right breeding?

Throughout the night Marcia's thoughts skittered. She found it impossible to focus. She went back and forth, trying to analyse the facts. But they kept slithering away from her.

Jack Palmer had explained to them that Phoebe's Instagram account, the one Marcia followed, with the picture of Phoebe at the sherry party in her gown, was just her vanilla account.

Vanilla! The look on his face as he'd pronounced the word made the hairs prickle on the back of her neck. It confirmed every instinct that she had about him, but she held her tongue.

He knows where Phoebe is. She remains convinced of it. Somehow he's tricked her, lied to her, trapped her. But the police would deal with him. She'd make bloody sure of that.

Palmer had shown them Phoebe's other Instagram account. PhoReal. She also has a YouTube channel and a website. Marcia was shocked, but not by the existence of these platforms. What upset her is that Phoebe had never told her about it. Why did her daughter assume she would have disapproved of her becoming an influencer? She could've helped. Given tips and advice. For heaven's sake, she has an office of bright young people who are experts in this sort of thing. It made no sense. Why hadn't Phoebe come to her?

Once they'd got rid of Jack and Simon, it was after midnight but Marcia continued to explore the platforms. And they were good. Even as a toddler, Phoebe was photogenic. She was building a social media brand. Her slogan was: *I have a life, not a lifestyle.* Many of the posts were quirky pictures of herself doing challenges — a difficult yoga position while drinking a glass of champagne. There were random philosophical quotes and snippets of poetry between pictures of Phoebe in unusual places — leaning on a skip in some derelict urban backstreet, standing on Waterloo Bridge at night but wearing sunglasses. The captions were cool and ironic. The styling was excellent.

Marcia felt proud. She understood why Phoebe had done this. Her daughter was showing initiative. There was nothing wrong with that.

But the further she dug into the website, the more revealing the pictures became. Phoebe in a bikini, then skimpy underwear. It was all still quite innocent. But then a box popped up, inviting her to become a private subscriber. For £10 a month she was being invited to see her daughter 'get real' on Patreon. Or she could opt to become a 'close friend' of PhoReal and access more private content. As the pictures got more risqué, it became clear why Phoebe had kept the enterprise secret.

Marcia's heart had sunk. She knows how competitive it is to make a splash on social media. Too many pretty young girls. How do you stand out? The answer is by doing or showing something more provocative. A little soft porn, done in a girly and romantic way, would get attention, would attract more likes. The look Phoebe was presenting was upmarket and a cut above reality TV with its sleazy dating shows. The content was intelligent and informed, but also beguiling and sexy enough to hook them. It was hard to avoid the conclusion that her daughter was collecting followers by pimping herself out.

The more she looked, the more it sickened Marcia. And she can see Jack Palmer's influence. He and Simon and all their slick, rich friends would've egged Phoebe on. It's the sort of prank they would love. And back in the summer, Phoebe wanted to be one of their gang. She was eager to impress them. That must be how it all began. They persuaded her that this was the way to build a career. They probably also advised her not to tell her mother.

Harry was still sleeping when Marcia left the hotel. She had to get out and walk, even if the stupid shoes crippled her. Saint Laurent. She paid over eight hundred pounds for them, although she can no longer remember why.

She wandered through the town and followed the path across the misty water meadows. The grass was heavy with dew, benches too wet to sit on. She stood for ages staring at a family of swans on the river. The perfect tranquillity of the scene felt like an affront. She was seething. But it was all trapped inside with nowhere to go.

She had to face the prospect that perhaps Palmer's theory was right. Had Phoebe had been targeted by one of her social media followers? She still suspected him, but this was another possibility, another unknown factor to grapple with, and it was out of her control. How could she have protected her daughter from this?

Phoebe had been selected via the internet. Someone she thought she knew because they followed her online, some sick psycho, targeted her and waylaid her when she was out jogging. This sort of things happens; she's read about it. The very thought brings her out in a cold sweat.

Marcia takes out her phone. Her brain is so fuddled she can't remember the name of the police officer, the tall, scruffy girl, too attractive to be a cop. She was a DS. She looks under D in her contacts list. There it is, DS Boden.

She clicks on the number. It's answered on the second ring.

'Jo Boden.'

Was her name Jo? Marcia can't remember if she ever knew that. And PhoReal? Why did Phoebe call herself that? It's stupid. The words, the provocative images, all jangle in her brain.

'Good morning,' she says, to steady her nerves. 'It's Marcia Lennox here. The mother of—'

'Yes, I know, Mrs Lennox. What can I do for you?'

'I've found out some things, some issues I wasn't previously… and I think—' Her voice cracks and she finds she can't hold back the tears.

'Of course. I'll come to you. Tell me where you are.'

Marcia looks around her. Where is she? She's been wandering for ages. Where the hell is she? She must get a grip. Stop crying. Now!

'I'm outside Asda,' she says. 'My feet are killing me. These stupid shoes. I need to buy some trainers.'

15

Sunday, 11.10am

Boden finds Mrs Lennox sitting on a wall at the edge of the supermarket car park. She looks forlorn, barefooted, and applying blister plasters to her heels. There's a shoebox on the ground beside her and a pair of socks. She's intent on the task in hand; her feet are raw and blistered in several places.

'Looks painful,' says Boden.

Marcia Lennox's gaze flies up to her face. She seems disorientated.

'Sorry,' says Boden. 'Didn't mean to startle you.'

'I'm fine,' says Mrs Lennox. 'Could you throw these in the bin over there?'

She picks up her shoes and holds them out.

Black high heels, pointed toes with a suede finish. Extremely elegant.

'They look expensive,' says Boden. 'Are you sure you want to throw them away?'

'Of course I'm sure. Otherwise, I wouldn't ask you to do

it. They're ruined anyway.' The tone of voice is petulant but superior.

What is it about Marcia Lennox, Boden wonders? Why does this woman surround herself with such an emotional ring of steel? A missing daughter would upset any mother. No one's going to criticise her for that. There are people who use attack as a form of defence, especially when desperate; as a police officer, Boden has seen plenty of that. But there's something else here, and she can't quite put her finger on it.

The shoes are muddy, but nothing that a damp cloth wouldn't fix. Boden picks them up by their strappy backs and carries them over to the bin. Someone will have a lucky find.

Marcia Lennox puts the socks on and then removes the new trainers from their box. It strikes Boden that she walked into the store and picked the ones with highest price tag.

Boden looks around. Questioning an upset and volatile Mrs Lennox in the middle of a car park isn't a great idea.

'Fancy a coffee?' she says. 'Then you can tell me what's on your mind.'

Mrs Lennox nods. 'I was about to suggest it.' She puts on the trainers and ties them with a firm double bow.

The box and other packaging she folds neatly. 'Do you suppose they have recycling?' she says. 'I always insist we recycle. If everyone did their bit, then the planet wouldn't be in such a mess, would it?'

She chucks out the posh shoes, but wants to recycle the box?

Boden smiles. 'I agree.'

Mrs Lennox meets her gaze; it's a look of defiance. Why? Because she resents needing Boden's help? Because she regards being in control as vital to her survival? What kind of life lessons have led her to that? Perhaps she's just scared because she's facing the stark possibility that her daughter isn't coming back? Her face is tight and drawn, eyes red-rimmed from crying.

Boden takes the box and deposits it in the recycling bin and then shepherds Mrs Lennox down the road to a coffee shop.

They find a table tucked away at the back. While Boden gets the drinks, she can see Mrs Lennox scrolling on her phone. As soon as she returns to the table and sits down, Marcia Lennox places the phone in front of her. The latest iPhone, of course, with a gold back.

'This is my daughter's Instagram account,' she says. 'I would have told you about it before. Except I didn't know about it.'

'Okay,' says Boden.

'It seems Phoebe was trying to establish herself as an influencer. In the process, she may have attracted some unwanted attention.'

Boden gets out her notebook. 'You think she's been targeted by an online predator?'

'I don't know what to think. But it's something that can happen, isn't it? She's a very attractive girl.' Her delivery is clipped, as if even suggesting it risks making it true. And that thought is choking her.

'You didn't know about this before? How did you find out?'

'Jack Palmer. And my stepson, Simon.'

Boden notes down the username of the account. PhoReal. Sounds rather juvenile. And Jack Palmer again. He keeps cropping up.

'They called you?' says Boden.

'They turned up in Cambridge last night.'

Intriguing. Boden pauses and takes a sip of her coffee.

She has a plan. Of sorts. CCTV is often the key to

cracking a case, and it could offer them a quick breakthrough here. But she decides on a circuitous approach. No point in freaking Marcia Lennox out more than necessary. Once she shows her the possible sighting of her daughter, she'll be reactive.

Boden prevaricates.

'Are they still here?' she says.

'I suppose so.'

'Do you know where they're staying?'

'Probably the Hilton too.'

Boden notes this down. She writes slowly hoping Marcia will drink some of her own coffee. But Mrs Lennox has her hands clasped in her lap. She's staring at Boden like a fire-cracker about to go off.

'Has Jack Palmer ever been to Cambridge to visit your daughter since she's been here?' says Boden.

'No, I'm sure he hasn't. Phoebe would've told me.'

'And they're no longer involved?'

'No, I told you. She finished it.'

Boden takes out her own phone. Not the latest model. Nowhere near. She cleans it on her sleeve.

'Can I show you a picture?' she says. 'This is a single image we've taken from some CCTV footage. I'm afraid it's quite grainy.'

It's the best shot they have of the young man in the hoodie just before he bumped into Phoebe Lennox, if it is her, outside Sainsbury's.

'Do you recognise this man?' says Boden.

Mrs Lennox picks up the phone and peers at it. 'Who the hell is he? Has he taken Phoebe?'

'Just tell me if you recognise him?'

'No.'

Boden takes a deep breath. 'This is not Jack Palmer?'

Mrs Lennox laughs, if you can call it that. It's more like a bitter cackle.

'No,' she says. 'Jack's quite tall. Blonde wavy hair. More Greek god. I think that's how he sees himself.' She turns back to the phone. 'This young man looks mixed race, I'd say.'

'Hmm. I would too,' says Boden.

It was a bit of a punt. Much easier if it was Palmer, but, hey. It was only a guess.

'This is just a potential witness,' she says. 'But you've never seen him before?'

Mrs Lennox glares at the screen. 'No, I don't recognise him. A witness to what?'

'Have you or your husband been approached by anyone saying they know where Phoebe is and can help?'

'You mean asking for a ransom? We would've said, obviously.'

'People sometimes think they can handle it best alone. If you could check with your husband?'

Marcia Lennox gives a curt nod.

Boden takes the phone and scrolls to another image. The runner in the khaki leggings and matching vest. This time she plays a short video clip and hands it to Mrs Lennox.

'Is this Phoebe?'

As she watches the clip, Marcia Lennox's face seems to crumple. Her right hand flies to her mouth, struggling to hold back her sobs. But they erupt anyway.

'Oh my god,' she gasps. 'Oh my god…'

16

Sunday, 2.15pm

Marcia has walked for miles to clear her head. Her meeting with DS Boden wasn't long. All the stupid young woman would tell her is that the police have 'a potential witness', who Phoebe spoke to. He could be another student. The police are going round to all the other students at Phoebe's college to see if anyone knows him, which seems a rather haphazard approach to Marcia.

But the thing that's killing her is the video clip the officer showed her of Phoebe out jogging. This could be the last image she ever sees of her daughter. She's wearing the leggings and matching top that Marcia bought her back in the summer.

Marcia's parents were 'weddings and funerals' Christians. By the time she was in her teens, she was a confirmed atheist. Anything else seemed ridiculous. But as she walked away from DS Boden, and through a crowd of milling Chinese tourists gawping at King's College Chapel, she prayed. It was more like a desperate plea to any available deity. Bring Phoebe back, make it all right, and she'd believe anything. Convert to anything. If this was a test, a challenge, whatever it was, she'd got the message. She'd spend the rest of her life working in a shelter for the homeless, if only she could get her daughter back.

The new trainers have helped, cheap but serviceable. Still, by the time she walks back into the lobby of the hotel, she's exhausted and dehydrated. But punishing her body hasn't helped. She needs water to drink and a shower. Food too, although she can't face eating.

She lets herself back into the room with the keycard. The television is on; Harry is lounging on the bed watching a Formula One Grand Prix, cars roaring round the track.

He jumps up as soon as she enters.

'Where the hell have you been,' he says, clicking the TV off. 'And why haven't you been answering your bloody phone?'

Marcia has ignored his calls. But she's not about to admit it.

'I went for a walk,' she says. 'I need to take a shower.'

She goes to the fridge, takes out a bottle of water and cracks it open.

'Well, we should've checked out of the room by two,' says Harry.

'Why?'

'I only booked it for one night.'

'Then re-book it.'

'Don't you think we should head back to London?'

Marcia is peeling off her top. She stops in her tracks. 'No, Harry, I don't. Our daughter is missing.'

'And the police are looking into it. I spoke to Louisa again. Her father talked to the Assistant Chief Constable, and they've mobilised a full team with a Detective Chief Inspector co-ordinating the search.'

'So we just go back to London and leave them to it?'

Harry sighs. 'What possible good are we doing here?'

'What if they... I don't know, need us? Need some information.'

'They'll contact us. Being here, stuck in a hotel room, there's absolutely no point. It's not going to help.'

'Harry, I need to be here.'

What if they find her? What if she's hurt? What if they find a body in a ditch? What if... Scenarios flit through her brain on a loop. She can't say any of this.

She finishes taking off her top and folds it. 'I need to be here,' she repeats. 'You must make your own decision.'

'Darling,' he says, in his most whinging voice. 'Don't be like that. Obviously you're worried. And so am I.'

Worried? She feels like she's about to explode. 'You mean, as in slightly anxious?'

'No, poor choice of word.'

'Very poor,' she snaps.

He's scanning her and seems nervous.

'I've been sitting here waiting for you to come back and I've been thinking...'

And catching up on the bloody Grand Prix!

But she says, 'While I was out, I met up with that young DS. She showed me a video clip they've got from the CCTV in the town. It's of Phoebe out jogging. She wanted me to confirm her identity. And she had a picture of a young man Phoebe stopped and talked to.'

'Well, there you are,' says Harry. 'The police are doing their job. That's something, isn't it?'

'But where the hell is she? She went out for a run and

disappeared into thin air. And you just want to go home? For Chrissake, Harry!'

'It seems to me to be the most sensible thing to do. We're not achieving anything here.'

'And would it be the most sensible thing if it was Simon or Eddie missing, your two precious sons?'

'I don't see what you're driving at. I make no distinction between her and the boys. I never have.'

Marcia doesn't intend to say it, but somehow the words tumble out.

'Yes, but at the end of the day, they're yours, your flesh and blood, and she isn't, is she?'

They stare at one another across the hotel room. Marcia has her hands on her hips, a defiant stance even though she's just wearing her bra and jeans. It feels like a frozen moment, skating on thin ice towards the yawning fissure in their marriage that's always been there, just out of sight. She can tell from the shock on his face that she's found her mark.

When Harry Lennox married Marcia, she was a single parent with a small child. Harry himself was a divorced father. His record as a parent, with his own sons, was not good. The chance to have a second crack with Marcia and her perfect little girl appealed to him. Phoebe took his name and became his daughter. And Marcia knows it's true, he has never made any distinction between her and the boys. Phoebe has been the one indulged. Harry has been a better father to her, giving her more time and attention that Eddie and Simon ever received.

Harry puts his hands in his trouser pockets and turns away. 'Well,' he says, 'if that's what you think.'

It's what she thinks when she's this angry, when she's wild and mad with fear. He must realise that. She knows she should recant, apologise, step back from the brink. The spite and need to lash out at him seems to have come from nowhere. His ego can be fragile. She usually takes that into consideration; it's how their marriage has survived. Attacking Harry won't bring Phoebe home. But her head's a jumble, she can't leave Cambridge. It's impossible. He should know this.

'I need to stay here,' she says. 'And now I need to take a shower. Could you phone the reception desk and tell them we'll be keeping the room?'

She unzips her jeans and takes them off.

'Okay,' he says. 'But it's Monday tomorrow and I've got important meetings. I'm driving back to London.'

'Fine,' she says, as she walks into the bathroom and closes the door.

She turns on the shower, strips off her underwear and gets in. The steamy jets of hot water engulf and soothe her. Where does he think Phoebe is? It's almost forty-eight hours. Is he not imagining all the horrendous things that could've happened? Is he deluding himself that the police will find her and it will all turn out to be a silly misunderstanding?

The shower gel and shampoo provided by the hotel are passable. She scrubs herself and washes her hair. She steps out and envelopes herself in the towel. It was foolish to accuse him. She must explain her fears and make him see. Still, it's his fault for being stupid.

She opens the bathroom door and walks out into the room. But Harry is gone.

17

Monday, 6.50am

During her Sunday morning walk, Carol had noticed an old tumbledown barn, and that's where she took refuge when she ran. Half the roof had collapsed, but the walls were stone and solid. Through the broken door she had a broad view across the fields. It was isolated and would be hard to approach without being seen, which made it a good hiding place. There, she had a chance to calm down and think.

How could he have tracked her down?

Rosa? Surely not.

She'd made it clear to her probation officer that she was estranged from her family. And she had good reason. Rosa was sympathetic, but hinted that she thought Carol was paranoid. Rosa's mantra was: *make peace with the past.* Easy to say.

Carol knew the truth. This was not paranoia. And she should've known.

The time she served in prison was tough. In one way, it

was also safe. The walls and the razor wire provided protection from what was waiting for her on the outside. Freedom was always going to be risky. But she'd allowed herself to believe that after all these years, it would be all right.

It wasn't all right. She realised that now. He'd made his position clear. If he still had breath in his body, he'd come after her.

But what now? She's spent a cold, damp night huddled in a corner of the barn, turning over the options in her mind.

She listened to the owl screeching as it hunted, and the scurrying of rats; that didn't bother her. She's always been relaxed with animals. They went about their business and meant you no harm. Other people were always the problem.

She could try going on the run and hope the authorities pick her up first. That might work. But they might put it down to the mental stress of getting out and give her another chance. She knew the parole system; they'd twist the rules, so it didn't look like they'd failed. To ensure they banged her up again, she'd have to do something bad. A serious violation of her licence.

A part of her mind balked at that. A court convicted her of murder, but she wasn't a bad person. There was the incident in Bronzefield when she lost it, but that was the exception. Otherwise she'd been a model prisoner. It's what Mum would've expected of her.

In the end, as dawn breaks, she decides to go to work. Being in the middle of a field of cabbages or carrots, surrounded by twenty Romanian pickers, is the safest place for her right now. She senses the gang and Vasile take care of their own. With any luck, if push comes to shove, they'll include her.

As she returns to the smallholding, she finds the place

bustling with activity. Two pickups are standing, engines running, people clambering into the back.

Vasile is hyper; issuing instructions and giving directions.

He waves his arm at Carol and shouts. 'Hey, wanna make some money? We got rush job, big bonus.'

Why not? Safest place.

'Yeah,' says Carol.

Vasile points. 'In truck.'

Carol climbs aboard. The half a dozen other pickers make room for her. The vehicles roar off up the lane. Carol hangs on, the wind buffets her, but the rush and speed are liberating.

By seven thirty, she's in an enormous field of celery.

Vasile has been hired as a subcontractor on this mega-farm. It grows vegetables on a vast scale and is short-staffed on one of its rigs. Carol overhears her boss's conversation with the English farm manager. The regular crews the farm uses are Polish or Lithuanian. The manager's tone and Vasile's obsequious manner suggest that Romanians are way down the pecking order. But this is an emergency and an opportunity for Vasile's crew to prove their worth.

At one end of the field, an enormous mobile factory processing unit is ready to go. A fellow picker hands Carol a lethal-looking machete. The rig starts up and they begin.

Working in a line, the pickers move along next to the rig. They bend, grab a celery stick, chop it off at the base, cut the top, hack off the leaves and place it on the moving conveyor belt that carries it up into the processing area of the rig where it is sized, washed and wrapped. The whole cavalcade moves forward through the muddy field at a slow shuffle.

Carol soon gets the hang of the repetitive process, but keeping up with the others is hard. It takes all her concentration and determination to keep pace with them. Her hands are not as dexterous, she fumbles, and her back is killing her. But she grits her teeth. Physical pain she can handle. She focuses on the job.

The first hour is the hardest. But after a while she settles into a rhythm. And eventually the harsh physical labour frees her mind from fear. She has no mental space for anything but chopping celery.

18

Monday, 9am

The morning briefing begins on the dot. Two DCs and another analyst have joined the team. Boden watches DCI Hepburn stride to the front of the room; he's suited and booted with a maroon silk tie, which means he knows they're under scrutiny. What is he thinking? If they find a body and this breaks, he'll be facing the media?

Boden worked the whole weekend, as did Prisha. The download of Phoebe Lennox's phone arrived from digital investigations late on Sunday. Scott Mackie came back in on Sunday afternoon when he got wind that this could turn into a major case. They're still waiting for the DI to return from his sickbed.

'Right,' says Hepburn. 'Thanks to everyone who's worked double shifts on this. To summarise: Phoebe Lennox is eighteen. She's a first-year student who disappeared around 5pm on Friday. This is what we have: CCTV of her out jogging; an encounter with a young man, who we've yet to identify; no reasonable explanations for where she could've gone and why. She took nothing with her. Plus, we have an ex-boyfriend, who is of interest. Scott, you've been looking at the boyfriend. Can you tell us more?'

Jo Boden sighs. Here we go again. Knee-jerk reaction. He goes straight to Mackie. But she's the one who spent most of Sunday afternoon digging into Jack Palmer's background. And when Mackie finally appeared, she despatched him to the Hilton to see if Palmer had come to Cambridge by car.

Mackie stands up with a swagger. He shoots a glance in Boden's direction and smiles.

'Yes, boss,' he says. 'We became interested in the car Jack Palmer drives. He lives in London, he's currently in Cambridge, and he's been staying at the Hilton since yesterday. But we're wondering if this is a bit of a ruse and he was also here on Friday at the time of Lennox's disappearance.'

Boden and Prisha exchange glances. They'd wondered about this first. The obvious lines of inquiry are the hoodie that Phoebe Lennox talked to outside Sainsbury's, and the ex-boyfriend. They've been digging into the data on the phone and sorting it into categories. But there's tons of it. Prisha has been going through the posts by PhoReal, the influencer; it's a huge task and raises the question: was she identified and targeted on social media?

'I went to the hotel, and I got lucky,' says Mackie. 'It seems Palmer's stinking rich. He drives a Ferrari Portofino. A red one. It was in the hotel garage. I saw it, very cool. I got the registration and confirmed the ownership. We can get on to the National ANPR Data Centre and see if he was here on Friday. And then put a marker on the car. Find out where he goes. Could lead us straight to her.'

Mackie beams as if he's cracked the case and is waiting for the applause. Hepburn folds his arms. Boden waits.

'Well,' says the DCI drily. 'As far as I'm aware, at present, Mr Palmer has committed no crime, apart from being stinking rich, and is not, to our knowledge, a member of an organised criminal group. What grounds do we have for targeting him?'

Mackie's face falls. He stares. 'Oh, yeah, and we'll need a surveillance authority. Of course.'

Boden smiles to herself. They'll need that for a marker on Palmer's car and future updates. But they could do a one-off check on the past data without it.

She watches Hepburn. Maybe she's misjudged him? Mackie walked straight into the trap. She could almost feel sorry for him. But Hepburn's making a point. This could turn into a high-profile case. And he wants everything by the book.

She clears her throat and says, 'Perhaps I can help, sir.'

Hepburn gives her a thin smile. 'Yes, Jo. I wish you would.'

Boden stands up and holds her notebook in front of her. 'Jack Palmer is twenty-seven, privately educated then went to Oxford. Qualified as a lawyer but works for a City investment bank, which was set up by his great grandfather and in which the family retains an interest. As Scott has already said, rich. Last summer he was romantically involved with Phoebe Lennox. But she dumped him. Her parents say he admitted to putting a spy app on her phone. So he could be stalking her. An initial trawl through the texts on her phone reveals that he often contacts her several times a day. It's banter. She doesn't always answer him. There's a sense she is holding him at arm's length. Nothing conclusive in that, except he has form. At Oxford, aged twenty, he was charged with sexual assault against a fellow student. Charges were dropped, she accepted a financial settlement and signed a non-disclosure agreement.

His college reversed a decision to expel him after representations from his family.'

Hepburn smiles and nods. 'Thank you, Jo.' He looks at Mackie. 'I'd say that constitutes grounds. DC Mackie, you may liaise with Hendon and track his Ferrari. And get on with it. Clock's ticking. If she got in his car, if we even suspect it but can't prove it, I want to know ASAP.'

'Yes, boss,' says Mackie. He sits down, looking sheepish.

The DCI turns back to Boden. 'Okay,' he says. 'Let's invite Mr Palmer in. Helping with our inquiries. See how he reacts. Nothing heavy. Are you ready for that?'

'Yes, sir,' says Boden. 'More than ready.'

She smiles to herself. Thank you Mackie, for being a fool. Now at least she has the chance to show the DCI what she can do.

19

Monday, 10.05am

Marcia wakes with a start. A moment of panic. Where is she? It takes several seconds for the heavy drapes and the anonymous lines of the hotel room to register. She's in Cambridge. Is it still night? She climbs out of bed, pulls back the curtains and the room floods with light.

The sudden brightness startles her, and she shields her eyes. Her mind is full of dread. For long hours, she scrolled through pictures of her daughter on social media. Her vanilla Instagram account; Phoebe the diligent student. And then the other posts of a young woman flaunting herself to get attention.

After that, she tossed and turned, half-sleeping, half-waking, her brain brimming with dark fantasies.

She slept in the hotel bathrobe. Her mouth is dry, and she has a niggling headache. When she moves, she gets a shooting pain up the back of her neck. Too much tension.

She needs coffee and a shower.

Her phone says it's after ten. That's crazy. She never sleeps this late. She checks for messages — a slew of work-related texts and emails, but nothing from her husband.

Harry is a sulker; it's one of his less attractive traits. But he'll come round.

Marcia uses bottled water from the fridge to fill the reservoir in the coffeemaker. As she takes a couple of swigs, she notices there are the four G&T cans in the bin. Explains the headache. She never drinks. Hates the loss of control. And feeling like this.

Concentrate. She can't collapse now. Her daughter needs her.

She begins a new list.

One: get some new clothes. She'll need fresh underwear, a couple of tops and some smarter trousers. Harry must stop being silly, return to Cambridge, and bring her something decent to wear.

Two: she must contact the DCI, who's in charge, and arrange a proper meeting. Harry said he was going into the office, so his best bet will be to come back on the train. She looks up the King's Cross to Cambridge service. There's a fast train every half hour, and it takes forty-eight minutes. If he can make it to the station in the next hour, he could be back in Cambridge before midday.

She rings his mobile. He doesn't pick up.

She sends a text: *I'm arranging a meeting with the senior policeman. I need you to be here.* As an afterthought she adds an *x*. He doesn't deserve it. He walked out and abandoned her.

The message delivers. She waits.

She presses the button on the coffeemaker and watches it. Her brain is nattering with impatience. It takes a good thirty seconds for the element to heat up, then it gurgles and delivers a stream of dark liquid into the mug. The other thing she needs is Xanax; there are only two tablets remaining in the blister pack in her bag.

She picks up her phone and looks at it. Nothing. She takes a sip of coffee. He's being ridiculous. And that leaves her no alternative.

She scrolls to find the office number of his PA and clicks on it.

One ring and it connects.

Marcia dives straight in.

'Hayley,' she says. 'Good morning, it's Marcia. Is my husband there? It's rather urgent.'

'He's in with Tom, Mrs Lennox. But I will see if I can get his attention.'

Moments pass. She never drums her fingernails. Why ruin a good manicure? She wonders about the Xanax. Should she take one of them now? Or wait, in case she can't get any more? Take some painkillers for the headache. Sensible.

The line clicks; the PA's transferring the call.

'Marcia.' He sounds irritated. He's the one who should apologise after stomping off like some moody teenager.

'I'm arranging a meeting—'

'I've already spoken to him.'

'What?'

'DCI Hepburn. The officer in charge. We spoke on the phone this morning. You may think that I have no concern for our daughter's welfare, but that's not true. He seems a very capable chap, and he's assured me he and his team are working flat out to find Phoebe.'

'Well, what did he say?'

'I've just told you.'

'Yes, but what are they actually doing?'

'Marcia, you have to stop. They're not about to share the

details with us. We have to trust that they know what they're doing.'

'But what if—'

'I am as concerned and worried as you are. Whatever you say, she is my daughter.' The tone is haughty and aggrieved. Her heart sinks.

'Harry, I didn't mean to—'

'Oh yeah, you did. But when you ride roughshod over people's feelings all the time, it has consequences. I've tried my level best with you, Marcia.'

She hates it when he does this. Me, me, me. Oh, poor bloody Harry! It's always about him.

But she takes a breath and reins herself in. 'I was upset, and I lashed out. I'm sorry. But surely the important thing here is Phoebe. That should be our focus.'

She hears him snort. He wants a righteous rant, to dump all his pent-up feelings on her and she's undercut him.

'Well,' he says peevishly. 'I don't see what else we can do. And if you want my honest opinion, I think she'll turn up. I will have words with her when she does. But I don't believe she's been kidnapped off the streets of Cambridge by Jack or anyone else.'

This is Harry all over. If something doesn't suit him, he denies it's real. He retreats.

'Harry, think about it. What if someone bundled her into a car? This stuff happens.' Marcia hears the whine of desperation in her own voice, and she hates it.

'In the middle of Cambridge at five o'clock in the afternoon? People everywhere, CCTV cameras? If there was any evidence of it, the police would've found it. And they haven't.'

'He told you that?'

'He knows what he's doing, Marcia.'

'But he didn't tell you that?'

'I don't know what you want from me or what you expect me to do. The police will sort this out.'

Marcia sighs. She wants him to be with her, to hold her in his arms, to stroke her hair and whisper words of comfort.

'You're not coming back to Cambridge?' she says.

'I can't. I told you, I've got meetings back to back all day. The world can't stop because Phoebe's gone off and done something daft.'

Something daft?

'Harry, no one's heard from her or seen her. She's got no money, no phone—'

'I'm sorry. I have to go.'

The line goes dead. Marcia stares at the phone.

She can feel her heart pounding in her chest and she wants to scream.

But she gets it. This refusal to even consider that something bad has happened to their daughter, that's his way of coping. He can't let it be real. In the privileged bubble of Harry's world, bad things don't happen, not to him. The idea is too horrific. He won't accept it.

And now the depth of his pain hits her. He's hurting as much as her. She wishes she could reach out and comfort him.

But there's nothing either of them can do.

They're both waiting for their lives to be upended by the news no parent ever wants to hear. You see it on the television news from time to time: *the body found in undergrowth on the outskirts of Cambridge has been identified as—*

It feels like there's a dense choking smog rolling towards her. Soon it will swallow her up.

20

Monday, 11.15am

The interview room is in the bowels of the building, close to the custody suite. It's small and claustrophobic. Boden gives Jack Palmer about five minutes to absorb his depressing surroundings.

The cameras in the interview room live-stream into the office network. She looks at him on her desktop. He shows no sign of impatience. He's tall and muscular, an expensive linen shirt and faded jeans. His hair is shaved up the back and sides, but with a mass of blond curls on top. Boden wouldn't call him classically good-looking; his face is long and lupine. But he's still handsome.

Mackie is her back up for the interview. She hopes that another large, testosterone driven male in the room might challenge Palmer enough to unnerve him. But Mackie has been instructed to leave the questioning to Boden. Hepburn will watch from his office.

The two officers walk in and take their seats.

'Sorry to keep you waiting, Mr Palmer,' she says. 'I'm DS Boden and this is my colleague, DC Mackie.'

'Not a problem, Sergeant,' says Palmer with a warm smile. 'I want to do whatever I can to help find Phoebe.'

'And thank you for coming in so promptly. Can we offer you a coffee?'

'I'm fine.' He laces and unlaces his fingers. Fidgety. Possibly not as confident as he appears.

'Right,' says Boden. 'Let's begin. Have you been in touch with Phoebe in the last few days?'

'The odd text.'

The odd? Prisha has counted twenty-five over three days.

'She didn't mention that she intended to go away for the weekend?'

'No, not at all. Beginning of term, loads going on. Why would she?'

'It's our understanding, from Phoebe's parents, that you placed some sort of spy app on her phone. Why did you do this?'

Palmer lounges back in his chair and tilts his head. 'I should probably begin by explaining something of the background to all this and my relationship with the family. Would that be okay?'

He glances from Boden to Mackie and back, asking permission and waiting.

'Please do,' she replies.

He smiles. His eyes rest on Boden's face. She can feel his focus on her and a few pheromones. It would be easy to be charmed by Jack Palmer. He is fanciable, and he knows it.

'I've been close friends with Simon since primary school,' he says. 'I went to both his houses lots. Phoebe is nine years younger than us, and I watched her grow up. Simon's father, Harry, is a lovely bloke, very chilled, I always got on well with him. Marcia, his stepmother, is a different proposition. She's quite uptight and opinionated. As boys, she always made us take off our shoes. No rough play indoors. She hates any kind of mess or disorder. With Phoebe, she's always been overprotective. Wouldn't let her do anything risky. And, as I'm sure you can imagine, the older Phoebe got, the more this became a problem. Phoebe fell off her bicycle when she was about fifteen. Nothing serious, but her mother banned her from riding it again. Then when she was seventeen and wanted to learn to drive, Marcia refused to let her. Said she must wait until she was eighteen. She finally passed her test in the summer.'

'You're saying you think Marcia Lennox is controlling when it comes to her daughter?'

'I was being polite, but yes. Phoebe used to kick off in reaction, but only ever minor stuff. And she'd get grounded for silly things.'

'Like what?'

'When she was sixteen, she went to a pub with some school friends, using a fake ID. I mean, come on, everyone does it, but Marcia went ballistic. Like it was some kind of personal betrayal and Phoebe was about to turn into an alcoholic. Harry had to weigh in and calm Marcia down.'

'Calm her down? Would Marcia have hurt Phoebe?'

'Oh God, no. No one, including her, could lay a finger on her precious daughter. Phoebe's her princess and Marcia wanted to keep her in a gilded cage. But Phoebe soon learnt to play along with her mother to get what she wanted. She's clever, did well at school, got into Cambridge. But by then, both Simon and I knew Phoebe was lying to her parents about quite a lot of stuff. Presumably you know about her Instagram page and YouTube?'

'Why didn't she tell her parents about that?'

'I think Phoebe just wanted some space in her life where Marcia wasn't trying to control everything she did. Which brings me to the spy app. Simon and I discussed it. We thought there was a good chance that once she was at uni, Phoebe would go wild. Now she didn't have Marcia on her case 24/7. It worried us. We decided to keep tabs on her.'

'In a brotherly way?' says Boden.

Palmer grins, 'Yeah, okay. You're going to ask me about my involvement with Phoebe back in the summer. We had a house party in Ibiza. My parents have a place there. I was surprised Marcia let Phoebe come. Anyway, it was just a bit of fun. And it was no big deal. I wasn't the first guy Phoebe slept with, if that's your next question. You've seen the pictures. She's gorgeous. She's been turning heads since she was fifteen.'

'Perhaps Mrs Lennox could see that, which is why she was protective?'

Palmer nods. 'That's a fair point. But Phoebe could take care of herself, believe me. She wanted to go to uni unencumbered. And I accepted that. We're just friends.'

'She dumped you?'

'It wasn't like that. It was only ever a casual thing. We were both happy to move on. By mutual agreement.'

'But you still texted frequently?'

'Only as mates. I text all my mates.'

'You weren't upset?'

He chuckles. 'She's a beautiful girl, but she's high-maintenance.'

'I'm never sure what that means,' says Boden.

'In Phoebe's case, it means living in a whirlwind. It never ever stops. She's always got some new scheme. She'll calm down, eventually. But I like an easier life.'

He glances at Mackie for the first time and smiles. Some attempt at male solidarity?

'Was Cambridge her choice or her parents?' says Boden.

'Oh, hers. She's ambitious. I think Harry would've preferred Oxford, which is where he went. Not sure where Marcia went. Somewhere else, I assume.'

'When's the last time you saw her, Mr Palmer?' says Boden.

Palmer scratches his head. 'End of September, maybe three or four weeks ago. She was about to leave for uni and a whole gang of us went clubbing.'

'You haven't visited her in Cambridge?'

'No.'

'Marcia Lennox thinks you may be obsessed with Phoebe.'

He shakes his head and sighs. 'That's just not true. Marcia's never liked me.'

'Why do you think that is?'

Palmer frowns. 'I'm not sure. Sometimes she's chippy about people who are wealthy. I think it makes her uncomfortable.'

'She and her husband seem well off by most people's standards. Why would that worry her?'

'Well, yes, but my family is in banking. It's serious money. And yeah, it's been easier for me than most people. But I can't help where I was born. And I appreciate how lucky I am.'

Boden looks down at her notes. 'There was an incident when you were a student at Oxford. You were charged with sexually assaulting a fellow student. Although the charge was dropped.'

Palmer sighs and shrugs his shoulders. 'I was twenty. I got steaming drunk, and I behaved in a completely horrible and unacceptable way. The girl involved, Eleanor, was very upset at the time. And rightly so. But, once we sobered up, I apologised unreservedly, and she was generous enough to forgive me.'

'Did it help that your father was generous enough to pay her some money?'

'Okay, I know what that looks like. Looks like we bought her off.'

'Did you?'

'Eleanor is brilliant, but her family had no money. She was struggling financially, racking up debt. My father paid her fees for the rest of the course. Seemed like the decent thing to do. But she has forgiven me. She got married last year to a friend of mine and I was an usher at their wedding.'

Boden watches him, the body language has become a little more tense. But he's still making direct eye contact. She's trying to get a sense of him, a subliminal feel for the man underneath. But she's not sure. He's confident and over-entitled. Smart enough to know what the police want to hear. He could be telling the truth. The story is plausible enough.

Or they could be dealing with a charming psychopath.

'Where do you think Phoebe is, Mr Palmer?'

He inhales and folds his arms. 'I just don't know. I wish I did. Phoebe can be unpredictable. And I worry her online success has made her a target.'

Boden waits a moment. Jack Palmer dips his head and swallows hard. 'But I'm really worried about her. You will find her, won't you?' He looks up, straight at her, tears glistening on his long, sandy lashes.

'We're doing our best,' says Boden. 'Thank you for coming in, Mr Palmer.'

Once he's been escorted out by a uniformed officer, Boden turns to Mackie.

'Gut reaction?' she says.

Mackie huffs. 'He's a lying creep.'

21

Monday, 12.35pm

'Oh, my god! Is she dead?' Marcia blurts out the question as soon as she opens the door of her hotel room and finds DS Boden standing there.

Boden seems startled. 'No, Mrs Lennox. Can we come in? Just a quick chat.'

Marcia stands back and lets the police follow her into the room. The sergeant has the same young Asian girl with her, DC Something-or-other.

Now she's embarrassed. She doesn't want them to see the state she's in.

'You remember my colleague, DC Chakravorty?' says the sergeant. 'She's noticed something on the CCTV that we want to ask you about. Is that okay?'

Marcia rakes her fingers through her hair. She's drunk too much coffee; it's made her jittery. In the end, she didn't take a shower. Since her conversation with Harry on the phone, she's been pacing and trying to figure out what to do. She's still wearing the hotel bathrobe she slept in.

'Of course,' she says.

The fight has gone out of her, in terms of the police. Perhaps Harry is right and they do know what they're doing? She needs to get her head straight. But everything is spiralling out of control. She's stuck in a nightmare and can't wake up.

The DC takes an iPad out of her shoulder bag and opens the cover.

'We're going to show you a short sequence from the CCTV footage we've gathered,' says the sergeant. 'And it's of your daughter.'

Marcia swallows. At least it's not a body. Not yet.

'Is that okay?' says the sergeant.

'I assume you've got a reason,' she says stiffly.

The young DC holds the iPad out for her to view and presses play.

On screen, Phoebe is running along the pavement; her lovely, loping stride makes it appear easy. The sight of her brings a lump to Marcia's throat. Concentrate!

The road is well lit, Phoebe zigzags around other pedestrians. Harry's right, busy streets. Surely someone will have seen what happened. People wouldn't just stand by and ignore a kidnapping.

'Here's the thing we noticed,' says the sergeant.

Marcia stares at the screen. What are they talking about? It's just Phoebe running.

'I don't see what you mean.' She feels desperate. Is she being stupid?

'Let's take another look,' says the sergeant.

The DC rewinds the clip and replays it.

This time the sergeant adds a commentary. 'She's running

along the pavement. Going at a good speed. And here we go. She puts her hand up to her ear. As if she's adjusting or checking some kind of earpiece. She takes her hand down and, although it's difficult to see, there is something dark in her ear.'

'She's got the same Bluetooth earbuds as me. They're black. They hook over the ear,' says Marcia.

'And you use them to listen to music while you run?'

'Yes. I do.'

'Well,' says the sergeant. 'We assumed that because Phoebe's phone was left in her room, she wasn't listening to music.'

'She always used to.' It was the idiot tutor who'd persuaded her not to. But Marcia decides not to mention that.

'Could she be listening to her music on another device? An old iPod or perhaps she has a smart watch?'

'She has a playlist on her phone she made for running. That's how she's always listened. She used to share tracks with me.'

Another everyday thing that's become a poignant memory. The tears are welling. She doesn't want to cry in front of these young police officers. Not again. It's too shaming.

'We think she is running to music,' says the sergeant. 'Which raises the question, could she have a second phone?'

'A second phone?'

'Quite a few people do. If she has two, perhaps a newer one recently acquired, then it makes sense she left the other one on the shelf. Do you think she could've bought herself a new phone? Would she have the money to do that?'

Marcia's head is aching. A new phone? And she didn't tell her?

'Is there a limit on her credit card? Do you know what it is?'

The two police officers are staring right at her. It's unnerving. It's as if they suspect her of some wrongdoing. But perhaps this is how the police always look at people.

'I don't,' she says. 'I'd need to ask my husband. Harry is quite strict with her. She has her allowance and she must pay her own bills. But, I suppose, yes, she could've bought a new phone.'

Her thoughts are reeling. More secrets. More subterfuge. Why? Did Phoebe not trust her?

'I understand this is all very difficult, Mrs Lennox.' The sergeant seems to be reading her mind. 'But when you're eighteen and you first go to uni, it's a big thing. Most people don't tell their parents everything. It's not really lying. It's about finding your feet.'

Marcia stares at the sergeant. What does she know about it? What does she know about Phoebe? About how hard it's been.

'Do you lie to your mother?' she says sharply.

The sergeant gives her a wistful smile. 'I used to. Not anymore.'

The young DC pipes up. 'I try not to lie to my mother. But there's loads of stuff I don't share with her, because I don't want her to be upset or always worrying.'

What are they talking about? Her relationship with Phoebe is completely different. She's not like them. She wants to say that. But she says nothing.

They're watching her with expressionless faces. She feels accused, accused of being a terrible mother. But she's not some whining nag who dumps her anxiety on her daughter. She's always protected Phoebe from that. Kept her intimate thoughts and fears to herself. The past, the mistakes she's made, that's her burden, not her daughter's.

The sergeant seems to be waiting for her to speak. So she says, 'What does any of this mean?'

'We're not sure yet.'

'That she could've gone off and done something daft? That's what my husband thinks.'

'You know your own daughter, Mrs Lennox. Does she go off and do unpredictable things?'

'If you'd asked me a few days ago, I'd have said no. Absolutely not. Phoebe's sensible. But even if she has got another phone, why hasn't she called or texted to tell us?'

'Does she have any reason to be upset with you?'

'No!'

'Not some kind of disagreement, where she might be sulking and want to teach you a lesson?'

'No.' She sighs and adds, 'I don't think so. The last time I saw her was three weeks ago. We brought her up, and I helped her unpack.' She presses her fingernails hard into her palm. The sharp stab of pain helps her focus.

'I'm sorry we have to ask these things,' says the sergeant. 'But we need to examine the possibility that Phoebe doesn't want to be found. People run away all the time, often just temporarily. It's by far the most common reason that people go missing. Foul play is only involved in a minority of cases, which is the good news.'

'She has not run away!'

'I'm just telling you the statistics, because I want you to think carefully about anywhere your daughter could've gone, for any reason.'

'Of course I've been asking myself that.' Marcia sits down on the bed. 'And I'm at my wits' end.'

The two detectives exchange looks.

Then the sergeant says, 'Just one other thing before we go. How close is Phoebe to your stepson, Simon?'

'Simon? Well, they've always got on. I think she prefers him to Eddie, that's Harry's elder son. Eddie's geekier and more reserved. But Simon's much more easygoing. And slightly closer in age.'

The sergeant nods and exchanges another glance with the DC.

'Okay,' she says. 'That's really helpful.'

'In what way? I don't understand.'

There's something they're not telling her. What has Simon got to do with this? Has he helped Jack kidnap Phoebe? Could he know where she is?

'Oh,' says the sergeant. 'I just mean this whole conversation has been helpful.'

It sounds polite and vague because they don't want to tell her the truth. They turn towards the door. They're about to leave. Marcia feels a surge of panic.

'But... what happens now?' she says. 'What am I supposed to do? Should I stay here?'

The sergeant turns. 'That's up to you, Mrs Lennox.'

'Up to me? How?'

'My advice would be, go home. We have all your details and we will keep in close contact.'

'Do you think something bad's happened? I'd rather be told. If you're looking for a body—'

'If we believed she was dead, we would tell you. Trying to find someone who's disappeared is a laborious process. We have all kinds of information to sift through. But we're putting a lot of resources into this.'

Marcia swallows down a tear. 'That's because you've been leant on, isn't it? I should apologise for that.'

The sergeant smiles. 'Don't. If it was my daughter, I'd do

everything I could. Try to move heaven and earth. We all would. What you have to do now is the hardest thing. Go home and wait.'

Marcia nods. 'Thank you.'

The sergeant nods back. 'We'll be in touch.'

22

Monday, 12.40pm

Lacey is bunking off school. Mondays are the worst day of the week. Teachers hungover and snippy, the most boring lessons, everyone feeling pissed off and mean. She walked down the lane to the school bus at the usual time, then doubled back over the fields and slipped into the barn. Now she's tucked away between the bales, warm and snug with Daisy for company.

The weekend was crap. Everything has gone wrong. At first she couldn't believe it. To say she was disappointed is an understatement. She's been betrayed. None of this could've happened without her. Steve knows that. Yet he acted as if she wasn't there. As if she didn't matter. She was just a kid. Someone to be ignored. He's used her. They all have.

She's already eaten her packed lunch and half the Celebrations tub of chocolates she stole from the cupboard. She felt she deserved something. Her mum stockpiles this stuff;

she has a larder full of canned food and two extra freezers in the outhouse to prepare for the Day of Judgement.

Most of the morning Lacey's been online and chatting. At least there she's appreciated. She has friends who understand. And everyone agrees she's been treated like shit.

people let you down babes
fuck's sake don't I know it
stay strong lol

On Friday night, she had such hopes. But the old man took over. It became all about him. Usually he sits back and lets her mum do the talking. Mum is a preacher and an elder in the church. He never says much, just nods a bit and listens. Every bloody Sunday they have to go. Twice!

Mum's big on forgiveness and salvation. But you only get forgiven if you repent, admit your sins and join the church. And not any church. All the others are bogus. To be one of the Lord's chosen and be saved on the Day of Judgement, it must be this specific church. Lacey has always wondered why, in the entire world, God should decide to gather his chosen flock in an old wooden hut with a leaky roof in Essex. But Mum says he glories in the meek.

Well, Dad wasn't being very meek on Friday. It was like he was transformed. Okay, it was his birthday. Lacey bought him socks. Not that he showed the least interest in that. He went on and on about how he'd prayed for this day.

He may have prayed for it. But prayer didn't do it. Lacey did. She made it happen. And that's been ignored.

And Uncle Brian sat in his armchair, like the slimy toad he is, lapping it all up.

Lacey wonders if she should run away, disappear into thin air. Then they'd all sit up and take notice. Or maybe they wouldn't even care. But where would she go?

She takes one last look at *PhoReal*. It's been the focus of her life for months. She scrolls through the pictures. She's is so beautiful and special. Always telling you such cool things. And posting little messages and poems that are obviously for Lacey. You can be who you want to be if you dream big enough. It was like becoming friends with a movie star. This is the Phoebe she wants to remember.

They only found her because of Lacey. Without her, they'd never have known. But now she realises she's been conned. Steve was lying all along. No one gives a stuff about her.

She cuddles Daisy. But the dog whines. It wants biscuits from the celebration tin. Lacey pushes the greedy little shitbag away. Everyone's in it for themselves. She hates them all, her family, the whole world. She hopes her mum's right and the Day of Judgement comes soon. Blow it all up with fire and fury so there's nothing and no one left. That's the best thing. It would serve them all right.

23

Monday, 3.55pm

Marcia Lennox took the train back to London. Her panic subsided; it was impossible to sustain. Her exhausted brain craved sleep, but it wouldn't come. For most of the journey she gazed out of the window at the flat East Anglian landscape, the heart of agribusiness. Vast fields stretching away to the horizon, acres of plastic poly tunnels producing year-round fruit and vegetables.

She hates the countryside; it depresses her. The mud, the mess, the awful smells. Heaps of rotting manure, the acrid stench of chicken farms, once smelt, never forgotten. When she goes outside, she likes her surroundings to be civilised. Richmond Park is lovely. The deer run free and if some of them end up on a plate in a high-end restaurant, it's not something she needs to think about.

She ordered a private hire car to drive her home from King's Cross. Harry has an account. She rarely uses the tube anymore if she can avoid it. That's in the distant past, struggling up and down steps with a baby and a buggy. The occasional helping hand, but most people barging by.

She didn't expect her husband to be at home and he wasn't, which was a relief. Stripping off her clothes, she took a long, hot shower.

Her hair is still wrapped in a towel and she's wearing a silk kimono when the doorbell rings. Her first impulse is to ignore it. But the caller is persistent. It could be important.

She opens the door and gets a shock. Louisa Muirhead, Harry's first wife, is standing on the doorstep smiling at her.

'Sorry if I've caught you on the hop,' she says. 'I wondered if we could have a chat.' She makes it sound as if popping round is a regular occurrence.

In all the years of her marriage to Harry, there have been half a dozen encounters between the two wives, always at large social gatherings: christenings, weddings, funerals. They've never spoken more than a dozen words to one another. Louisa's attitude to her successor has been one of disdain.

But here she is with a look of friendly expectancy.

'Do come in,' says Marcia. What else can she do?

With her hair wrapped in a towel, she feels like a washerwoman which is probably how Louisa would see it. Her predecessor may be much older, tall and gangly, a large-limbed woman who makes no attempt to disguise her grey hair. But even in what looks like an old Barbour, she exudes a confidence and dignity that Marcia envies.

She steps into the hallway and looks around, 'Oh this is lovely,' she says. 'And I'm sure this is nothing to do with Harry. You have such good taste, Marcia.'

What the hell does she want? To come and gloat?

Marcia paints on a smile. 'Thank you. Can I offer you a cup of tea?'

Louisa flaps her hand. 'Just point me towards the kitchen and I'll make it. You probably want to dry your hair.'

Marcia opens her mouth and shuts it again. How can she say no?

'Down here, is it?' says Louisa, pointing.

'Yes, the china's in the cupboard at the end.'

More hand flapping. Louisa is already off. 'Don't worry, I'll find it.'

Marcia turns and sprints up the stairs two at a time. She rips off the kimono, flings it on the bed and blow dries her hair in record time. She puts on a skinny sports top and leggings that show off her slender, athletic figure. Stand the two women side by side and it should be clear why Harry divorced one and married the other. She reminds herself of this, but it doesn't help.

When Marcia enters the kitchen, she finds Louisa perched on a stool at the breakfast bar eating chocolate biscuits from a packet. She's made a pot of tea, found two mugs and taken a carton of milk from the fridge.

'I expect you're rather surprised to see me,' she says, peering at Marcia over her scarlet-framed glasses, which match her lipstick.

'Harry and I are very grateful that you persuaded your father to intervene on our behalf.'

'Oh, my dear, he didn't need persuading. He adores Phoebe. We all do. Is there any news?'

'No.'

She takes a stool on the other side of the breakfast bar and almost jumps out of her skin when Louisa reaches across with her bony, bejewelled hand, grabs Marcia's arm and squeezes it.

'The family is right behind you, my dear. We want you to know that. Awful business.'

'Thank you,' says Marcia. She's determined not to cry. Not in front of Louisa Muirhead.

Louisa pours her a mug of her own tea. She slops some of it on the counter. Marcia wants to get a cloth and wipe it up. But she resists.

'I wanted to talk to you about Simon,' says Louisa. 'He's got himself in a bit of a spin.'

'Oh?' says Marcia.

'The police questioned Jack Palmer this morning. But I expect you know that.'

Marcia says nothing. She has no intention of admitting her ignorance. What's going on? The police did ask her about Simon.

'I make no secret of the fact I've never liked my son's friendship with that boy,' says Louisa.

This is the first Marcia's heard of it.

'Especially after that business at Oxford.'

'What business?' says Marcia.

'I thought Harry would've told you. Jack tried to rape some poor girl, but he was too drunk to get it up. They charged him with sexual assault. But his father bought the girl off.'

Marcia takes a moment to digest this. Her daughter has slept with a rapist?

'Of course, when people have that sort of money,' says Louisa, 'there's not a lot to be done. But I told Harry to speak to our son. And I told Simon in no uncertain terms that he should steer clear of Jack Palmer. But he thinks I'm a nagging old bat and refuses to listen.'

Marcia feels sick. Harry let Phoebe go to Ibiza and stay in the house of a rapist? He even persuaded her to go along with it, against her better judgement.

'The problem is, Harry is far too soft with the boy,' says

Louisa. 'He doesn't like arguments and unpleasantness, takes the easy way out. Well, I'm sure you know this. How long have you been married now?'

'Sixteen years.'

Louisa nods, sighs, and takes a sip of tea.

It's impossible to tell what she's thinking. And Marcia doesn't care.

'Why is Simon in a spin?' she says.

'He regards Phoebe as a sister. I think he's worried that Jack may well have done something, and people will assume he knew about it.'

She means the police. She's worried her precious son is next on their list.

'Done what?' says Marcia. 'Does Simon know where she is?'

'Absolutely not. I have asked him straight and insisted he tell me the truth.'

'Are you aware Jack's been stalking Phoebe? He put an app on her phone.'

Louisa sighs. 'Oh, how awful. Well, I'm sure Simon knew nothing about that.'

'He did. He came with Jack to tell us about it on Saturday. That's how we found out she'd disappeared.'

Louisa takes off her glasses. She pulls out a tissue that she has tucked up her sleeve. Marcia has a sudden flash of memory: her mother always tucked a cotton hanky up her cardigan sleeve. There's a tightness like a fist in her chest. No, can't think about that now. She pushes the thought firmly away.

Louisa polishes her glasses with the tissue and shakes her head.

'Marcia,' she says. 'I am really sorry. I don't know what to say.'

'Well,' says Marcia. 'The matter is in the hands of the police. And I expect they will want to speak to Simon.'

She meets Louisa's gaze and has the small satisfaction of seeing the worry in her eyes. It will only be a fraction of the pain she's suffering. But life never deals a fair hand, she already knows that.

24

Monday, 5.15pm

'What we seem to have here, boss,' says Boden, 'is an interesting little romantic triangle. Jack Palmer, Simon Lennox, and Phoebe.'

'She's been having it off with her half-brother?' says DCI Hepburn.

'If you go back to the summer, that's what we're getting from the texts. Her and Jack. Her and Simon. And possibly all three of them together.'

The DCI raises his eyebrows and looks at DC Chakravorty. 'How the other half live, eh Prisha?'

'Sir,' says the DC, shifting nervously from foot to foot.

They're in Hepburn's office, standing in front of his desk. The room is small and functional. He's by the window, hands in his pockets, staring out. It's already dark and lights are on in office windows across the street.

Boden is exhausted. She's dreaming of a soak in the bath followed by a curry and catching up with the latest episode of

Strictly. Sad life of an overworked and lonely cop. Don't think about that. This could still be her big break.

Hepburn shakes his head.

'But this all seems to have been going on before she came to Cambridge,' says Boden. 'We can't find any direct reference to either Jack or Simon visiting her in the last three weeks. Although the way they talk to each other in the texts, it's ambiguous. It's all teasing, adolescent stuff.'

'Where's Mackie up to with the car?' says the DCI. 'A Ferrari, wasn't it?'

'It seems he has two,' says Boden.

'Two cars?'

'Two Ferraris. A Range Rover Evoque. And a BMW M3 Sport.'

'Bloody hell!'

Boden meets his gaze and smiles. 'As you say, boss, how the other half live. But we've also been moving on with the CCTV and the hoodie.'

'The hoodie?'

'She bumped into him outside Sainsbury's. Was it just a casual encounter with someone she knew, maybe another student? So she stopped to say hello. We couldn't tell. Then Prisha found another sighting. She's no longer jogging and she and the hoodie are walking side by side down Market Street and having some kind of conversation.'

'Do we think he's a student?'

'He's not known by anyone at her college. At least no one can identify him from what we have. But the shot is grainy, and he has his hood up. We could ask the university to let us go through their database and try to match him to a mugshot.'

'Manually? That'll take forever and a day.' Hepburn sighs. 'Brings us back to the possibility of kidnap for ransom. How rich are the Lennoxes?'

'Not billionaire rich,' says Boden. 'There are better targets in the Cambridge student population than Phoebe Lennox. Plus, I think the mother would tell us if they'd been approached.'

'How was your chat with her?'

'She's freaking out, fears her daughter's dead. I'd say she has no idea about what was going on between Phoebe and Simon.'

He folds his arms. 'Okay, what do we reckon? Is she dead? Sex games gone wrong with the two boys? They're now trying to cover it up?'

'I think we shouldn't forget the spy app, boss. They were trying to keep tabs on her. Which suggests she was moving away from them. There are two things that ring true to me in the Jack Palmer interview: he says her mother's overprotective, which is my impression, and Phoebe is quite a number, who likes to get her own way. What if she was playing Jack and Simon off against one another? Someone got upset?'

'Brings us back to the cars,' says Hepburn. 'Do we know what Simon drives?'

'Nothing registered in his name.'

He sighs. 'Cases like this are a nightmare. Is Phoebe Lennox locked up in some penthouse somewhere? Or is it a no body murder? Or are we all being led up the garden path because Ms Lennox is pissed off with her parents and kicking over the traces?'

Boden shrugs. 'What do you want us to do?'

'You two have done enough for now. Go home. We'll see what we can get on the cars overnight, all four of them. Keep on with the CCTV. And review the situation tomorrow morning.'

'Okay, thanks boss.'

'And I should say,' Hepburn adds. 'I'm impressed with both of you. Good work.'

Boden smiles, glances at Prisha, who beams and stares at her feet.

'Thank you, sir,' says Boden.

Praise from the boss. She'll take that. She decides to pick up that curry on the way home. Thai? Yeah, that new place she noticed and has been meaning to try.

25

Monday, 6.30pm

Carol can hardly move. Her limbs are lead weights and her boots are caked in mud. She half climbs, half tumbles out of the back of the pickup. A helping hand, rough and calloused, reaches out to steady her. He gives her a gap-toothed smile, says something she doesn't understand. But she smiles back. She's part of the gang. She's proved she can do it.

It took the entire day to harvest one field of celery. The clocks had gone back, by four-thirty the light was fading. But they carried on, with the aid of the lights on the rig, chopping, slicing, loading the trundling conveyor belt, and by five-thirty they had the job done.

The day passed in a blur. Two tea breaks, a lunch break, but the rest of the time Carol was just part of the line of pickers, moving steadily forward and feeding the massive processing rig.

Vasile drove the crew into Diss and pulled up outside the fish and chip shop. He was in good spirits; they completed the job on schedule and got paid. Cash in hand. He went inside and ordered, returning with carriers of food, which they shared out and ate in the back of the pickup.

Carol couldn't remember the last time she had chips from a chip shop. Prison food wasn't that bad, and she was used to eating what she was given. But the tangy combination of salt and malt vinegar took her back to another time and place. Fish and chips were the family's Friday night treat, so Mum didn't have to cook. The first time Dad gave her a gherkin, she spat it out. Like a sour little cucumber, she hated it. But they all laughed. And then Dad put one in front of his teeth and made a monster face. Back then, before Mum got ill, he was a different man, a different dad.

Would Alan have ever taken his kids out for a treat on a Friday night? Unlikely. It used to give her nightmares. The memory of him sprawled across the bed, spluttering, as he choked to death on his own blood. But she didn't think about him too much anymore. She'd paid the price. She had no regrets.

After they'd eaten their fish and chips, someone suggested the pub. The touristy establishments in the town centre didn't welcome foreign farmworkers. But Vasile knew a place in the back streets where they were happy to fill their empty tap room with a gang of pickers who had money in their pockets.

Helped out of the back of the truck, Carol follows the others inside.

The building is Victorian, and in need of renovation. Dismal decor, low ceilings and a smell of stale beer. But the barman is welcoming, tells them not to worry about their muddy boots. The floor is chequered linoleum and has a tacky feel to it. Carol worked in pubs like this, pushed a heavy mop over floors like this, where the dirt is so ingrained that it's hard to make an impression. But she feels at home.

The first round is on Vasile, everyone orders pints with a chaser. Carol sticks to lager and it comes in a straight glass. This is the first time she's been in a pub for years. The glass reminds her of Dad. He liked a drink. Even as a kid, she knew he liked it a bit too much.

She sits in a corner and watches the others telling jokes, teasing each other. She may not understand the language, but she feels included. They laugh a lot and she likes that. Laughter is infectious, it lifts the spirits even when you don't understand the joke.

They begin a drinking game. It's easy to understand. You balance a beer mat on the edge of the table; the idea is to flip it up and over and catch it. They go round the table and take it in turns. Miss and you down a whiskey chaser.

Carol sips her lager. For the last five years inside, she's been on the Twelve Step programme; getting clean from drugs has been an enormous struggle. She started smoking dope with Alan when she was thirteen. From then on, her drug use escalated. She knows now it was how he controlled her. It was her escape from feelings she could neither face nor understand. She drank, but preferred getting high. The hankering remains; but now she only thinks about it two or three times a day instead of all the time.

The beer loosens her, eases her aching muscles and her anxiety. But she still has a serious problem. Now she's out, she's exposed. The threat is real and not some paranoid fantasy. Her refuge with the gang is only a temporary reprieve. Still, there's no harm in enjoying it.

One of the girls she bunks with gets out a packet of cigarettes and invites Carol to join her. They go outside to smoke. The door of the pub opens onto the narrow side street.

Carol tries to limit her tobacco consumption to a few roll-ups a day. But warm with booze, she accepts a luxurious king-sized filter tip from Daria's packet. They light up and stand side by side on the chilly pavement.

Daria wants to improve her English. Carol knows this is why the girl is sharing her cigarettes. But she doesn't mind.

'Is hard work, no?' says Daria.

'Tough, but I'm getting used to it.'

'Getting used to?'

'It's what you say when you do something a lot, maybe it's hard, then as you do it more, it becomes easier.'

Her entire life has been about things she's had to get used to and accept.

Daria nods and repeats the phrase under her breath. 'Getting used to.'

Carol smiles. Daria is bright and energetic. Carol wonders what sort of family she comes from. Are they happy? Do they worry that she's far from home? Her mother must be proud of her.

She's about to ask the girl where she comes from when the door to the pub opens. A lad comes out, early twenties followed by two girls of a similar age. They're all English and Carol has already noticed them sitting at the end of the bar. They seem to be regulars who know the barman.

The lad is lanky with a pock-marked face and a shaved head; he's had too much to drink.

Carol meets his gaze and smiles.

But he glares back at her and says, 'Yeah? What you looking at, you stupid bitch? Come over here, taking our jobs. Fuck off back where you came from!'

He staggers, and one girl grabs his arm.

Carol considers her options. It's a moment of decision, she knows that.

She puts the cigarette in her mouth and draws deeply. The end glows red. She removes it from her lips and lunges at the lad's face, pressing the red-hot tip of the cigarette into his cheek.

He shrieks with pain and reels backwards, collapsing to his knees and holding his cheek.

Daria stares at her, slack-jawed.

Carol drops the cigarette on the pavement and grinds it underfoot.

All she has to do now is wait.

26

Monday, 8.15pm

Marcia Lennox hadn't eaten all day, so she made herself a mushroom omelette with a green salad and a few cherry tomatoes. She'd watched Louisa Muirhead consume half a packet of Harry's favourite chocolate biscuits. However distraught she was, Marcia can't imagine having such a lack of self-discipline. But Louisa seemed unconcerned about the biscuits, at least. She remained fixated on her son, Simon. It felt like there was something she was trying to say but couldn't.

After Louisa had left, Marcia texted her husband several times, telling him she was home and wanted to talk, but received no reply.

She tidied the kitchen, put the dishwasher on and wandered round the empty house. Harry had left a shirt and some underwear in the hamper. She transferred these to the washing machine with her own clothes from the weekend and turned it on.

Now she finds herself in Phoebe's room. She sits on the bed, scrolling on her phone through her daughter's posts. She keeps coming back to this. It's a flimsy thread. But it connects her to Phoebe.

And she's been discovering new clips. There's loads of footage to explore.

Here's Phoebe, dancing along the pavement. It's night, a London street and the entrance to a club. She addresses the camera directly.

'Hey, gang. Here we are! And, trust me, it's gonna be awesome!'

She spins the camera round for a brief glimpse of a lavender neon sign. Below it, a door, a queue of people, a burly doorman with an earpiece.

The camera flips back to Phoebe's grinning face. 'But no waiting in line for us,' she announces. She beckons with her index finger and laughs. The doorman waves her through and a wall of sound hits as she walks through the door into the club.

Marcia follows. She's immersed in her daughter's world. The thud of the music, the kaleidoscope of lights. Greeting friends. As good as being there. She's so engrossed, she almost misses it.

The front door slams.

It drags her back to the present. She clicks the phone off and hurries downstairs in time to see the back of her husband disappearing into the kitchen. By the time she gets there, he has the fridge door open and is taking out a bottle of wine.

He stares at her for a moment. 'Oh, you're back.'

'I did text.'

He looks away. 'I've been busy.'

He means he decided to ignore her. Is he still pissed off because she accused him of not caring enough about Phoebe?

She can sense the tension in him. He wants an argument. Usually he avoids them. But she's weary and battered. Why can't he put his arms around her and say everything will be all right, even if it is a lie?

He takes two wineglasses from the cupboard and holds them up. She nods. He places them on the kitchen counter and pours the wine.

'You won't believe who came round this afternoon,' she says.

'Louisa.'

Of course he knows. He may have even sent her.

'I gather the police interviewed Jack Palmer,' she says. 'They must be investigating him.'

'Yes, Marcia, because you put some absurd notion in their heads about him being obsessed with Phoebe.' The tone is testy.

'Is it absurd?'

He takes a swallow of wine and says, 'Oh for God's sake, when did you become such a prude? Kids have sex. She's of age. Why is it a problem for you? Ever since Ibiza you've had it in for Jack.'

She stares at him. 'I don't understand.' He seems to blame her for something, but what?

He shakes his head, takes off his suit jacket and slots it over a chair back.

'Jack's a young man,' he says. 'His career, his future prospects could be ruined, because he's become involved in a police investigation. Yet he came to us and told us she was missing. It makes no sense he would've harmed her.'

'Maybe he was trying to be clever in order to cover up what he's done.'

'Oh, don't be stupid,' Harry huffs. 'You've been watching too much television.'

Why is he attacking her like this?

'Come on, Harry, Louisa told me he tried to rape some girl at Oxford. You knew that. But you let Phoebe go to his place in Ibiza.'

'He didn't rape anyone. He just got very drunk and silly. And there is no way I would've put my daughter in harm's way. If anyone's to blame for pushing Phoebe into doing something risky, it's you.'

'Me? How can you say that?'

'You were very frank with me the last time we talked. Now I'm being frank with you.'

'This is so unfair.'

'Is it? Now the police are wasting valuable time and resources focusing on Jack. When they should be out there looking for Phoebe. And you, your selfishness and inability to let the girl grow up, has caused that.'

She can feel his rage, and it's scary. This is not Harry. He drains his glass, plonks it on the counter and refills it. Marcia hasn't touched her drink. She stares down at the amber liquid. She has no idea how to answer him. Where is all this coming from?

'And now Simon could get dragged into this,' he says. 'This is a mess. None of which is helping find Phoebe.'

'I don't see why you're worried about Simon. Louisa insisted he doesn't know where she is or what Jack might've done.'

'Are you really this naïve? Or just wilfully blind.'

What's he talking about? She doesn't get it. But the spite of this remark stings. He's looking at her with hatred in his eyes. Her knees feel weak, but she's determined to stand her ground.

'Harry,' she whispers. 'This is not my fault.'

He shrugs, drinks more wine. He's demolished his second glass.

'At the end of the day,' he says, 'she is your daughter, yours not mine that's true, and so I've not questioned the way you've brought her up. God knows, I've done my best.'

'I know you think I'm over-protective—'

He turns away, he's not even listening.

'I suppose once she left home,' he says, 'things were always going to come to a head between us. It was inevitable.'

What's inevitable? The knot in her stomach is tightening. This sudden attack is completely unjust.

'For fuck's sake, Harry,' she says, 'she hasn't left home, she's disappeared, and no one knows if she's alive or dead.'

'There's no need to shout.'

'I'm not shouting, I'm trying to make you listen.' She reins herself in. Don't give him what he wants.

'You always turn everything into such a melodrama, don't you?' he says. 'Because when you lose control, you also lose any sense of reality.'

'The police are searching for Phoebe because she disappeared off the streets of Cambridge. That's real.'

Breathe slowly, keep calm.

'I'm not talking about what the police are doing. I'm talking about what you're doing, what you always do. You make everything about you.'

'What? How can you say that? I'm just worried sick about my daughter.'

He walks over to the floor to ceiling windows.

Out there it's black. Beyond the patio, the garden is invisible. The windows reflect the room. He turns back to face her. He's created a space of several metres between them. It's deliberate, this distancing. This is planned, something he's rehearsed.

She senses what's coming before it hits, like a wind rushing towards her.

'I'm sorry, Marcia,' he says, in a formal voice as if he's addressing the Board. 'I can't do this anymore.'

'What do you mean?'

'This. Us. What we've become.'

'What have we become?'

'Two strangers who don't understand each other.'

'I understand you. I've given you your freedom, haven't I? As wives go, I'm pretty tolerant.'

She's a damn sight more than that. This has been the trade-off and a choice she was prepared to make.

She takes a step towards him; he takes a step further away.

'It's too hard. I can't do it anymore,' he says. The tone has become apologetic. He doesn't want this to be his fault. Harry's always the good guy.

'Why now?' she says. 'Because I have to say, your timing is not great.'

'I know. And that can't be helped. But I think it's better to be honest.'

She laughs. This is all too absurd.

'For a man who lies as much as you do,' she says, 'that's an interesting statement.'

He shakes his head. 'You can't help yourself, can you? Sarcasm to put me in my place. This is just typical of you.'

Marcia takes a breath. Her heart is thumping, but she wills herself to stay calm.

'Who is she?'

'I don't know what you mean?'

'I know you, Harry. You wouldn't be walking out on me

unless you had somewhere else to go. You've decided it's time to trade up, have you?'

His chin juts. She's hit the nail on the head.

'I wonder about you, Marcia. Where you're coming from. The way you see the world, it's all quite basic and sordid, isn't it? Because that's who you are.'

He skirts the edge of the kitchen and lifts his jacket off the back of the chair.

'You may as well tell me who she is. I'll find out, eventually.'

He puts the jacket on, straightens the lapels, then shrugs. 'Her name's Marie-Claire. She works for us, she's an analyst. She's French and very bright. Speaks five languages.'

'And she's thirty to thirty-five and you're pushing sixty, which is why you're right, it is sordid.'

He walks towards the kitchen door.

'I've done my best to make this marriage work,' he says. 'All you've done is accuse me of loving Phoebe less than my own sons. Which is completely unfair.'

He has the look of a sulky schoolboy.

Marcia watches him adjusting the cuffs on his nine hundred quid suit and something inside snaps. 'Are you really going to make that your excuse for this? I've been unfair to you. Oh poor, poor Harry! You self-centred, spoilt, lying piece of shit!'

He smiles. He's made her lose it and got the row he wanted. Now it's her fault.

'I think we're done here,' he says with satisfaction. 'Goodbye, Marcia.'

He strolls out of the door. She picks up his wineglass and thinks about throwing it after him. But what would be the point in that? She'd only have to clear up the mess.

27

Carol was awake most of the night. The police cell has a high, barred window, but amber light from a streetlamp flooded in, creating patterns on the wall. The bunk was hard, the blanket inadequate, but she didn't care. She was back in familiar territory, under lock and key, and she knew the drill. Just do what you're told. No decisions to make. She'd found a safe haven.

About seven o'clock, the custody sergeant brought her a mug of tea. Institutional brown, hot and sweet.

'You all right?' he said gruffly.

'Fine,' she replied.

'That little toe rag, he's known to us. He's got form. Robbing pensioners is his speciality. Offering to get their shopping. Then making off with the money. He's charm personified.'

Carol sipped her tea and stared at him.

'Your mate, the girl you were with, she says he provoked

you. He was mouthing off. Racist stuff, which I can well believe. We're gonna have a word with your probation officer when she turns up. See what we can do. Can't promise anything.'

He gave her a nod and smile and disappeared.

Carol's heart sank. This was not the plan.

Yet again she considered her options.

Attack a police officer? Bite him, maybe. She'd seen enough inmates kick off and go berserk. They'd write it up as a mental health thing. She could feed some crazy shit to the doctors about hearing voices and wanting to stab people. That would do it. She'd get put away somewhere secure.

The custody sergeant returned and brought her a ham sandwich for breakfast. She looked at him. He was tubby with a bald patch, but he had a kind face. She couldn't bring herself to do it.

She thanked him for the sandwich.

It occurred to her that perhaps she could tell Rosa the truth. They'd come looking for her, as she always knew they would. But then what? How could she prove it wasn't paranoia?

She finished the sandwich.

And now she waits. She's good at waiting; it's a skill she's had years to perfect. She wishes she had a book to read. Mum used to read to them when she was little. She lost the habit of reading in the bad years, the druggy years. But in prison she got it back.

When the door to the cell opens again, it's Rosa, lugging a shoulder bag stuffed with a laptop and files. She's late for every appointment and always has too much to do.

She pauses on the threshold and shakes her head like a disappointed parent. 'Carol,' she says. 'What the hell is this about?'

Carol shrugs. 'Lost my rag.'

Rosa plonks the bag down and pushes her glasses up her nose. 'Have you used?'

'No. I had a drink in the pub after work.'

'Were you pissed?'

'No.'

'Then why?'

Carol sighs. It's wearisome, this need to explain your feelings, justify your actions. She hates it, never sees the point.

'I dunno,' she says.

Rosa sits down on the bunk beside her. 'I think you do. You're out, you've got a chance of a fresh start. Why do you want to go back to prison? Change is scary, I realise that.'

Carol watches her young, animated face. She wants to help; she's bursting with it, with hope and goodwill. This makes her stupid. It was probably her that told them.

'You're lucky the police have decided not to charge you. And that's because Vasile and the girl you were with are maintaining this was self-defence. They're trying to protect you, Carol. They like you. Are you going to let them down? Are you going to let me down?'

Those big brown eyes are gazing at her expectantly.

'You don't understand,' she says.

'Okay, explain.'

Carol sighs. 'Someone came looking for me. Luckily, I was out for a walk. Because no one's supposed to know where I am.'

Rosa frowns. 'Are you sure about this?'

'How do they know where I am? Did you tell them?'

'No. A member of your family did contact me. I didn't tell them anything. They may have got news of your release from victim liaison, but that's all. It's possible they've got some information from the prison. There should've been a note on your file. But the system isn't foolproof.'

'Tell me about it.'

'You killed a family member, didn't you?'

'You've read the file.'

'I'm sure you're remorseful.'

Carol glares at her. 'No I'm not,' she says. 'I lied to the parole board, told them what they wanted to hear. I killed my cousin. He was a drug dealer, a pimp and a thug. He deserved it. Now just put me back inside where I belong.'

Rosa sighs and tilts her head. 'I have read your file. If you'd had a better lawyer, the charge would probably have been reduced to manslaughter. Nowadays you wouldn't get a life sentence. You were the victim of abuse and—'

'Rosa, shut the fuck up! I don't wanna talk about it. It's done!'

'I do understand.'

'No, you fucking don't!'

Rosa folds her arms. 'Well, you can swear at me all you like, but I won't let you give in.'

'What difference does it make to you? Just fill in the form and ship me back.'

'Okay, you've got a cynical view of the world. I can see why. So let's go with that. Everyone's out for themselves. And I won't let you do this, because I'm as stubborn as you. I don't want to fail.'

'I can believe that.'

'Fine.'

The young probation officer is glaring at her. She's tough for her years. A black woman who's made it through the system.

'Why do you even do this job?' says Carol.

'Because I like it. And I make a difference. Listen to me.

You've done really well. Stuck to the Twelve Step programme, not many do. You've got a chance here, Carol.'

Yeah, to end up dead in a ditch. That's the part she doesn't get.

'You don't understand,' she says.

'If you give me some evidence of who you say is threatening you, I will ask the police to investigate.'

She thinks about the cards. The flowery cards she's received every single year to remind her of that grim anniversary. But he's always been cunning. It proves nothing.

'Oh, like that'll work,' she says. 'The cops'll protect me. What planet are you living on?'

'My job is to do what's best for you. And to respect your wishes. It's unlikely your family or anyone else know where you are. And they won't get any information from me. But you have to make this work too.'

'How?'

'First, how much of this is real and how much is in your head?'

'You think I'm paranoid?'

'Carol, you've been away for seventeen years. Out here in the world, things have moved on.'

It's true. She feels she's emerging from a time warp. It has been weird, coming out and seeing all the things that've changed. Clothes, cars, haircuts. Random reminders of what she's missed.

Rosa smiles. 'You're still viewing the threat to you as it was in the past. Back when you were convicted. And that's causing you huge anxiety. It stops you from getting on with your life.'

She's right about that too. But what about the cards? Could be he wants to torment her?

'What you're saying is get over yourself?'

Rosa shrugs. 'That's a bit brutal. I'm saying let's move forward cautiously, but with pragmatism. You've found some new friends. If you need someone to watch your back, you could do worse than trust them.'

'Why would they help me?'

'I've told you. They like you. Is that so impossible to believe?'

28

Tuesday, 9.15am

Marcia woke up alone in the super king-size bed; the house was eerily quiet. She had no idea what to do with herself, so she went to work. For most of her adult life, working has been a refuge and a place to retreat when things got chaotic.

She'd texted her PA, Lawrence, the previous day with news of Phoebe's disappearance. She'd asked him to keep it to himself and make some excuse for her absence. This was a reflex action. She hated people making a fuss or, worse still, their sympathy and pity.

As she walks into the office, she scans the room nervously, but everything seems normal. The smell of morning coffee, the quiet buzz of conversation. Several people greet her and she returns their smiles. Only Lawrence is surprised to see her. He's followed her instructions.

She goes straight to her corner office, puts her briefcase on the desk and adjusts the blinds.

Lawrence follows her in.

'Any news?' he whispers. She shakes her head.

'What can I get you?'

She wants to say: a lawyer. That's top of her to-do list. She's spent the night worrying about Phoebe, watching more clips of her on YouTube, and fuming about Harry.

How has he wrong-footed her like this? Why didn't she see the signs? After sixteen years of marriage, she thought she knew all his little tells. If anything, prior to Phoebe's disappearance, he was being rather sweet.

The last time they'd had sex was on the Sunday morning after they'd returned from driving their daughter up to Cambridge. It was perfunctory, but he'd brought her coffee and croissants in bed afterwards, and they'd chatted about a trip to Siena at the end of October. Harry had a client with a villa outside San Gimignano he was happy to loan out.

Now someone else, Marie-Claire with her five languages, would accompany Harry on these little jaunts. Maybe she already has. On his last business trip to Dubai, Marcia had a sense that he wasn't alone when he called her. He had nothing to say to her, but blamed a busy schedule and tiredness.

She feels a fool. She is a fool. To end up like Louisa Muirhead, a discarded wife who wasn't smart enough to work out how to hold on to her husband.

Why has he visited this apocalypse on her now? Does he have so little care for her? Did reminding him he wasn't Phoebe's real father tip him over the edge? It's hard to believe he could be petty.

She realises Lawrence is speaking to her.

'Sorry,' she says. 'I'm not with it this morning. Couldn't sleep.'

'Is there anything I can do to help?' says Lawrence. 'Anything at all, just say.'

Marcia meets his gaze and smiles. He's worked for her for

five years. She trusts him more than any of the people she calls friends.

'Keep any hassles at bay for me,' she says. 'I need to make some calls.'

'Of course.'

Lawrence leaves, closing the door. Marcia gets out her laptop and sits down at the desk.

Last night, after Harry walked out, she'd done some digging. The name and the fact she works for Harry's company meant it took about thirty seconds to track down Marie-Claire Gagneux. Since then, she's chased her replacement all over the net.

What she's discovered is her age: twenty-nine, three years younger than Harry's eldest son. Even in the context of her husband's known extra-marital tastes, this is shocking. Her education: the Sorbonne and Harvard Business School. What does a clever young woman want with a raddled old dog like Harry? And numerous pictures of a beautiful, smiling, blonde who could be Phoebe's older sister.

How could anyone not be jealous? Marcia knows she should stop looking, but she can't. She was twenty-eight when she met Harry. He was forty-one. Then it didn't seem wrong to be luring him away from his wife and children. The marriage was dead, that's what he told her. They argued all the time. He was doing his wife a favour by moving on. Is he using the same line with Marie-Claire?

She feels sick and couldn't face breakfast. All she's had is coffee and Xanax, and she knows she needs to be careful with that. The doctor before last had warned her about dependency and refused her any more prescriptions. She got a new doctor, but she knew he was right.

Focus. She takes out her phone and calls DS Boden.

When the detective answers, she sounds like she's walking and eating.

'I'm just on my way into the office, Mrs Lennox. But there have been no developments overnight.'

'How do you know if you're not there?' And why isn't she there? Is this a part-time effort?

'We work shifts, but I've been keeping in touch. Can I phone you back when I've spoken to my boss?'

Marcia has the urge to say something cutting. But she stops herself. Maybe Harry's right. She's a bitch who mistreats people. Is this the woman she's become, a spiteful shrew? Only after she's hung up does she recall. She wanted to ask why they were interested in Simon.

It's the fourth day. Where is Phoebe? Where! She wants to scream out her desolation. She's alone and abandoned. But displays of emotion rarely help. She learnt that a long time ago.

29

Tuesday, 10.25am

Boden and Mackie stand like sentinels on either side of DCI Hepburn. He's sitting at his desk. All three of them are watching Simon Lennox on the boss's computer screen. Simon is hunched over the table in the interview room, foot rapidly tapping, chewing his nails.

'Looks to me like he's bricking it,' says Mackie. 'Plus he's come dressed as his granddad.'

Simon is wearing a tweed jacket with leather elbow patches, a check shirt and chinos.

'It's what posh boys like him wear,' says Boden.

She raises her eyebrows at Mackie; yeah, she is smarter than him. He gives her a sulky look back. Rattling his cage is one of her few pleasures.

DCI Hepburn steeples his fingers. 'Let's swap the interview techniques round,' he says. 'Strikes me he might be a bit of a mummy's boy. Jo, you're the strict parent who won't take any nonsense. Scott, you're his new best friend.'

Mackie frowns. 'Really, boss? I'd prefer to give him a good spanking. I mean seriously, doing it with your own sister?'

Hepburn sighs and looks up at Mackie.

'I wasn't being serious, sir. Just black humour.'

'Mackie,' says the DCI. 'Four days down the road, this girl could well be dead. Let's behave like we care.'

Mackie looks at his feet. 'Sorry, sir.'

'We could be talking about an offence under the Sexual Offences Act,' says Boden. 'Presumably you want him cautioned?'

'Yes,' says the DCI. 'And if he knows we talked to Jack Palmer without a caution, that might frighten him enough to open up and tell us what they've really been playing at, the three of them.'

'Okay,' says Boden.

There's a tap on the door and DC Chakravorty enters.

'Morning, Prisha,' says the DCI. 'What have you got?'

'On the cars. Nothing, I'm afraid. We've got the Ferrari that entered Cambridge on Saturday. But nothing before that. Not that we can find.'

Hepburn folds his arms and shakes his head.

'Could be another car we don't know about,' says Boden.

'But there is something else, sir,' says Prisha. 'I've got copies of her credit card statements. She bought a brand new iPhone 11 on Tuesday at a phone shop in Lion's Yard. She paid £1149 by card.'

'That's something,' says Hepburn. 'Get on to the retailer. We need the service provider and the number. Then we'll see if we can get a cell siting. Impress upon them the urgency.'

'Sir.' Prisha hurries out.

. . .

Boden and Mackie walk down the corridor towards the interview room.

'Listen,' he says. 'I know I can be a dickhead—'

'Now we both know.'

'I'm trying to apologise, Sarge. We got off on the wrong foot. And I'm sorry.'

Boden stops and turns to face him. 'Be nice to Prisha,' she says. 'She's nervous, but she's got the makings of a top-notch detective. She works hard, and she's meticulous. And if she gets promoted to sergeant before you, you'll be glad you stayed friends with her. Okay?'

He nods, smiles and gives her a mock salute. 'Okay. Fancy going for a drink sometime?'

'No, Mackie. You're not my type.'

'You like women? That's cool.'

'No, I like men. The grown-up sort.'

As they enter the interview room, Simon Lennox jumps to his feet. Schooled in manners, if nothing else.

Mackie beams at him and slips into role. 'As you were, mate. Everything all right? Can we get you a coffee?'

Simon's looking at them like a frightened rabbit.

'I don't understand,' he says. 'They said I was going to be questioned under caution. Because of the Sexual Offences Act.'

'We're not arresting you, Simon,' says Boden. 'But you may want a lawyer present.'

'What sexual offence?' he says. 'I'm in love with her. I was going to ask her to marry me.'

'You can't marry your half-sister,' says Boden. 'That's the sexual offence, contrary to the Sexual Offences Act 2003.'

Simon huffs. 'She's not my actual sister. Half or otherwise. My dad is not her biological father.'

Boden sighs. Expect the unexpected and never assume.

That's the first thing her old boss told her when she became a detective. The complications of modern families.

'Okay, let's sit down and talk about this,' she says.

Simon sits and the two police officers take the chairs opposite.

'I wouldn't get romantically involved with my own sister,' says Simon. 'That's gross.'

'Your father, Harry Lennox, is not her real dad?' says Boden.

'No, she was about two when Dad and Ma got together.'

'Ma?'

'Short for Marcia. Family joke. Most of my life Phoebe was this annoying little kid. Then suddenly, she wasn't. She used to flirt with me all the time. But I would never've laid a finger on her. Ma would've killed me. Literally.'

'We know from her phone you two were involved,' says Boden.

'It was in Ibiza in the summer. Jack was, well, being Jack. Dad told me I had to look after her. I told Jack to back off. And he did. And me and Phoebe, we sort of, y'know. It happened.'

'Do you know where she is, Simon?'

'No. I swear.'

'Jack's a good friend of yours, isn't he?' says Mackie. 'How did he react when you told him to back off?'

'He was cool. He said fine. But Phi, is, well, flirty. She's a gorgeous girl, likes the attention I guess.' He seems uncomfortable. He can't sit still.

'Are you saying she played you off against each other?' says Boden.

He stares at his bitten nails. 'Yeah, I suppose.' He's avoiding eye contact and his right foot drums the floor.

They're getting to something here. Boden knows she must press him.

'Did she continue to sleep with him too?' she says.

This hits the mark. Simon flinches. He's silent for a moment. Perhaps he's remembering the pain of it? A girl he was in love with having sex with his best friend? He exhales and says, 'She thought it was all a game. I told her how I felt and she'd just brush it off. She never took me seriously.'

'Must've upset you, mate.' says Mackie. 'Girls can be manipulative. Not fair, is it?'

He wipes his nose with the back of his hand. 'No, it isn't,' he says bitterly. His head dips, his shoulders shake, and he begins to cry.

'Let it all go, mate. You'll feel better.'

'None of this is my fault,' wails Simon. 'Phoebe's a bloody nightmare. You tell a girl you love her, and she practically laughs at you.'

Boden looks up at the camera. The boss is watching, and she knows what she must do.

She turns to Simon and says, 'Simon, I'm going to caution you before you say any more. But I should tell you again, you may want a lawyer present. Do you understand?'

He blinks at her. 'Not really,' he says.

30

Tuesday, 10.45am

Marcia takes a taxi to Knightsbridge. She's not sure what she's going to say. The cab drops her a block away from the auction house where Louisa Muirhead works.

She could've phoned or texted but felt compelled to come in person. Why? Because she needs answers.

Louisa studied art history at university; to her parents this was the highbrow but unthreatening education that would suit a girl expecting to marry serious money. Harry Lennox, a stockbroker's son, was not quite what Sir Edwin expected for his only daughter. But with his father-in-law's connections, Harry's career in the City prospered.

When they got divorced, Louisa didn't need a job, but took a junior role at a leading fine art auctioneers. She rose rapidly through the ranks and is now Global Head of Post-War and Contemporary Art. Her breadth of knowledge is intimidating, and her capacity to sell obscure artists for eye-watering sums made even Harry sit up and take notice. Louisa has never married again.

Marcia stares up at what she supposes is the Georgian facade of the building. Louisa would know. Old is just old to Marcia. Older things are dirty, which is not something she likes. The steps are edged with wrought-iron railings and there are two small ornamental trees, one either side of the front door.

She gives her name at the desk.

Don't let the nerves show. Anyway, she'll probably be fobbed off.

She isn't. Within five minutes Louisa comes sweeping down the magnificent staircase and greets her like an old friend.

'Oh, my dear,' she says, brow furrowed with concern. 'Is there any news?'

'No,' says Marcia. 'I'm waiting for the police to call me back with an update.'

'It's just so awful.'

Louisa shepherds her into a small anti-room hung with rather gloomy paintings in heavy gilt frames. No doubt worth a fortune.

'The reason I'm here,' says Marcia. But she can't continue. She dips her head. She's used to walking in anywhere, head held high, steel in her backbone. But, somehow faced with Louisa's effortless confidence, she crumbles.

Louisa sighs. 'Yes, I heard something was in the wind. Harry is being Harry. His brains always were in his trousers.'

Marcia meets her gaze. 'You must think it serves me right.'

That's awful! Sounds like grovelling.

'No, I don't indulge in schadenfreude,' says Louisa. 'Life's too short. And, in the long run, I'm glad Harry left me. I have my sons, I have a rather interesting job and I have my freedom. Once I got used to being a spare part at dinner parties, I found it suits me rather well.' She adds with a sly grin. 'And I haven't lacked for male company when I've wanted it.'

'Still, I feel I ought to apologise to you.' She is grovelling. Why? Stop it!

'Apologise? Whatever for? My dear Marcia, women steal each other's husbands all the time. We like to believe we're above all that. Sisterhood, some such nonsense. But I went to an expensive girls' boarding school on a blasted heath where hockey was a blood sport played in the cold and mud. And I learned early on what complete bitches we can be to one another. I suppose it's genetic. We have to get the best deal we can for our young, the best provider we can. And it's other females who get in the way of that.'

'Wow,' says Marcia. 'I thought I was cynical.'

'Realistic. And I presume you're here because you're angry and in need of a suitable firm of lawyers to exact financial revenge on Harry.'

'Is it bad of me to ask you for that?' she says.

She wasn't going to. But it's a plausible excuse when what she wants to ask about is Simon.

'No, it's sensible, and it's what I would do. Divorcing me cost him a fortune, as I'm sure you know. The firm I used knows all the tricks men like Harry employ to hide their assets.'

'I can't believe he's doing this now. With Phoebe missing—'

'Seems cruel, I know. But Harry lives his life in blinkers. The Phoebe missing compartment and the marriage compartment he would keep separate. I'm sure he is extremely concerned for Phoebe.'

'It's a shock, not having him there to rely on. Especially at the moment.'

'Well, according to Eddie, his hand may have been forced.'

'How do you mean?'

Louisa sighs. 'You won't want to hear this, but better you know. The girl concerned, I gather she's French, is pregnant. She's been pressuring him to make a decision.'

A baby!

Marcia manages to stay upright, although she feels as if she's reeling. Louisa takes her arm and guides her to a chair.

Her mind spins back to when she and Harry were first together. She wanted a child with him, wanted it desperately, but he said no. Even now she's only forty-three, it's still possible, if that's what he wanted.

'My guess is he was caught out. Men like Harry become more ridiculous the older they get,' says Louisa. 'That's my opinion. My dear, you are looking very pale. Are you all right?'

She's not all right. And if she's lost Phoebe, she never will be again.

'I thought if I just ignored his indiscretions, he'd always come home.'

Louisa shrugs. 'I've female friends who take that view. Sometimes it works. My theory is that in Harry's case, the philandering is to compensate for the fact he'll never make it to the top. At work, I mean. It's about how other men see him.'

'He's done fairly well.'

'My father calls him a loyal lieutenant. Hasn't got it in

him to go for the top job. He's the laid back party boy who gets all the women and everyone loves him for that.'

'I wish we'd talked years ago.'

'Would you have listened? When we met at social gatherings, you always walked away as soon as you could.'

'I thought you hated me.'

She always gave an excellent imitation of it.

Louisa laughs. 'I wouldn't say hate exactly. Your superior attitude annoyed me. And you are rather good-looking. That annoyed me too.'

Louisa's phone buzzes. She glances at it.

'Excuse me,' she says. 'I need to take this.'

Marcia gets up and goes to look at one of the large gloomy landscapes, while Louisa answers her phone.

She's adrift, although it's probably shock. Harry's having a baby. All the moorings that held her life together have snapped. Phoebe's gone. Harry's gone. She has no idea what to do with herself. In less than four days, her entire world has imploded.

Louisa has turned away, but Marcia can't help overhearing.

'Darling, just calm down.' Louisa is saying. 'You've done nothing wrong. Now, listen to me. You say nothing else. Nothing at all. I will speak to granddad and we'll sort this out.'

As Marcia listens, a shiver runs down her spine. She's speaking to Simon. The police have got him. Sounds like they've arrested him.

How could she be such a fool? Why would Louisa Muirhead be nice to her? Now it all makes sense.

Louisa hangs up and faces her. She's frowning. Behind those red glasses, the eyes are small and ferrety. That mean crimson mouth. Now she'll try to talk her way out of this.

The lethargy evaporates. She came for answers. To confirm a truth, she unconsciously knew. Phoebe always was in danger.

Their eyes meet, and Marcia's rage explodes.

'Fuck you!' she says. 'You knew the police had Simon. You think you can play me with all your upper class bullshit!'

'Marcia, listen—'

'No! No way.' She spins on her heel to walk away.

'He would never hurt her, Marcia. It's not in him. He just been a rather silly boy—'

Marcia swivels to face her again. *Wilfully blind.* Harry accused her of that. And he's right.

'He's not a silly boy,' she says. 'He's a man. And he's nine years older than her. Are you telling me that your son has seduced my teenage daughter, who's barely eighteen?'

'That's a vast oversimplification. Phoebe is a very sophisticated young woman. She knows how to—'

'Where is she? What has he done to her?' She must be shouting. A concerned security guard appears in the doorway. Louisa waves him away.

'He doesn't know. I swear.'

Marcia's heart is thumping. She knows Louisa is lying. But there's nothing more to say. She strides out of the door.

31

Tuesday, 10.50am

Boden follows the DCI into the incident room. They now have half a dozen officers working on the case with several civilian analysts to back them up.

'He collapsed in a heap,' says Boden. 'Said he wanted to call his mother. And we stopped it there.'

'Well, we can expect the heavy mob to be arriving soon,' says Hepburn. 'But you did the right thing. There would've been no point in an inadmissible confession.'

'Maybe it's more complicated than that, boss. He kept blubbing and saying, I should've protected her.'

'You think he's covering up for Jack Palmer?'

'That doesn't make sense either. He hated the idea that she was still sleeping with his best mate.'

'Crime of passion, then? In which case, a good lawyer will advise him to come clean. Is someone babysitting him? I don't want any complaints about how we've handled this.'

'Mackie's with him at the moment. He's followed your

instructions, and that helped loosen Lennox up. Mackie's quite good at role playing.'

Hepburn smiles. 'Don't let him annoy you too much, Jo.'

She shrugs. 'He doesn't, boss. We're fine.'

DC Chakravorty is sitting at her workstation in front of several monitors. Hepburn and Boden come up behind her.

'Right, what have you found, Prisha?'

'It was Carly, not me sir,' she says, pointing to the analyst sitting opposite. 'But we've been following through.'

She taps her keyboard, and two still images appear on her screen side by side. 'These were the two important sequences that we linked first.'

Hepburn and Boden lean over her shoulder and peer at the screen. Prisha presses play.

The video sequence on the left is pixilated and grey. Two figures moving side by side.

'We think this is Phoebe and the hoodie. And they're about to disappear through a door. This, we've identified, as one of the entrances to Grand Arcade multi-storey car park.'

Prisha stops that sequence and clicks over to the other side of the screen. 'And here's the static camera at the car park exit. This is four and a half minutes later.'

The camera looks down on to cars passing below. The automatic barrier rises for each vehicle to pass through.

Prisha freezes a frame. 'Now here we're looking down through the windscreen of the car from above. We can see some of the lower body of the driver and the passenger. We've enhanced this as much as we can. What do you see?'

'Her legs,' says Boden. 'And it looks like she's wearing khaki leggings, like Phoebe.'

'Yep, that's what we think,' says Prisha. 'We pulled the registration of the vehicle off another camera covering the exit. It's a Mitsubishi pickup, and it's registered to a Steven Jarman, lives just outside Saffron Walden.'

'Bloody brilliant,' says Hepburn. 'Bloody brilliant.'

Within fifteen minutes the team is assembled for a full briefing. The discovery energises everyone. The slow, meticulous work has created a breakthrough. Now they need to drive through and crack it.

Hepburn paces at the front of the room. 'Okay, listen up. This is taking the inquiry in a very different direction. Steven Jarman, tell us about him, Jo?'

She's sitting next to Prisha with her laptop open, scanning entries on the Police National Computer.

A few keystrokes and a mugshot pops up on the monitor at the front of the room. A handsome face, mixed race, dark hair with a zigzag razored on one side.

'He's got form,' says Boden. 'Started young. Possession of class A drugs with intent to supply. Suspected connection to a County Lines gang. Did time in a young offender's unit for that. He's twenty-two now. Nothing recently. Could be Phoebe knows him because he supplies drugs to students? He lives forty minutes away. Cambridge could be his turf? Looks like he persuaded or somehow tricked her into going with him in his car. But why?'

'Kidnap for ransom,' says Mackie from the back. 'He sells her coke, becomes her dealer. He knows her folks are rich. Makes his move.'

'Four days, why haven't the parents heard?' says Hepburn.

'They're lying?' says Mackie.

'Make them sweat?' says Boden.

'Perhaps he's her secret boyfriend,' says Prisha.

Everyone turns to look at her. 'Just saying,' she adds. 'There's no evidence she went under duress.'

'That's a good point,' says Hepburn. 'We shouldn't assume anything. We have an address outside Saffron Walden. I'm asking the Essex Major Crimes Unit to put up a drone so we can get a closer real-time look. What have we seen on Google?'

'It's a farm,' says Boden. 'Down a track off the main road.'

'Off the beaten track. What is it? Just a farm? Is it being used by a County Lines gang? We can't discount that,' says Hepburn. 'But we need more intel and to see what the drone shows up.'

'With respect, sir,' says Boden. 'Waiting might come at a price. If she's there, she could still be alive. I think we should go in and try to get her. Anything else is too much of a risk.'

Hepburn scans the room. Boden wonders what he's thinking. Ticking all the boxes? No comebacks. The Lennox's high-powered connections versus risking his officers' lives? It's a judgement call. And he's right, they don't have enough information. They go blundering in, it could end badly. Her guess is he'll wait.

He sighs, folds his arms. Then he says, 'Right, we'll ask Essex for back-up. Jo, you and Scott go and check it out.'

Boden is surprised. She can feel Prisha nervously swivelling her chair.

The DC jumps up and says, 'Can I go too, sir?'

Hepburn looks at her for a moment. 'Okay. You've earned it.' He turns to Boden. 'But are you hearing me, Jo? Proceed with caution. We have no idea what we're walking into here.'

Boden nods. 'I'm hearing you, sir.'

32

Mackie is driving. Foot down in the fast lane of the M11, blues flashing. Boden likes this feeling; the adrenaline, the buzz. Prisha sits in the back, balancing her iPad.

'Drone's sending some aerial shots,' she says. 'I can see two vehicles parked in front of the house. One could be Jarman's truck.'

'He's there,' says Boden. 'Does it look like a working farm?'

'What, you mean like sheep and stuff?' says Prisha.

'Not much livestock round here anymore,' says Mackie. 'Agribusiness, big fields of crops.'

'I think I can see a tractor. Oh, but it's got no wheels.'

They turn off the motorway north of Saffron Walden and a B road leads them to the entrance of the farm track. A tactical aid unit from the neighbouring force, Essex, and a sergeant from their Major Crimes are waiting for them.

Boden introduces herself to her counterpart.

He shakes hands. 'Local intel says it's a family farm. Bit run down. But nowadays it's hard to tell. Want us to lead you in?'

'Yeah, that'd be great,' says Boden.

The cavalcade sets off down the rutted lane. It's about a mile long and ends with an open gateway and a sign: Elm Tree Farm.

They drive into the yard, everyone piles out. The back-up team fan out round the building.

Boden walks up to the front door. She's flanked by Mackie and Chakravorty. Everyone's tense but ready. This is the moment of highest risk. What's behind the door?

It's wooden, freshly painted, with a brass knocker. She lifts it and raps hard three times.

A couple of moments pass and the door opens.

A small, stout black woman peers out at them. She has grey, crinkled hair tied in a bun and a sizeable silver crucifix round her neck.

She frowns and says, 'Good morning.'

Boden holds up her ID. 'Detective Sergeant Boden. We're looking for Steven Jarman. Is he here? May we come in?'

The woman looks confused. 'My son is here,' she says. She's scanning the yard, seeing the van and the uniforms. 'My good Lord, what is this about? What has he done now?'

'Can we come in, Mrs Jarman?' says Boden.

'It's not Jarman, it's—' she sighs and shakes her head. Then she opens the door wide.

Boden goes in, followed by Mackie.

The woman is pointing down the hallway. 'The kitchen's down there. We're just having a cup of coffee.'

The place is neat, a well scrubbed wooden floor with an old-fashioned patterned runner. Another crucifix on the wall. The hall is poorly lit, but it leads into a large farmhouse kitchen, with a Rayburn cast-iron stove in an open stone fireplace. In the centre of the room there's a long deal table. Several people sit around it.

A white man, in his seventies, stands up. 'Is there a problem?' he says.

But Boden isn't looking at him. She's staring at the girl sitting opposite him, sipping her drink. Long golden hair gathered in a loose plait, blue eyes.

It takes Boden a moment to believe what she's seeing.

'Phoebe Lennox?' she says.

The girl stares back at her. 'Yes,' she replies.

'Are you aware that you've been reported missing?'

'What?'

'Police from two counties have been looking for you since Friday.'

'That's ridiculous! I'm not missing, I've been here,' she points at the man. 'Visiting my grandfather.'

Boden glances at him. He's still standing at the head of the table but he's unsteady; his hand shakes.

'Your parents and your college have been extremely concerned. They reported you missing.'

The girl huffs in annoyance. 'Oh bloody hell, I was going to email Dr G. But I got this new phone last week and I haven't transferred all my contacts.'

An excuse or a lie? If it's an iPhone, wouldn't the data transfer automatically?

Boden moves on. 'How did you get here?'

The girl points at a young man who has retreated into a corner of the room. He matches the mugshot. 'I came with Steve.'

'You were out jogging and you bumped into him outside Sainsbury's at around five pm on Friday.'

'How the hell do you know that?'

'Why did you leave Cambridge with him then?'

Phoebe stands up. She's wearing an old sweatshirt and a pair of jeans that are held up by a belt and look borrowed. 'I'm sorry, officer,' she says, in a superior tone. 'I don't think that's any of your business.'

Boden looks at her.

'In this case, given the reports we have received, Ms Lennox, I need to establish why you are here and if you were brought here under any form of duress or deception.'

The old man is still standing. He sighs. 'Phoebe, I think we should answer the officer's questions. She's only doing her job.'

Boden turns to him. 'And you are, sir?'

'Derek Cook. You've met my wife, Celia. This is a complicated family matter. Phoebe is indeed my granddaughter, but she's only just discovered that.' He shakes his head then adds, 'My daughter and I are estranged.'

'She always told me her parents were dead. She's lied to me for years,' says Phoebe sourly.

'Steven is my stepson,' says Cook. 'He and my daughter, Lacey, planned this reunion as a surprise for my seventieth birthday, which was on Saturday. Lacey's fourteen; she's at school.'

Boden nods.

'Do you mind if I sit down?' says Cook.

Another elderly man sits at the table. He has a walking frame next to him.

'We're not in the best of health, are we?' says Cook, giving his companion a nod and a smile. 'This is my brother. Farming's not an easy game. I don't farm any more. Most of the fields we rent out.'

Boden glances at the other man. An older and much fatter version of Derek Cook. No smile. He sits stock still, as if moving is painful; only his wheezy breathing is audible.

She turns back to Phoebe.

'Have you got your new phone?' she says.

Phoebe reaches into her jeans pocket and pulls it out. 'Okay,' she says. 'Granddad's right. I suppose I have gone off the grid deliberately. I didn't mean to cause a fuss. But I was angry with my mum. Still bloody well am! And I thought I'd make a video of the reunion for my YouTube channel. I've got loads of followers. I got the new phone for the filming. This one's got three lenses: ultra wide, wide and telephoto. I was going to post it and send her a link. Shock her, I guess.'

'I think you've done that. Perhaps you could call your parents. Now, if you wouldn't mind.' Boden makes sure this sounds like an instruction.

Still, Phoebe seems reluctant. She doesn't like to be thwarted. She glances at her grandfather.

'You should,' he says.

She shrugs, 'Okay. But on one condition. Can you and your colleagues go out and come in again? Then I can film you.'

'There's a lot more of them outside,' says Celia.

'Oh, wow!' says Phoebe, clapping her hands. 'Excellent. Can I film them too?'

'Absolutely not,' says Boden. 'And I suggest you get back to Cambridge and explain yourself to the college authorities.'

Phoebe grins. 'Oh, Dr G's a pussycat. She'll be fine.'

Boden watches her for a moment. No apology, no contrition. Nothing. A spoilt brat.

'I'm really sorry for the trouble we've put you to, Sergeant,' says Derek Cook.

At least he has some manners.

. . .

Boden, Mackie and Chakravorty walk back to their car.

'Well,' says Mackie. 'There you have it. Posh parents panicking.'

'Shut up, Mackie,' says Boden.

'She's a bit arrogant though, isn't she?' says Chakravorty.

'Yeah, but hot as hell,' says Mackie. 'I wouldn't say no, I can tell you.'

'She wouldn't look at you twice,' says Chakravorty.

Mackie smiles. 'Oh, you're getting cheeky, aren't you? Miss big boots detective.'

Prisha grins. He pulls a face back at her.

Boden shakes her head and sighs. 'Well, a result's a result,' she says. 'Though I don't think the boss'll be thrilled at what this operation has cost.'

33

Tuesday, 12.30pm

Marcia Lennox walked and walked; it took the best part of an hour for her temper to cool. The streets of Knightsbridge were a blur — pedestrians, cars, bikes, buses — as the argument with Louisa raged on in her head. Eventually she finds herself in Hyde Park. In the green and quiet of trees and shrubs, she becomes calmer.

Her pace slows as she skirts round the edge of the Serpentine. A breeze ripples the surface of the ornamental lake.

Finally she comes to a standstill, energy drained, and sits on a bench. Several fat, overfed geese waddle towards her, hoping for some tidbit. She shoos them away. They shit on the path.

She wants to find some way out of this morass of conflicting feelings, but she can't. Her phone vibrates in her bag. She pulls it out: Harry. She rejects the call. He's the last person she wants to talk to.

The phone vibrates again. Typical Harry. Me me me. He'll persist until she answers.

She clicks accept. 'What's the problem, Harry? You've spent one night at the new girlfriend's, but she's puking her guts up with morning sickness and you've realised being a daddy again might not be a bed of roses.'

'I've just spoken to Phoebe. She phoned me.'

His tone is neutral, but there's a catch in his voice.

For a moment she can't speak. Her whole body shudders. Shock. Relief. Mistrust. This isn't some cruel joke?

'She phoned you? When?'

'Just now. The police found her and told her to.'

Relief cascades through her, followed by questions.

'Oh, my god? Is she okay? Where the hell is she?'

'Elm Tree Farm, Marcia. Ring any bells?'

The words reverberate like echoes from another life.

She realises she's holding her breath.

Harry ploughs on, his tone snippy and critical. 'Apparently she's discovered her long-lost grandfather and is making a little film about it for her YouTube channel.'

Her lungs scream for air, the pain is intense. She must let go.

She gasps, 'She's… there? How?'

'I wondered that. Because according to you, he died years ago. Wasn't that the story? Drank himself to death after your mother died of cancer. Very sad. But not true. And you accuse me of lying.'

Disbelief becomes panic.

'I need to speak to her.'

'Good luck with that. Because she doesn't want to speak to you.'

'Have you got a number for her?'

'Y'know, Marcia, I feel sorry for you, I do. I'm going to give you some advice. Stop and think carefully about how to handle this.'

'Harry, I must speak to her.'

'Listen to me, I'm trying to help you. Whatever relationship you had with your daughter, you've wrecked it. She feels like you've denied her the chance to know her real family. I mean, why would you do that to her? I guess you had your reasons. But if you want to regain her trust, you need to back off, give her some time and space, and wait for her to come to you.'

How has this happened?

'You don't understand, Harry. That's not possible—'

'Well, it wouldn't be, would it? Have you listened to a word I've said?'

'Please. Just give me the number.'

'You can't force her to talk to you.'

'We must get her home, Harry.'

'Marcia, there is no we anymore. She'll always be my daughter. But she's a grown woman. We both have to respect that.'

She takes a deep breath. Focus. Convince him.

'Harry, I hear what you're saying. But there are things you don't know about.'

'Clearly.'

'It's not safe for her to be there.'

'Well, the police turned up. Quite a lot of them, I gather. They had every opportunity to assess the situation and I'm sure if there was the least danger, they would've removed her and taken her back to Cambridge with them. They didn't. Now, I've got to go. Think about what I've said.'

She swallows hard. 'I'm begging you. If you've ever cared about me the least bit, text me her number.'

'Oh, for God's sake, Marcia. Don't guilt trip me! I've cared about you. Of course I have. I've loved you. But we're not those people anymore. And it's not just me that's changed. You must know this in your heart. Last few years, we've just been going through the motions. It's not been a marriage.'

'And whose fault is that?'

'I'll take my share of the blame. But not all of it. You're so closed and inaccessible. No one gets near you.'

'I don't understand what you mean. I've tried to be a good wife.'

'That's the trouble. It shouldn't be an effort. You're tense all the time. Popping Xanax like they're sweets. You never relax, you never drink more than half a glass of wine. And you never laugh. What do you think it's been like living with you? For me. And for Phoebe. You're always on the cusp of annoyance. Everything's got to be how you want it. No mess, no genuine emotions. I'm not a perfect man, far from it. But I need some warmth. Someone who cares.'

'I care. I love you. I've always loved you.'

Silence. She hears him sigh.

'Marcia, you're just not... there. There's no getting close to you. We have sex, it's like you're thinking about what to make for dinner or some issue at work. And since Phoebe left, it's been ten times worse.'

She stares out across the water. A muddy beige with ducks bobbing on the tiny waves. Cyclists. A mother pushing a buggy. She's shivery and nauseous. How can she answer such accusations?

'I'm sorry you feel like that,' she says. 'I didn't know.'

'I'm sorry too,' he says. 'Sorry it's ended like this.'

More silence. She listens. Hopes. Neither wants to be the first to hang up.

'Well,' he says. 'I've got a lunch. I need to go.'

The line goes dead. She stares at her phone.

Thirty seconds later, it pings. A text pops up from Harry. With a phone number.

34

Tuesday, 1.15pm

Phoebe Lennox strolls through the quad, hair loose and flowing. She and Steve Jarman have entered the college by the back gate. She's still wearing his borrowed jeans and sweatshirt; they're cheap and tatty, but she's liking the look.

He's following her like a faithful hound, her new protector. He seems to regard himself as a big brother. A vast improvement on Eddie and Simon. Eddie's married now but has always been a self-important nerd. Simon was fun until he fell in love with her. Then he became a pain.

Phoebe turns to face Steve. He's cool and those muscles are no joke. They need to ditch the brotherly thing. His eyes are dark and sexy. The way he stares sends a shiver right through her.

'Okay,' she says. 'I need to see my tutor, do some grovelling. You can wait here.'

He folds his arms. 'When are you going to make the call?'

'Stevey, I've got a lot going on here, in case you haven't noticed. This shitstorm is not of my making.'

'Just saying, you promised the old man.'

'And I will deliver, compadre. But I left her a message, and she said she'd get back to me.'

'Yeah, well, I know what these people are like. Bloody social workers are all the same. They fob you off.'

She reaches out and touches his forearm, runs her finger along the snake tattoo. She suspects he has tats all over. 'I know this matters to granddad. I've made a promise and I intend to keep it. I'm going to make this happen for him. Like we agreed.'

He gives her a lopsided smile. So hot! 'Be sure you do,' he says.

She smiles back. 'Just wait here. This won't take long.'

Most of the tutors have their rooms in the oldest part of the building. The treads on the stone stairs are worn in the middle from generations of feet. She runs up two at a time to the top floor and isn't out of breath. She raps on Dr Grayson's door, waits for the instruction to come in, and then opens it.

Dr G is a fan, she knows this. Ever since primary school Phoebe has had the knack of charming her teachers. But the tutor is sitting at her desk, fingers laced with a stern expression on her face.

Phoebe plonks down in the chair without waiting to be invited. She runs her fingers through her hair and sighs.

'Look, I've fucked up,' she says. 'And I can only—'

'Have you called your parents?'

'Yes, I called my dad.'

'I've just spoken to your mother. She says she's having problems getting in touch with you.' Grayson pushes her glasses up her nose. She looks ultra pissed off.

Phoebe tilts her head, tries to seem penitent.

'Yeah,' she says. 'I've got this new phone, and it's been playing up. I think the battery's faulty. I may need to send it back.'

Does Grayson know she's lying? Unlikely.

On the drive from Saffron Walden back to Cambridge, her mother called her repeatedly. Phoebe didn't pick up and in the end she blocked her. Serves the stupid cow right. Maybe now she'll get the message.

'Everyone has been extremely concerned about you, Phoebe.'

'Yes, I know. But I didn't realise there'd be such a fuss. And it's not my fault.'

'I understand you told the police officers that came looking for you you'd gone off the grid? Wasn't that the term you used? And it was deliberate. I've spoken to Detective Chief Inspector Hepburn, and I had to apologise for the time and resources that the police have wasted. I hope you apologised to them too.'

'Of course.'

They still got paid, why would they give a stuff? She tries to look contrite. Is this over now? She's got things to do.

But Grayson sighs and says, 'The senior tutor and I need to discuss the best way forward for you now.'

'What do you mean, way forward?'

'I have some serious doubts about whether you're suited to academic life here. Possibly you're not quite ready.'

The spiteful bitch!

'You're not going to send me down? That is completely unfair. I mean what have I done? I discovered that the grandfather I thought was dead is alive, and I went to visit him for his seventieth birthday. He's not in the best of health, it seemed like the ethical thing to do.'

'I will not debate ethics with you. And your family situation is obviously complicated.'

'My mother lied to me and that's very upsetting.'

'Yes, which is why I think you should go home—'

WTF!

'I don't want to go home! I've only just got here.'

'Well, what do you want, Phoebe? You don't appear to want to study. It's early days. But the essays you've written for me are rather thin. You missed your supervision on Monday because of this jaunt. Have you attended any lectures?'

'Of course.'

'I don't recall seeing you at my introductory lecture on Milton.'

'I sat right at the back.'

Grayson raises her eyebrows. 'Did you?'

The stupid woman doesn't believe her. Front it out.

'I'm not a liar, Dr Grayson.'

The tutor shakes her head and sighs. 'Don't try to play me, Phoebe.'

'I swear, I'm not.'

'You're a very confident young woman. And there's nothing wrong with that. I applaud it. But there's a fine line between confidence and arrogance. And you seem to have ended up on the wrong side of it.'

Phoebe meets her gaze. What the fuck has turned Dr G against her? Ma must've bent her ear with some sob story.

She dips her head. She's feeling shaky. This is not going to plan. Can they boot her out for this?

'I'm sorry you think that.'

'Okay, I'm going to offer you some options. Number one, you go home, sort out the situation with your family, perhaps get some counselling, and we will consider readmitting you next year.'

'You mean next October? Like twelve months from now? Go home until then?'

Tears are welling, panic is rising. The thought of it! No way!

Dr G pushes a box of tissues across the desk towards her.

'The college takes seriously the mental health of our students and when someone isn't quite managing—'

'I'm managing fine. Let me prove it to you. Please.' This is totally fucked!

'That would be option number two. You're a clever young woman. But I need to see proof you can approach your studies in a mature way. I want to see that in your essays, the breadth of your reading, your attendance at lectures and your participation in seminars and supervisions.'

'You will.'

She takes a tissue and blows her nose. Flicks her hair out of her eyes for good measure.

Grayson is watching her from behind those awful glasses, deciding whether to buy it.

The tutor sighs. 'I realise a social media career is attractive and a springboard to bigger things. Half my third years seem to be more concerned about their social media profile than finals. But, for you, for now, it will have to wait.'

'I've been stupid. I understand that. I got sidetracked. It won't happen again.'

'And phone your mother. Anger can lead us to some dark places. When I spoke to her, she seemed upset and desperate to talk to you. Whatever this is about, you need to hear her out.'

Phoebe nods. Fat chance! She's blocked.

'Okay. I expect to see you at my seminar on Paradise Lost tomorrow afternoon.'

'I'll be there.'

Grayson smiles. 'Good. We'll see how you get on. If you can turn this around.'

If? It's a threat. She's being threatened!

Phoebe runs down the stone staircase at full pelt and erupts into the quad.

Steve is sitting on a wall at the edge of the formal garden. She takes a deep breath and walks towards him.

He gets up, scans her and smiles. 'Oh dear, did teacher tell you off?'

'Don't be bloody stupid. Piece of piss, I told you. Let's go.'

As they walk away, she's brooding. Does Grayson think she's not managing? She got sixty-five percent for her last essay; that's hardly thin. Then it occurs to her: she's the one who's been played. The sneaky cow knew which buttons to press; and Phoebe panicked and fell for it. So annoying! And she hasn't even read Paradise Lost, which is long.

'What about the phone call?' says Steve.

'Yes, all right! First, I need a bloody drink.'

35

Tuesday, 1.25pm

Marcia is walking up through the park towards Paddington
intending to get a taxi. She's rung the number Harry sent her.
Repeatedly. One ring, then straight to voicemail. She suspects
Phoebe's blocked her. She's also spoken to Doctor Grayson,
the idiot tutor, who wasn't much help. But she said she was
expecting to see Phoebe, which means her daughter's gone
back to Cambridge. That's some relief.

She's still wobbly. Her head's a jumble of warring
emotions. What do you do when the fear that's stalked you
for years becomes a reality?

Marcia has spent her adult life putting as much distance
as possible between herself and Elm Tree Farm. But in the
last hour it has burst back into her consciousness. Even after
all these years, the picture in her mind's eye is vivid.

The majestic row of elms with their crows' nests, which
gave the place its name. They succumbed to Dutch Elm

disease; she remembers them being cut down. The buzz of the chainsaws that dismembered them, the crash of falling branches. The crows screaming. Clutching her mother's hand and watching her cry. Her mother cried a lot.

Later she understood why. Her grandfather's prizewinning dairy herd was culled back in the sixties, before Marcia was born. The old man had to butcher two hundred pedigree cows, his life's work, because of an outbreak of foot and mouth disease. And it destroyed him, too. He gave the farm to his daughter and son-in-law, then put a shotgun in his mouth and blew his brains out. Her mother found him. She once told Marcia that the place was cursed. And she was right.

How did Phoebe end up there? It's not possible. The last time she saw her father he was passed out drunk in his own vomit. She assumed the booze would've killed him years ago.

As she moves forward, putting one foot in front of the other, she feels desolate and overwhelmed. Harry has abandoned her for no good reason. He's trying to make it her fault, but few women nowadays would've put up with his serial adultery.

She needs help, but she has nowhere to turn. Her life has been based around her husband, her daughter, and work. She's never been the sort of woman to make close friends.

She wonders about calling Lawrence, her PA. He would be sympathetic. But is that what she needs?

In the end, desperation drives her to phone DS Boden.

She's surprised that the police officer even answers.

'Hello, Mrs Lennox. I assume Phoebe's called you.'

'No. She phoned her father. But she's blocked my number. I just need to be sure she's all right. Because I'm still really worried about her.'

'She seemed fine to me.'

'I didn't mean to lie to you. It wasn't deliberate. I thought my father was dead. He was a serious alcoholic. I wouldn't have expected him to survive.'

'Families can be complicated. I'm sure Phoebe will come round.' The police officer is being polite, which is something.

'Has she gone back to Cambridge?'

'I believe so.'

Marcia hesitates, then she says, 'You'll think this is me being paranoid, but I think he could pose a serious threat to Phoebe.'

Stay calm, be reasonable. Don't sound like a madwoman.

'Your father, Derek Cook?'

'Yes.'

'Why is that, Mrs Lennox?'

'I can't... really explain.'

She does sound like a madwoman.

She hears the sergeant sigh.

'Well, okay, in the past, if he used to be a drinker, I get that your father could've been a violent man. Did he abuse you?'

'Not exactly. He drank himself into a stupor and checked out.'

'He was neglectful?'

'Yes, but...' She takes a breath. This is ridiculous. How can she even begin to explain? It's impossible.

'You haven't seen him for many years?'

'No. I left and I've never been back.'

'Let me tell you what I saw, going there now,' says the sergeant. 'First, he seemed perfectly sober. Are you aware he's married again?'

'Married?' Who the hell would've married him? That's ludicrous.

'I would say that his wife is a lady of strong religious

175

faith. They have a teenage daughter. He also has an older stepson. It was his stepson who Phoebe met in Cambridge.'

A daughter? A teenage daughter!

She says nothing. It's all too bizarre.

'I understand it was his seventieth birthday on Saturday,' says the sergeant.

She dredges her memory. Twenty-sixth of October? She can remember her mother's birthday in August. But not him. Everything about him she's blocked out.

'Would that be right?' says the sergeant.

'I don't know. I can't remember.'

'Mr Cook said that you were estranged. It sounded as if he regretted that. I would say he's not in the best of health. Perhaps you should go and see him for yourself, Mrs Lennox? I realise you might find that difficult. But I think that would help you resolve this matter with your daughter.'

Why are these bloody people so patronising! She has to rein in her temper.

'You can't do anything to help me?' she says.

The panic is rising again. Threatening to engulf her.

'What do you expect us to do?'

'Stop her going there again.'

'Mrs Lennox, this is not a matter for the police. Your daughter was reported missing. We took steps to locate her and confirm she was safe. But she's an adult and has every right to go where she likes and do what she wants, within the law. We have no power to tell her what to do because you're worried about her?'

'Even if she's in danger?'

'Do you have any grounds for saying that, now in the present? It sounds to me as if—'

Marcia hangs up and throws her phone onto the grass. She wants to scream. She can't. Get a grip!

She clenches her fists, pressing her nails into her palms until the pain is too much to bear.

36

Tuesday, 1.30pm

Phoebe's only been in the town three weeks, but she's already figured that *Barney's,* near the Corn Exchange, is the bar to frequent. It's expensive; cooler students go there, but not the general rabble. It has great tapas and is often full of performers from the nearby concert venue. She's seen a couple of famous faces.

She perches on a stool at the high bench facing out through the window. Steve puts his hands in his pockets; he has a now-what expression on his face.

'I'll have a large G&T,' she says. 'Hendrick's and don't let them put any crap in it. Slice of lime, not lemon.'

He tilts his head and gives her a long-suffering look.

'What?' she says. 'You expect me to go to the bar?'

She pulls out twenty quid and hands it to him.

He sighs. 'Okay. Now, make the call. You promised.'

She gets out her phone and holds it up. 'I'm doing it, okay.'

He walks off towards the bar. She watches him go. Those shoulders tapering down to his tight little arse. It's hard to take her eyes off him.

She's slept with quite a few boys. This is 2019, and she's not some naïve virgin waiting for love. But truth is, it's always been a let-down. Either a frantic fumble that's over too quickly or just plain boring. She wonders if there's something wrong with her. But who can she ask about that? She's hunted around online, but what's out there is total rubbish.

She thought someone older would know what they were doing. But Jack was rough, and not in a good way. He wanted her to try all kinds of stuff she didn't like. She agreed to a threesome with him and Simon; they all got high, and that made it super weird. Afterwards she was covered in bruises and she felt sick. It was at the villa in the summer, and everyone was having such a great time. She didn't want to be uncool and spoil it by making a fuss.

Talking to girlfriends about sex is awkward. It's so competitive. How do you admit that you've never actually come with a boy, you can only come when you masturbate? She'd be a laughing stock if that ever got out.

Maybe with Steve it'll be different? He gives off a real charge, like a coiled spring. Gets impatient with her when she teases him. That's such a turn on.

She sighs, looks at her phone, finds the number and calls it.

Two rings, and it goes to voicemail.

'Hi, Rosa,' she says. 'It's Phoebe Lennox again. Sorry to hassle, but I'm really keen to speak to Carol, hear her story. The prison told us she might be working for a vegetable picking gang in Norfolk. We went round loads of places at the weekend, but we couldn't find her. Just a chat, nothing intense, I promise. I'm really hoping you can persuade her for me. Thanks.'

She hangs up. Job done.

If she's honest, this long-lost-family thing is not what she expected. It's turned into a complete hassle. They're all a bit thick, and quite Goddy. But the meat in the sandwich was always going to be Carol, getting her to talk on camera. The cops wouldn't be filmed, which was a pain. Plus, now she's got herself on the wrong side of Dr G. More hassle.

There's a queue at the bar, but Steve has shouldered his way in. He's the only interesting thing to have come out of this. He'll have to be her consolation prize.

But this total fiasco has made her nervous and unsure of herself. Front it out, Ma always says. Don't let them see how you really feel.

She thinks about her mother. Ma has always been a complicated woman. But why did she have to lie about all this? It's pissy. She suspects it's snobbery. And the Carol thing. Ma thinks people are always judging her, which means everything must be right: her clothes, the house, her perfect daughter. Try playing that role 24/7. But who would give a stuff if they found out she grew up on some dingy farm in the backend of Essex? It's ridiculous.

Dad says she should talk to Ma, give her a chance to explain. And, of course, he's right. He's always been the voice of reason in their family.

Cambridge has been her dream and her goal for years. It's been a slog; no one can say she hasn't worked for it. But everything has got muddled up. Too much has happened all at once. Now she's in trouble with Dr G and could get sent down. She wants to cry. Or scream. Or both.

The gin is about to arrive. Focus on that. Then she'll call Ma.

She glances out of the window and does a double take. Simon is standing on the pavement staring in at her. She can't believe it! When's this shitshow going to end?

Why the hell is he in Cambridge? He's coming in. And he appears to have his bloody mother in tow!

Simon walks across the bar towards her; his jaw is hanging open, and he looks like a wounded puppy.

'What the hell, Phoebe!' he says, pulling her into a hug. 'Just spoke to Dad. Are you all right?'

'Fine,' she says, pushing him away. 'It was all a misunderstanding. I don't know why anyone thought I was missing.'

Louisa is behind him. She doesn't look happy. There's an imperiousness to her that Phoebe's always found scary. She reminds her of a horrible teacher she had at primary school.

'Hey, Louisa,' she says, with as much enthusiasm as she can muster. 'What are you two doing in Cambridge?'

'You are such an awful brat, Phoebe. Have you any idea how much trouble you've caused?'

Phoebe is taken aback. This is bloody rude, even for Louisa.

'I'm sorry,' she says. 'I don't know what you're talking about.'

'I had to come to Cambridge to get my son out of jail. The police were about to arrest him. He came looking for you.'

This makes no sense whatsoever.

Phoebe frowns. 'Arrest him? Why?'

Louisa shifts her vintage Chloé bag from one shoulder to the other. 'Because they thought he could be involved in your disappearance.'

'That's ridiculous.'

Louisa huffs and shakes her head.

'Mum, it's not her fault,' says Simon. 'Jack should never have put that thing on her phone.'

Phoebe glares at them. 'What thing?'

He looks sheepish. 'We were worried about you, y'know.'

She's aware of Louisa staring at her, as if she's some kind of criminal.

Can this get any more irritating? 'Why is everyone worried about me?' she says. 'I'm not a bloody child. I'm eighteen.'

Simon sighs. 'Jack put an app on your phone, so we could check you were all right.'

Phoebe laughs out loud. 'Oh, right! He's such a control freak. I might've known. Do Ma and Dad know about this?'

'Yes, it's what set it all off,' says Simon. 'The app told us the phone hadn't moved, and you hadn't used it.'

She shakes her head and laughs again, though it's far from funny. Front it out. 'Yeah, cause I got a new one! What? Now I can't get a new phone without starting a major panic?'

'Y'know Phoebe,' says Louisa, with icy calm. 'You're a bright girl. But you'd do well to think about the impact of your behaviour on other people. You're totally self-centred.'

This is totally unfair! She wants to scream. Louisa can be a right cow. No wonder Dad divorced her.

'My behaviour? None of this is my fault, Louisa. None of it.'

Why can no one see that?

'You need to talk to your mother.'

She knows this, but it won't be because snooty Louisa bullies her into it.

She wants to give a cutting reply and bites her tongue. But the old hag seems to read her mind.

'Everything's not about you, Phoebe,' she says. 'And

what you may not know is that Marcia and Harry have split up.'

'Don't be ridiculous. What are you talking about?' This must be a lie, but why is she being spiteful?

'It's true. I spoke to Marcia this morning. I've never seen her this upset. But that was about you being missing. What you've put that poor woman through, put us all through.'

'You saying this is because of me too?' Phoebe is flabbergasted.

'No. I'm saying if you want to be treated like a grown-up, you need to behave like one.' She turns to her son, 'Come on Simon, I want to get the two o'clock train. I need to get back to London.'

Louisa turns on her heel, sticks her nose in the air and walks out. What a cow!

Simon is gawping at her like the fool he is. 'Sorry, Phi. She's a bit upset. I'll text you. We'll talk. You're right, this is down to Jack.'

He scurries off after his mother. She watches them go.

WTF! When is this nightmare going to end? Her eyes well with tears.

Steve is walking across the bar towards her. He's carrying a bulbous glass and a bottle of beer. She swallows hard, wipes her eyes.

'Who was that?' he says.

Phoebe takes the glass; it's loaded with ice and beaded in moisture. She takes a large mouthful of gin.

'No one,' she says.

37

Tuesday, 1.45pm

Marcia sits on a bench at the edge of the park. She has no idea what to do or where to go. She's well-dressed, her hair cut in an expensive, collar-length bob, and she has credit cards in her purse. But inside she feels like an outcast, like some homeless bag lady that no one cares about. Everything she believed was solid in her life is shattering, like fine bone china smashing to smithereens on a stone floor.

She's been abandoned. That's the reality.

Harry will want to sell the house. Or perhaps he intends to evict her and move her replacement in? Turn one of the back bedrooms into a nursery; the quiet one overlooking the garden. That was her plan years ago. A sibling for Phoebe. A playroom in between for both children to share.

Harry had vetoed all that. No more sleepless nights and shitty nappies, he said. He wanted them to have fun.

Was it ever that much fun? Yes. At first it was a glorious adventure. Harry is such a charmer; he has the gift of making you feel the most special person in the world. They did things and visited places she'd only read about in glossy magazines. He loved spoiling her and seeing her pleasure as she opened his latest gift. Secret trysts in fancy hotels. Snatched weekends away. Throwing caution to the wind. Harry was great at all that.

She never expected it to last. But when he proposed, she realised it was what she needed. Security for herself and her child. A live-in nanny instead of a child minder; a cleaner who did the ironing too; a private school with all the extras; skiing every winter; holiday cottages and villas in exotic locations. And she worked hard at this marriage, worked at parenting, worked to advance her career; hadn't she earned these things?

Perhaps she's been fooling herself. It was always a fragile and fleeting thing. But it lasted much longer than she expected; that's what her efforts achieved. Perhaps she should be proud of that.

Her phone vibrates, making her jump. The number that she's called forty-six times.

She answers it immediately. 'My god, Phoebe! Are you all right?'

'Yes, I'm fine.' There's tension in her daughter's voice. She's not fine.

'Oh my god, Phi, I've been desperately worried. Where are you?'

Don't cry! Focus.

'Ma, I'm fine. I'm sitting outside a bar in Cambridge, although I have to say it's bloody freezing.'

Marcia doesn't trust herself to speak. But just hearing her daughter's voice is enough.

'Is it true,' Phoebe says, 'that you and Dad are splitting up? Because I know the stuff he does is a pain. That waitress at the wedding. There was no excuse for that, even if he was drunk. But he adores you, Ma. Don't boot him out. Give the silly sod another chance.'

Her gut is rigid from the effort to hold herself steady.

'It's not that simple, darling.'

'Okay, then let's make it simple. Here's the deal. I'll forgive you for lying to me, if you forgive him.'

The tears well up; she can't stop them.

'That's certainly a deal I'd take,' she says. 'But he's left me. For someone else.'

'Who?'

She can hear the incredulity in Phoebe's voice.

'A woman he works with. Her name's Marie–Claire, and she's pregnant.'

'Pregnant? Well, she's got him over a barrel. How could he be that stupid?'

'It might be more than that. I think it's what he wants.'

'Well, he said nothing to me when I phoned him.'

'I'm sure he was just relieved to hear your voice. My god, Phoebe, we were just… in despair.'

Phoebe sighs. 'Okay, look, I am sorry. I didn't mean… well, you know I didn't mean for you to worry. Or the police or any of that stuff. The whole thing's completely mad. And bloody Jack, he's such a tosser. You were right about him.'

Marcia takes a deep breath.

'Oh my darling girl, I'm sorry too. I never meant to lie to you. I thought my father was dead. Okay, it was an assumption. All I've ever wanted to do was protect you.'

There's a silence on the line. Then an audible sigh.

'But what about Carol?'

An icy shiver shoots up her spine. 'Carol?' she says.

'I know about her too. You've got a sister called Carol.'

'How the hell have you found out all this?'

'Well, when I started my Insta page. About six months ago. I didn't tell you because I wanted to show you what I could do. Impress you, I guess.'

'You don't have to impress me, Phi.'

'I used one of my baby pictures. The one of me in this basket thingy when I was just a couple of weeks old. And in the background, there's a fence. Like quite an unusual lattice pattern with red bits. This girl who was following me online said it looked like the place where she lived. On this farm. Then she sent me some pictures. And it was the same fence. We chatted. She said her second name was Cook, like ours used to be. Then I asked her loads more questions.'

Marcia realises she's holding her breath. She's dizzy.

'Ma, are you still there?'

'Yes. I'm here. What did you find out?'

'The girl's called Lacey Cook; she's fourteen. Her mum's Celia, and she's a nurse. She comes from Antigua and she worked at this rehab facility. Derek, your dad, was a patient there. He was older than her, but she ended up marrying him. She already had a son, Steven, but they came to live on his farm and Lacey was born. Seems you have a half sister and I have an aunt who's four years younger than me.'

What DS Boden said is true.

'I had no idea about this, I swear.'

'Lacey told her dad about me. And it sort of developed from there.'

'Phoebe, why didn't you tell me?'

'I thought… I don't know. I suppose I thought you'd be angry or try to stop it. Then I did a couple of Zoom calls with them and he told me about Carol.'

'What did he say about Carol?'

'She murdered her cousin and went to jail. And then I thought you would be pissed off with me. You had a sister in jail and you obviously wanted to keep it a secret. I could see why that would be embarrassing.'

'Not embarrassing. I needed to protect you.'

'Yeah, when I was a little kid, maybe.'

But she's still a little kid. Marcia knows she can't say that.

'I did some research, all the old press I could find about the trial. There wasn't much because she pleaded guilty. But she must've had terrible legal advice. He was awful. A drug dealer, who abused her. Did you know all that?'

'Yes. Listen Phoebe, we need to talk about this properly, in person. I'll come up to Cambridge.'

'What about your dad? He's been sober for years. Still goes to AA. And Celia is lovely. Okay, they're a bit religious, the happy-clappy sort. But he talks about forgiveness all the time. And making amends. That's why he asked me to help him with Carol.'

Forgiveness! The word sounds hollow.

'Help him do what?'

'She won't see him or have any contact. And now she's out—'

'She's out?'

A hot nausea sweeps over her.

'Last week,' says Phoebe. 'They let her out on licence. I've been talking to her probation officer and trying to persuade her to see me. I'll admit that to start with, it was about filming her. You know, justice for my aunt, the wrongly convicted murderer. That would get loads of attention. People love that miscarriage of justice stuff.'

'Please, don't do anything until you see me. And don't try to see her. I'll come up to Cambridge. I'll come this afternoon.'

'Can it be tomorrow? Because Dr G is on my case. Big time. I've got a seminar with her tomorrow at two. I've got the whole of Paradise Lost to read before then. We could talk after that.'

Marcia hesitates. Harry's right. Don't push too hard.

She clenches her fist, forces herself to take a breath.

'Agreed,' she says. 'But Phoebe, do nothing until we talk. Promise?'

'What are you saying? Is she dangerous?'

'Just promise me, darling.'

'Ma, I'm not going anywhere. It's just me and Paradise Lost.'

'It's too complicated for the phone. But we'll sort this out.'

'Look, I know it was impulsive. I regret that. But Steve came looking for me, we'd met on Zoom, and he said it was the old man's seventieth birthday. I only wanted to help him. He is my grandfather. It seemed like the right thing to do.'

'Calling me would've been the right thing to do.'

'Yeah, I see that now. I'm sorry. But hey, guess what? I bumped into old Louisa. I think the police questioned Simon about my supposed disappearance.'

'They did.'

Phoebe laughs. 'She was so pissed off. Should've seen her face. You would've loved it.'

Marcia smiles. Her irrepressible daughter. She longs to hug her, stroke her hair and hold her close.

'You're incorrigible,' she says.

'Must get that from you. But, hey, I'm sorry about you and Dad. I think he's a fool.'

'He still loves you, Phi. He's still your dad.'

'I know. But you're the important one. Always have been. And I am sorry.'

'I'll see you tomorrow afternoon.'

'Yeah, text me. Love you, Ma.'

38

Tuesday, 5.40pm

Yesterday had been pretty boring, and Lacey ended up on a real downer. Plus, she ate all the chocolates in the Celebrations tub and felt sick. So this morning she went to school.

It was an average day. The special needs class psycho kicked off in double maths and threw a chair at the teacher. By the time he'd been restrained and removed, half the lesson was over. The teacher was upset; who wouldn't be? The psycho's a big lad. Steve says his dad's in jail for GBH. Her mum says she should have compassion for the afflicted. But in the real world, outside the Church, no one ever does.

When she got home at quarter to four Mum had made some salted caramel brownies and a banana loaf, and she knew something was up. The only time her mother bakes is after she and her dad have rowed. Except they don't row like normal people, they *have words*. They take it in turns to put their hand on their heart and *speak their truth*. It doesn't happen often because usually the old man backs down as soon as he sees Mum's pissed off.

But something had happened this morning, while she was at school, and it was serious. They weren't even speaking. Her dad looked uncomfortable. No sign of Uncle Brian. Must be tucked up in his room watching porn on his iPad.

Lacey made herself a cup of tea. Her mother gave her a brownie. It was delicious. Mum's a brilliant cook when she wants to be. Lacey sat down to eat it. She scanned both her parents and waited.

Finally, her mother put her hands on her hips and said, 'The good Lord knows I have been a patient woman with you, Derek Cook. I have supported you, loved you, prayed for you. Borne your child.'

She shot a glance in Lacey's direction, which made her feel guilty. Though she wasn't sure for what. Being born?

'But the police! Coming here to our door like that. And not just one policeman. A van load. And detectives too.'

Shit!

'As a good, law-abiding Christian woman, how d'you think that makes me feel?'

Dad sighed. 'Celia, it was a misunderstanding.'

'All the grief I had with Steven when he was a teen. Now, I know you worked hard to be a proper father to that boy. And now he's a fine young man. And I give you credit for that, you know I do.'

Dad sat with his head dipped and the look of a whipped dog.

The fact Steve realised he could make loads more money selling coke than driving a delivery van or working in a chicken factory was hardly the old man's fault. Basically, he's a drug dealer. Except nowadays he was picky about his customers and took care not to get caught. He pretends to

Mum that he earns money selling Jacuzzis. She believes him; she's always been blinkered when it comes to Steve.

Lacey wondered where he was. Had the cops come looking for him? Detectives too; sounds serious.

'I don't think you can blame Phoebe,' said the old man. 'She had no idea they'd reported her missing.'

Bloody Phoebe. It was about her.

'Derek,' said Mum, in that long-suffering tone of hers, 'if Carol don't want to come home and receive a father's forgiveness, you can't make her. It will all happen in the Lord's good time. You've found your granddaughter. Be thankful for that.'

Lacey wasn't thankful. Phoebe had turned out to be a major disappointment.

First, she said not to call her PhoReal, that was just a social media thing. She thought it was childish. Friends called her Phoebe or Phi. Second, she only had eyes for Steve. After greeting Lacey and giving her an awkward hug, she didn't say another word to her the whole time she was there.

She talked to Mum and Dad, especially Dad, asked loads of stupid questions. She even tried to talk to Uncle Brian. He just stared at her like some dribbling idiot. Mum says the stroke has affected his brain. But Lacey reckons it depends who's around. He's a devious old bastard. When it's just her or Steve and he wants something, he has no trouble making himself understood. Him and Steve have long conversations about stuff.

Lacey finished her brownie and was about to leave when Mum said. 'I know Steve suggested it, but I don't think it's right to expect Phoebe to be a go-between. I think you have to be patient and keep these things separate.'

Dad shook his head. It looked like he was saying no or disagreeing. But it signalled him giving in. Still, his eyes were shifty. There was something he wasn't telling Mum. She didn't appear to notice.

Lacey needed to text Steve to find out what was going on. She ducked out of the back door.

Her mother's voice trailed after her. 'Lacey! Don't forget your homework.'

No maths homework tonight. Thanks to the special needs class psycho.

Daisy trotted after her, and they headed for the barn.

Once she was ensconced in her nest, Lacey texted her brother. Then she waited. The text delivered, but he didn't reply. Maybe he was using a burner. When he was out and about, he often turned his regular phone off. A sensible precaution, he called it. That's how the cops get people nowadays.

She wondered what to do until teatime. She checked into a couple of her regular groups, but nothing much was going on.

The straw was warm. The dog curled up next to her, and she dozed off.

Lacey wakes with a start; outside it's already dark.

In her dream she was out clubbing with Phoebe and it's like they were sisters, laughing and chatting. Telling each other all their secrets.

Then she remembers what Steve said to her, when she told him she was upset because Phoebe was ignoring her. He laughed and said: you got a real crush on her, haven't you? Like it was some creepy lesbo thing. And she felt awful.

She checks her phone; he still hasn't replied. But she hears a noise outside; a car is driving into the yard. He must be back. She wonders if he's on his own.

She climbs down from her perch, high up in the straw bales in the barn. The dog follows.

The outside light has come on in the yard and a car is pulling up. But it isn't her brother.

Not that many people drive into the yard. Sometimes people who rent the fields come to see her dad. Occasionally someone comes from Church.

It's not a church-goer's car. It's shiny and black; looks expensive. Steve knows all the brands of cars, but she doesn't. She knows a Land Rover, the cranky old heap her dad drives, and her brother's pickup.

She walks across the yard towards the visitor; Daisy trots at her heel.

A woman gets out of the driver's seat and stares at her. She's not a church-goer. Slim like a model, making it hard to tell her age. And wearing skinny jeans and a silk shirt. Too posh for round here.

The woman tilts her head and says, 'You must be Lacey.'

She nods.

'I'm Marcia,' the woman says. 'Is Dad around?'

39

Tuesday, 5.42pm

Marcia scans the front of the house. She remembers the stone facade of the original building and then the red brickwork of the Victorian extension built to one side. The downstairs sash windows have been replaced. Her mother always complained about the draught they let in. The front door is new, with a brass knocker. It looks as if someone polishes it.

Lacey is in front of her, she opens the door and shouts, 'Mum! Someone's here.'

Someone.

Following her in feels familiar, but also strange.

The drive from London took a couple of hours; she accepted the satnav's advice and took the longer but faster route on the motorway. For most of the way, she was still debating whether to do this. On the M11 she told herself she could carry on north to Cambridge. But when the exit to Saffron Walden came up, she made a snap decision. Now she's regretting it.

The hallway was always gloomy. It was the core of the old farmhouse and dated back to the late seventeen hundreds. The Maitland family had farmed the land since 1872. Her mother was Jill Maitland. When she left, Marcia considered adopting her mother's maiden name. She wishes she had. Better than Cook. But she had other pressing concerns back then.

A small, bustling woman appears in the kitchen doorway. Phoebe said she was a nurse, and that's what she looks like. Hair neatly tied back and strong, capable hands.

She stares at Marcia for a moment, then her face lights up. 'Well, well!' she says. 'He works in mysterious ways, his wonders to perform.'

The woman opens her arms and is about to launch forward. Marcia steps backwards to avoid a hug.

'Come in, come in! I'm Celia.'

'I'm Marcia.'

'I've seen the pictures.'

She allows herself to be shepherded forward towards the familiar kitchen. And it hasn't changed. The old Rayburn, the long deal table, given to her grandparents as a wedding present.

'You see, Derek,' says Celia. 'You pray for one daughter to return and he sends you the other.'

Her father is sitting at the head of the table, glasses perched on his nose, newspaper open in front of him. He looks old.

He stares at her in disbelief. 'Marcie?'

'Hello, Dad.'

What does she feel? Nothing.

His chair scrapes on the stone floor as he pushes it back and struggles to his feet.

She watches him stagger, age not booze this time, and he has tears in his eyes.

'I never thought…' he splutters.

Neither did she.

She walks round to the other side of the table to increase the distance between them.

He grasps the table's edge to steady himself. 'I've prayed for this day. And I thank the Lord.'

'Well,' she says coolly, 'if you've swapped whiskey and swearing for praying, I suppose that's an improvement.'

'I haven't taken a drink since the day Lacey was born,' he says. 'I knew I was being granted a second chance.'

Is he even going to introduce his new family? It seems not.

She glances at her new half-sister, an overweight teenager with a mass of unruly black curls and a surly expression. The girl stares back. A mixture of curiosity and hostility.

'I'll put the kettle on,' says Celia. 'And there are brownies.'

She raises her hand. 'Thank you, but no,' she says. 'What I want to say won't take long.'

'Please, sit and listen to me first,' her father says. 'You can spare five minutes, surely?'

Get in and out as fast as possible. That was her plan.

She sighs.

'I'm listening,' she says.

He lowers himself into his chair. Looks like he's in pain. Once he was solid muscle, could carry a calf looped round his shoulders. He puts his elbows on the table and clasps his shaking hands to steady them.

'He knows he's a sinner, Marcie,' says Celia. 'Just hear him out.'

'It's Marcia, not Marcie.'

197

'Sorry. Marcia.'

Celia steps back, moves over to the sink and fills the kettle.

Now he seems at a loss, hands shaking uncontrollably. Then he says, 'I had a new marble headstone put on your mother's grave. If you go down to the cemetery, you'll see it.'

'I don't need to visit her grave or have a piece of marble to remember her. Or what you did to her.'

Celia turns round from the sink to stare. She's apprehensive but curious. Lacey has settled on the old leather sofa in the corner with her dog.

He may have turned into a decrepit old man, but it doesn't change who he was. Or what he did.

'I wonder if your new family knows the whole story?' she says. 'Or do they think you're this soft old man, means no harm, always the victim. Poor old Derek, none of it was his fault.'

He shrugs. 'You can speak your truth. I have no secrets from them.'

'My truth? How about the truth? She had breast cancer, which had metastasised. It had spread to her bones. She was dying. And the GP sat you down at this table and he told you that. But you wouldn't listen. You poured yourself a large glass of whiskey and you told him to go to hell. Well, your exact words were: go fuck yourself. I was fifteen, and I was sitting over there.' She points at the sofa where Lacey is.

'You must understand, I couldn't bear to lose her.'

'You couldn't bear it? What about her?'

'I know I was selfish.'

'Selfish? More like downright cruel. The GP arranged for her to go to a hospice so her pain could be managed. You refused to let her go. Said it was too soon, she wasn't that sick. But you left me to bathe her, try to feed her, and comfort her while you drank. You wouldn't even go in her room.'

He dips his head, wipes his nose with the back of his hand.

'They sent a Macmillan nurse to help us. You threw her out. Drinking, ranting. I won't allow death in my house, you said.'

'I thought they were giving up on her. Filling her full of drugs that would kill her,' he says. 'I was desperate. I didn't want to lose her.'

'She died in agony because of you, because you wouldn't let her go. All I had to give her was paracetamol and codeine. You put all that on me.'

'And I am sorry for that.'

'Sorry doesn't quite cut it. You think you can buy forgiveness with a marble headstone?'

She's waited years to say this. The bitterness stewing inside her. Did she feel any relief? No. Just emptiness.

He's sitting staring at his hands. The girl is petting the dog; it reminds her of the Collie they had when she was a child. Celia is mumbling to herself, sounds like a prayer.

She needs to finish this and get out.

Then she hears a noise coming from the hallway. Something scraping the wooden floor? Celia rushes through the door towards it.

A bulky figure emerges through the doorway. Pot-bellied, wisps of white hair and a straggling grey beard. He's leaning heavily on a walking frame. He lifts it up and plonks it down in his slow progress into the room.

Celia fusses over him. 'Come on, lovey. Come and sit down. Look who's here.'

Marcia stares in disbelief. Uncle Brian. What the hell!

His eyes seem blank, he doesn't meet her gaze. There's

no recognition. His energy is focused on getting across the room to the armchair in the corner.

As she watches him struggle, she notices her father looking at her.

'He had a stroke. Few years ago now. We took him in, Marcie, because it was the Christian thing to do. He is my brother.'

She looks back at him in horror.

'And Carol is your daughter.'

'We must all put the past behind us,' he says.

'Why? Because you've got religion as your new excuse? You seriously think Carol will come back here? Never. Who can blame her? If you contact Phoebe again and try to use her to get to Carol, I'm going to the police. They've been here once. My husband is well connected, he knows people in government. Believe me, I can do it.'

The old man is looking at her with those watery blue eyes. Weakness personified.

'I'm not trying to make trouble for you, Marcie,' he says. 'All I want is to make amends before I die and beg her forgiveness. And yours. Look at me, seventy years old, but I may as well be ninety. I haven't got long. Is it too much to ask?'

'Yes. It is.'

She turns on her heel and walks out.

40

Wednesday, 8.15am

Phoebe opens her eyes. He's sitting on the desk chair looking at her. His boxers are super-clingy, hugging the muscles of his thighs. They leave nothing to the imagination. His naked torso is ripped, like a model in an ad. She wishes he'd let her photograph him. But he's curiously shy.

'Are all students as lazy as you?' he says.

She sits up, pushes back her hair and reaches out towards him. 'Stevey, come back to bed.'

'I don't call that a bed, it's more like a bunk. I ended up sleeping on the floor.'

She flaps her hand. 'Who said anything about sleeping?'

She tries to sound seductive. But he doesn't move. He continues to stare. His inscrutability is one of the things that makes him hot.

'What I'd like,' he says, 'Is a cup of coffee. Then we need to get on the road.'

She scrabbles on the bedside table, picks up her phone.

'It's not even half eight,' she says. 'You don't have to go yet, surely.'

'We need to go.'

'What are you talking about? Go where?'

'Back to Norfolk to track down Carol. That last place we went, I'm sure the woman knew her name. We should go back and check it out.'

They must've trailed round half a dozen farms and scuzzy caravan sites full of foreign workers. People who didn't speak any English had greeted them with suspicion. It was tedious.

'Stevey, it's a waste of time. Our best bet is to convince the probation officer. She's the only one who knows where Carol is.'

'She hasn't even called you back. I think we should keep looking.'

'No, I can't. Not today. I've got a seminar this afternoon. And I'm in enough bother already.'

He folds his arms and huffs. 'But you promised. You said if we go early. Check out that last place near Diss. We can be back by lunchtime.'

She rubs her eyes, sighs. 'C'mon, I'm sure I never did.'

'You did.'

Why is he being arsey about this? She can't remember what she said. After she spoke to her mother, they spent the rest of the afternoon in Barney's. And it was great. Well, she thinks it was.

'I guess I was drunk.'

'And that's your excuse for breaking a promise?'

'It isn't like that. And I'll make it up to you.'

She tries to think back to the sex. They did it. That much she remembers. But she was quite drunk. Which is a pity.

Under the duvet, she's naked; she pushes it back so he can

look at her. She has a good body; she knows that. If she can just entice him back to bed.

She tilts her head. 'Hey, don't be mad. I promised my mum I'd wait. She wants to talk to me.'

He stands up, ignoring what she's offering, and turns away, walking over to the window.

'What difference does that make?' his tone is tetchy. 'Aren't you old enough to make your own decisions?'

His shoulders are broad, defined muscles and silky skin.

She gets out of bed, goes over and puts her arms round him from behind. She presses her body against him.

'Let's not fall out,' she says.

He turns to face her, and he's got tears in his eyes. 'Derek's my stepdad. But I owe everything to him. I was a bad boy in my teens, but he never gave up on me. My mum can be difficult, but I could always talk to him.'

He's full of surprises. Hard one minute, then soft as a baby.

'I know what you mean.' She strokes his chest.

'Do you? Then you'll know I can't let him down. He's got Parkinson's and a dodgy heart. He could just collapse any time. Today, tomorrow. That would be it. He's gone. This whole thing with Carol. It weighs on him. He didn't protect her, and he should've. He needs to make amends. It's this AA thing. He thinks you can persuade her to see him. He's trusted you with this. I've trusted you.'

She gazes at him. His chin quivers like a little boy. The tears are running down his cheeks. He is gorgeous! She wants to hug him and comfort him. But he moves away.

'Steve, I'm sorry. I'll talk to Mum and then—'

'No! You haven't listened to a word I've said, have you?' He grabs his T-shirt and pulls it on. 'I guess we're done.'

She's at a total loss. He reaches for his jeans. She watches him. How can he be this upset? Has she caused this?

'Look, I didn't realise what this meant to you.'

'Why? Cause you think I'm some yob with no feelings? Boys don't hurt. Boys don't cry.' He wipes his face with the back of his hand. 'He's my dad. I promised him.'

'Okay, let's figure this out. I don't want to let you down.'

'Then don't.' Now he's begging her. 'I'll get you back in time for your thing. Read the stuff you need to read on the way.'

He's gazing right at her, those amazing dark eyes still liquid with tears. Letting him walk out now is not an option.

'Okay,' she says. 'Let's do it.'

What difference will it make? Ma said to leave it, but she never said why. She's just being a control freak. As long as they get back by lunchtime, maybe she need never know.

41

Carol is buttering bread. She's on her fourth sliced loaf. Alina is adding filling to make sandwiches. They're preparing lunch for the crew who are cutting cabbages on a farm a few miles away.

The police released her without charge late the previous afternoon, and Rosa drove her back to the smallholding. She was embarrassed and awkward. But a babble of incomprehensible voices greeted her with smiles and pats on the back. Vasile explained the gang were applauding her bravery. They'd all experienced insults, abuse and occasional violence from some of the more unpleasant locals; Carol had struck a blow on behalf of them all, and they appreciated it.

Her reward was an easy day, helping Alina out, but still on full pay.

Lunch is a mountain of sandwiches and a cauldron of homemade parsnip soup; Vasile will come back to collect it.

The two women work well together. Alina's baby dozes

in his Moses basket. It sits on a table in the old marquee which is their makeshift kitchen.

They listen to music on Alina's phone; the young woman sings along with the lyrics to improve her English. For Carol, she's relaxing company, dancing round the kitchen between jobs, cooing over her baby. Her happiness is infectious.

Carol smiles. 'What's his name?'

'His name is called David. In Romanian. In English. Same.'

'It's a good name. I knew a David once.'

She tries not to think about that.

But the look on her face gives her away, because Alina laughs and raises her eyebrows. 'Is maybe your boyfriend?'

Is she that transparent? But Alina means no harm.

'Long time ago,' she says.

Carol cuts the completed sandwiches and wraps them in clingfilm to make individual packs. She loads them into a plastic crate and places it next to the canvas flap which serves as a door.

As she puts the crate down, she notices a pickup driving up the lane. It's like the one Vasile drives, but as it gets closer, she realises it's not him. The vehicle will drive past; there are other properties further down the lane. But it slows and turns into their gateway.

Alina peers over her shoulder. 'Is people,' she says. 'Come before. Sunday.'

Her gut contracts with fear.

'You mean the ones looking for me?'

The adrenaline surges through her. Is there any point running?

Alina is scrutinising her. Frowning, she pats her arm and says, 'No worry. I do this. I make go.'

Carol retreats to the kitchen area and busies herself making more sandwiches.

The marquee is open along one side; the canvas is old and sagging. The hooks to secure this side have broken.

Carol keeps her head down, but she can see the pickup draw up.

The driver gets out first; twenties, male, mixed race. Far too tough-looking to tackle. Then a girl gets out of the passenger side. Tall and willowy with a mane of golden hair. She strolls towards Alina. There's a confidence and elegance about her that's arresting.

'Hey,' she says. 'Remember me? I came on Sunday to find Carol.'

Carol tries to keep her eyes down on her sandwich-making, but she's mesmerised.

Alina shrugs and says something in Romanian.

The girl gets out her phone and holds it up. 'An English woman, older than this now.'

Shit! They have a picture.

Alina shakes her head decisively. 'No, no English here. Romanian.'

'When we came before, you seemed to recognise her.'

'No. No English here. Go now.'

Carol realises the driver is staring straight at her. 'Can we ask her?' he says. 'Show her the picture.'

'She don't speak English.'

The tension in Alina's voice is betraying her. She's not a good liar.

The driver walks into the marquee; the girl follows. They're both studying her as they approach.

She keeps her eyes on her task. Does her best to ignore them.

An old picture? She's changed loads. Got fat.

'I think it's her,' he whispers.

They stop a couple of metres away.

'Carol?' the girl says. 'We don't mean you any harm. I'm Phoebe, I'm Marcia's daughter.'

Carol's heart misses a beat. Her eyes shoot up to look. She can't help it.

The girl is smiling. She was beautiful at a distance. Up close, she's stunning.

Carol swallows hard. My God!

Then she says, 'You look like your mother. Did she send you?'

'No, not exactly. We just want you to come home, Carol.'

She can't cry now. She absolutely can't!

'We?' she says. 'Marcie wants that?'

'Well, Granddad does. That is, your dad. Derek.'

A window in her mind snaps shut. It's what she feared. Of course it is.

'I have no dad,' she says. 'No family.'

'Carol, I know it's hard. He wants you both to put the past behind you.'

She knows nothing.

'When I discovered I had an aunt,' says the girl, 'I had to come and find you.'

Carol is hot. The panic is rising, threatening to overwhelm her. She must do something, but what?

She picks up the bread knife she's been using to cut the sandwiches. Points it at the girl. The driver is about to step forward, but Phoebe reaches out a hand to forestall him.

'I told you,' she says. 'You got this all wrong. I'm not your aunt. I got no dad, no family. But I know how to use a knife. And you come near me again, threaten me, ever, I'll slit your throat. You understand me? Now, fuck off!'

The girl's eyes flood with confusion. She raises a hand. 'Okay,' she says. 'Okay.' She backs away.

'And don't ever come back!' shouts Carol.

As she watches them walk back to their car, she notices Alina staring at her.

She lowers the knife and says, 'Some people want to kill me.'

42

Wednesday, 10.10am

Marcia is out shopping. Her knowledge of Cambridge is sketchy, based on a couple of visits, when they did touristy things, and went punting on the river. But she's wandering round the Grand Arcade and has found several interesting little shops that are not too shabby. There's a John Lewis which stocks some acceptable designer labels. She's already bought a pair of leather brogues from Russell and Bromley and a silly T-shirt that she hopes will amuse her daughter.

She walked out of the farmhouse the previous evening, got into her car and drove. For the first few miles her mind coasted. She fixed her eyes on the road. The dark, pot-holed lane, the main road with the glimmer of passing street lamps and finally the motorway. The car is a Mercedes CLS Coupé, nearly two years old. Harry bought it for her birthday.

Cocooned in the luxurious capsule of the car, she was safe from the taint of the past. She was leaving the mud and the mess and the stink of the farmyard behind. She was headed for an expensive hotel room and a rendezvous with her daughter. This is who she is now, a sophisticated business-woman driving a high-end sports car.

She slept well enough, with the aid of temazepam. She got up early, showered, sat in the fluffy bathrobe the hotel provided, and dealt with all the outstanding issues from work.

Lawrence had been filtering things, but there was still a slew of emails that demanded her attention. She was in no mood for any extraneous nonsense and ripped through them. She left him a message saying she expected to be back in the office on Thursday. Work has always anchored her; now it's the thing that will help her get her life back on track.

Cambridge is a pleasant town, and strolling around, she can quite see herself spending more time here in the future. Renting a small pied-à-terre is one possibility. Half the week in London, half the week here. She could play a bigger part in Phoebe's life. It's clear her daughter needs advice on how to build her social media presence. Some of the images she posts of herself need toning down. She should come over as attractive, but not sleazy. With a guiding hand, it can be fixed.

She stops for a coffee in a cool place that roasts its own beans. Bare brick walls and industrial ironwork. She can imagine that it's the sort of place she and her daughter might meet up in the morning before Phoebe goes to classes. Over time friends of her daughter would join them. An informal breakfast club? Some evenings she and Phoebe could go jogging together.

As she scans the passers-by—students, tourists, a cosmopolitan mixture of ages and ethnicities—the image of a broken-down old man drifts into her consciousness. Her father and his funny little wife. Her new, miserable half-sister.

Should she feel guilty for what she said to them? It was

spiteful. It was also true. But they're not part of her life and never will be. No way! And she's made it clear to them they must leave Phoebe alone. The notion of her daughter getting sucked into all that is horrible.

She did what she could for her mother. And for Carol.

She tries not to think about Carol.

But her sister lurks in the secret recesses of her mind, like a hungry ghost.

It's always been there; the fact that one day Carol would get out of jail. And then what?

She can't think about that. She must get on with her life. Keep moving forward. Don't look back. It's been her mantra: never look back. That's how she's survived.

She stands up, scoops up her shopping bags and strides out of the door. She needs to find a present for Phoebe, a gift to help her apologise and get their relationship back on track.

43

Wednesday 10.20am

Phoebe slumps in the passenger seat of Steve's pickup, shoes off, feet up on the dash. She's still quite shaken. Her thoughts are in a spin. Carol, and it definitely was her aunt, pointed a knife right at her. Threatened to slit her throat. And she meant it! It was unbelievable. It's obvious why Ma was worried. She knows what a monster her sister is. That she could easily turn violent.

How could she have been so stupid and naïve? Until now, her notion of Carol as a murderer was vague. The image she'd conjured in her mind was of a sad victim. The real Carol was a fat little thug with angry eyes. Spitting hatred. The whole encounter was awful. And she was only trying to help. It's all been a waste of time. And she's got into a heap of trouble!

They're on the A11, heading back towards Cambridge. Steve is driving and has said very little. He didn't even seem that surprised by Carol's behaviour.

She turns to face him. 'I don't know what I'm going to say to granddad.'

'Tell him what happened.'

'Don't you think he'll be upset?'

Steve shrugs. 'Maybe.'

'You don't seem very concerned. This morning you were crying like a baby and insisting we had to do this for him.'

He shoots her a sour look.

'Don't matter now.' He sounds irritated with her, which is ridiculous.

'What d'you mean?' she says.

He laughs, but his manner isn't loving. It isn't even friendly. 'You're such a spoilt little bitch, aren't you?' he says.

The words sting. Bastard!

'What? This isn't my fault. You insisted on going.'

He chuckles. 'Ah, poor Phoebe. Never your fault.' Now his tone is mocking.

Why is he being such a shitbag? She's losing her rag.

'Don't bloody take this out on me!'

He laughs again, indicates, and turns off the road into a garage.

'Why are we stopping?' she says. 'I need to get back to Cambridge.'

He draws up to the pumps and turns the engine off. 'And I need petrol and to take a slash. You'll just have to be patient.'

He gets out of the pickup. She watches him stroll towards the shop. He pulls out his phone and checks it. Absolutely no urgency! This makes her even more mad. She's tempted to steal his stupid truck and drive off. That would serve him right.

She glances across. He's taken the key fob, picked it up with his phone.

In frustration, she puts on her shoes and gets out.

The service station is set back from the road and surrounded by woodland. She recalls travelling this way earlier in the day. He told her it was the edge of Thetford Forest. The tall pines give the place a dank and gloomy feel.

Only a couple of hours ago, they were joking around and listening to music. Then she was with a gorgeous man she'd just slept with. Now he seems to have morphed into a resentful teenager.

She walks across the forecourt. It's busy. It stinks of exhaust fumes and diesel. The A11 is a major cross-country route. A dozen petrol pumps with cars and vans pulling up to them or moving off. A massive articulated lorry drives in front of her. As she steps back out of its path, she takes out her phone and calls Ma's number. Okay, she should've taken her mother's advice. But she plans to come clean and apologise.

Marcia answers. 'Phoebe?'

'Hey, Ma.'

A reply comes back, but the lorry is pulling up. It releases the air from its hydraulic brakes with a loud hiss which makes Phoebe jump.

She presses her finger in her other ear.

'Ma, I just need to get somewhere quieter.'

'Where are you?' Her mother's voice is almost inaudible. 'Because I'm in town doing some shopping and…'

It's impossible to hear.

'I'll call you back in a minute.'

She zigzags round several vehicles and crosses to the shop. To one side of the building there's a gravel car park and a cash machine on the wall. Several people are queuing. She skirts round them towards the back of the building where it will be quieter.

She's about to call her mother again when she sees Steve. He has his back to her. He's standing beside a white transit van talking to two men. One of the men notices her approaching and speaks to Steve, who turns.

A shiver runs through her; it's deep and visceral. Who are these men? They're large, rough looking types with shaved heads and tats. One of them wears a leather waistcoat like a biker.

Also, they seem to recognise her.

She stops and hesitates. But Steve is already walking towards her.

'Hey, babe,' he says with a smile. 'I was just coming.'

His manner has flipped again, back to friendly. It's clear he didn't want her to see this. What's going on?

It's all wrong. Should she run?

She turns back towards the shop, but he catches up with her and grabs her arm. His grip is hard. She tries to shake him off.

'Let go!' she shouts.

He releases her, holds up his palms in surrender.

'C'mon,' he says. 'What's the matter? I just bumped into some guys I know.'

'Guys? Maybe I'm biased but they look like, I don't know, gangsters to me.'

He laughs. Tilts his head and gives her that brilliant smile. 'Okay,' he says. 'Between you and me, they're drug dealers. Now and then they hook me up with some gear. I sell it on, make myself a nice little profit. We don't all have rich parents. But please, don't tell my mum.'

He grins and shrugs. 'I told you I was a bit of a bad boy. Isn't that what you like?'

'Why were you being such an arse before?'

He sighs. 'I'm sorry. I dunno. You just said what I was

thinking. What the hell am I going to say to Dad? I feel like I've let him down.'

Phoebe shakes her head. 'Carol is awful. Which makes sense, I suppose. People don't get sent to prison for no reason. She's a murderer.'

'I guess I'll just tell him that,' he says. 'Be honest about it. What else can we do?'

She smiles. Boys can be such a pain. Moody as hell. It's their first row. More of a spat. She scans him. He is gorgeous, and he's looking sheepish.

Relief floods through her. She was worried she'd upset him.

'I get it,' she says. 'This is stressful for you. Want me to come with you to tell him?'

He smiles and shakes his head. 'No, I need to get you back to Cambridge. Don't want teacher telling you off again, do we?

He slots his hands in his pockets and stares at the ground. He is so cute!

'And I'm really sorry,' he says. 'You're right, I am stressed, but I shouldn't take it out on you.'

She reaches out, strokes his arm. 'Before we go,' she says. 'Can I get a hug?'

He grins, throws his arms around her in an enormous bear hug and lifts her off her feet. He's strong.

She laughs.

He kisses her forehead.

44

Wednesday, 3.15pm

The formal gardens of the college are neat and well-maintained. The order and the symmetry appeal to Marcia. She's taken her purchases back to the hotel, and now she's free to wander and wait for Phoebe to come out of her seminar. She finds a stone bench that's catching a few rays of afternoon sun. For late October, it's a mild day. A covered walkway like a monastic cloister surrounds the college quad on two sides; it gives the place a tranquil feel, even though it's in the heart of the city.

Marcia remembers her own university years in London; the course was excellent. But her extra-curricula life comprised two menial jobs. It was a hard slog to study for her degree and survive. She wanted something better for Phoebe and looking around she's achieved that.

Money makes a difference; it isn't fair, but it is one of life's simple truths.

She thinks about Harry. When he proposed, he was

carried away with the romance of it all, and he only asked her to sign a skimpy pre-nup which a sharp lawyer should be able to pick apart. But what would be better, is not to get divorced. Just to stay married.

Surely she can persuade him of the sense in that?

Her marriage is the structure that holds her life together. It defines who she is.

She pulls out her phone and calls Harry.

He picks up after several rings and there's an ease and mellowness in his voice. A good lunch to woo a prospective client, laced with copious amounts of booze? Probably.

'Marcia,' he says. 'What can I do for you?'

'I wanted to let you know I've taken your advice. Phoebe and I are meeting up in Cambridge this afternoon. And I'm being careful and trying not to crowd her or be the possessive mother.'

'Good. Glad to hear it.'

There's a silence. She listens to his breathing. He's got his feet up in his office, pretending to be busy. But Harry's special skills come under the heading of client liaison; being pissed after lunch is not an issue.

'I've been wondering,' she says. 'Do you want a divorce straight away? It's rather final. And expensive. Should we take some time out to let the dust settle?'

She can hear him chuckling. 'Y'know, I could've predicted this.'

'Predicted what?'

'You're the only woman I know who doesn't think like a woman.'

Is this a compliment or an insult?

'I don't know what you mean,' she says.

'You're an odd combination. On the surface, rather up-tight and insecure, that's the female bit. But when your back's against the wall, you break the problem down and focus on what you can get. As ruthless as any bloke. Most women in your position would want to cut my balls off. They'd be sobbing to their friends. But you're not wasting any time on unnecessary emotions like that, are you?'

He knows nothing about how she feels. Focus, make the argument.

'I just know you, Harry,' she says. 'I'm thinking about the crying baby at four in the morning and the stressed out, hormonal new mum, who hasn't the time or the energy to be totally there for you. You're fifty-seven. It'll be messy and hard work and costly.'

'I'll get a nanny and some earplugs.'

'And what about a paternity test?'

He laughs. 'You're incorrigible.'

She smiles to herself. That's what she said about Phoebe.

'I'm just saying, you should give these things some thought. You've got this girl pregnant. You want to do the decent thing. But what about when the next gorgeous intern catches your eye? Will she put up with that in the way I have?'

He appears to be laughing.

'You've missed your calling,' he says. 'You should be a lawyer. Has it occurred to you I might be in love?'

That stings. His escapades have always been about sex. Nothing more.

'Are you?' she says.

He doesn't answer that.

'Okay,' he says. 'Since you've got me in a good mood, here's the deal. You get the house in Richmond to keep or sell. Contents apart from my personal stuff. Cash settlement of five mil, plus I'll pay for the rest of Phoebe's education and set her up with a flat in London after she graduates. No forensic accountants poking their noses in, I had enough of that with Louisa. No massive legal bill for either of us. Quick, clean, painless.'

Painless for him.

He is talking to her as if she was a man. For a moment she finds that hard to take. He has moved on. He isn't interested in her anymore, and he's not going to budge. When did this happen? And why didn't she notice? She can't answer any of these questions.

She swallows down her disappointment. But in her heart she knows it's what she deserves.

She played the game for as long as she could. But it was never going to last forever. Nothing does.

'Ten mil,' she says. 'And I get the cottage in Cornwall too.'

'You hate the countryside. Why do you even want the cottage?'

'Phoebe likes to go surfing with her friends.'

'She still can.' He sighs. 'I'll tell you what, if we can save on the legal costs, I'll make it seven mil. Now any lawyer will tell you that's a good deal. On the table for forty-eight hours. Isn't it better to be civilised about this?'

Civilised? She wonders what he means by that. Reducing their marriage, all the moments good and bad, that they've shared, to a simple financial transaction?

It sounds a ridiculous amount of money, and it is. But in Harry's world, it's cheap. Like an ageing mistress who's outlived her use and beauty, she's being paid off. This is how it's done.

'Tell me one thing,' she says. 'How long have you been planning this?'

'Oh, come on, Marcia, I didn't exactly plan it.'

'Okay, how long have you been involved with this woman?'

He sighs. This is getting tedious for him. 'Just over a year, I suppose.'

A year! A year ago they were talking about the travelling they could do once Phoebe went off to university. New Zealand maybe?

She has a lump in her throat. She can't stand any more of this. Haggling to put a price on the time and effort and toleration she's put into this marriage.

'Seven mil,' she says. 'Plus I get the cottage and the house.'

'Done,' he says. 'I'll get my lawyer to draw up the papers.'

He sounds as if he's pleased with that. He must think he's got off lightly. But she doesn't have the energy or the will for a fight.

'Okay,' she says.

'Well, take care of yourself. Give my love to Phoebe.' His tone is breezy, like a snake sloughing off its old skin.

She hangs up the phone and sits. Her marriage is over. It's not something she even saw on the horizon a week ago. Her life has been upended. And here she is, a fool and a failure. The shock of it reverberates through her.

Still, she has Phoebe.

She looks around.

A group of students is emerging from one staircase. This is must be Phoebe's lot.

She takes a deep breath. She needs to pull herself together and put on a brave face.

There are seven of them. Three boys, four girls. Bright, shining young people like her daughter. They're laughing and chatting with each other. But no sign of Phoebe.

She waits.

Moments pass. Perhaps she has the wrong place or the wrong time?

She gets her phone out and is about to call Phoebe when Dr Grayson, the idiot tutor, comes trotting down the stairs. She's clutching a bundle of papers and scurrying along like a demented hamster.

Marcia crosses the lawn towards her.

She calls out. 'Dr Grayson!'

The tutor stops and swivels. She sees Marcia and frowns.

'Ah, Mrs Lennox,' she says.

'I thought Phoebe had a seminar with you. I'm supposed to meet her.'

The idiot tutor pushes her glasses up her nose and nods. 'Yes, I thought Phoebe had a seminar with me too. But apparently not.' Her tone seems unnecessarily sarcastic.

'She didn't turn up?'

'No, she did not. And I have to tell you, Mrs Lennox, I gave her fair warning, but I'm at the end of my tether with her. I had to apologise to the police, on behalf of the college, after her recent escapade.'

'I should take responsibility for that. There were a series of misunderstandings. And I do apologise. But she did intend to be here today.'

The tutor continues to glare at her. A small person on a power trip? She has no choice but to suck it up for Phoebe's sake.

She smiles. 'There will be a good reason for this, I assure you. Phoebe told me she'd definitely be here. And my daughter is not a liar.'

Grayson heaves a sigh. 'Yes, she was kind enough to tell me that herself, that she's not a liar. However, we sometimes find, Mrs Lennox, that teenage girls like Phoebe, whilst intellectually bright, are not emotionally ready for this place. They're immature and easily distracted. Another bright bauble comes along to take their attention. I gather in Phoebe's case it was a rather good-looking young man.'

'What?'

'He spent the night in her room and they were seen leaving together this morning. One of the other students told me. Now, if you'll excuse me, I have a meeting.'

Grayson scurries off down the flagstone corridor.

Marcia stands stock still. She feels confused. Then panicky. Is this her daughter being silly over some boy? Or is it something else?

She rings Phoebe's number. It goes straight to voicemail.

45

Wednesday, 5.05pm

DS Jo Boden hates going on courses. She learns by doing. Spending the entire day sitting on a hard plastic chair in a stuffy room and listening to some suit from the National Crime Agency droning on about cyber-crime, feels like a penance. The DCI has assured her he doesn't hold her responsible for the time and resources wasted on a misper who wasn't missing. She's not sure she believes him. But she did her job and found Phoebe Lennox.

The course lasts for the rest of the week. Tomorrow it's electronic surveillance and data analysis; she can hardly wait. She wishes she'd opted for some time off instead. Prisha and Mackie both did that. But they have friends and family to spend time with. Boden has the job.

When she returns to her desk, she finds a scrawled note. Some woman waiting for her downstairs? Insists she needs to talk to her.

As Boden walks into the reception area, she sees Marcia

Lennox sitting on a bench and fidgeting with her phone. Her heart sinks. Of course. The perfect end to a bum-numbingly tedious day.

She paints on a smile and walks over.

'Mrs Lennox,' she says.

The woman raises her eyes. She's distressed, that's obvious. Her face is haggard and tear stained.

'I'm sorry,' she says. 'I didn't know what else to do.'

Boden tries to look sympathetic.

'How can I help?'

It takes Marcia Lennox a moment to compose herself.

'I know you think I'm this stupid, neurotic mother,' she says. 'I arranged to meet my daughter after her seminar. But she didn't go to it, even though she knew she had to, because the college is quite upset with her. And I've been calling and calling her for the last hour and a half. And I'm worried that this is all my fault, and she's got herself mixed up with the kind of people who... it's, well, I hardly know where to begin.'

Boden sighs. 'I've had a crappy day,' she says. 'I could do with a drink. There's a nice little wine bar down the road. Why don't we go down there, find a quiet table and you can tell me what's on your mind?'

Why not? The alternative is a takeaway and Netflix.

Marcia Lennox looks at her with tears in her eyes. The posh mask has slipped to reveal a nervous, frightened woman.

'Thank you,' she whispers.

They walk in silence to the wine bar. Marcia Lennox can't be much over forty and she's slim and fit. But it seems to Boden that since the last time they met, she's aged ten years. She walks as if carrying an enormous weight on her shoulders.

Boden finds a table, and Mrs Lennox insists on buying

the wine. She selects the most expensive bottle of Chablis on the list. Once it's poured, they sit facing each other in a narrow booth at the back of the bar. It's a cosy, oak-panelled place, filling up with thirsty office workers.

Boden sips her wine — which is rather good — and waits.

Mrs Lennox has calmed down.

'I expect you see me as this over-entitled, rich bitch with a snotty attitude,' she says.

'I wouldn't have put it quite like that.'

'Wouldn't you?' She gives Boden a rueful smile. 'I would, in your shoes.' She sighs. 'You visited Elm Tree Farm, where I grew up?'

'Yes.'

'It belonged to my mother's family. She was a teacher. My father came to work on the farm as a labourer. My mother's parents thought she married beneath her. That's how they saw things back then. Class mattered.'

In Boden's world, it still does.

But she says nothing and settles back in her seat. The wine is delicious, and she's content to listen. One reason she became a detective is because unravelling complicated messed up lives, including her own, has always intrigued her; it beats cyber-crime.

Mrs Lennox hasn't touched her drink.

'My grandfather had a prize-winning dairy herd,' she says. 'Foot and mouth destroyed that. When I was fifteen, my mother died of breast cancer. It was a terrible death. My father couldn't cope; he drank, left it all to me and my sister. She's two years younger than me. Before my mother died, she made me promise to look after Carol. Unfortunately, I didn't keep that promise.'

Her head dips. Tears spill on to her hand.

'Sorry,' she says, wiping them away. 'I haven't spoken about this before.'

'It's fine,' says Boden. 'Carry on.'

The carapace has cracked, and it seems to the detective that a different, more fragile woman is emerging.

'After my mother died, my father's older brother, Brian, came to live with us. My mother had hated him, refused to have him in the house. He was a lout, always buying and selling illegal stuff, and he bullied my dad. He saw the farm as a good place to grow cannabis. That's what he did. With my cousin Alan. They took the place over. My dad did nothing. Just kept drinking. Didn't stand up to them. I don't even think he wanted to. It was easy money. Easier than proper farming.'

'What happened to you and your sister?'

'Dad expected us to cook and clean. Service the men.'

Her jaw ripples with tension; it's clear this is hard for her.

'At the wake after my mother's funeral,' she says, 'my cousin Alan forced me to have sex with him. He said it was to comfort me.'

'He raped you? When you were fifteen?'

'He was nineteen. I couldn't fight him off. But I told my dad. Uncle Brian and Alan said I was lying. I was stuck up like my mother and just wanted to make trouble between the brothers. My father believed them. After that, I focused on getting out. I worked hard at school. An old teaching colleague of my mother's encouraged me and helped me apply for university. I escaped as soon as I'd done my A levels. But the problem was, I left Carol behind. She was nearly sixteen by then.'

She's clasping her hands on the table in front of her. The knuckles have turned white from the tension.

'It's all my fault,' she says.

'What is?' says Boden.

'What happened to Carol. Once I'd left, Alan turned his attentions to her. Him and his dad had moved on from cannabis to ecstasy and cocaine. Brian was arrested and got off several times. I returned later, I tried to get Carol to come and live with me in London. She wouldn't. She'd become an addict. That's how Alan controlled her. Then Brian finally got sent to prison for drug dealing. While he was in prison, Carol and Alan had a big fight. He was drunk, beat her up. Afterwards, while he was asleep, she stabbed him. She went to prison for his murder. Got a life sentence.'

Mrs Lennox pauses. She seems to be holding her breath. Her gaze goes across the bar into the distance. And back to another time, Boden suspects. Her hands tremble.

'Is she still in prison?' says Boden.

'No. She's just been released on licence. That's what Phoebe got herself wound up with, looking for her aunt. She's naïve. She doesn't know what she's dealing with. I'm worried that's where she's gone.'

'Have you kept in contact with your sister?'

'No. I haven't seen her since the trial. She pleaded guilty.'

'Do you think she blames you for leaving her behind?'

'I don't know.'

Boden scans her. Her chin is quivering. Is she scared of her sister? She's told her story. But there's something left hanging in the air, something else that she's not saying.

Boden can't help it. She's intrigued.

She gets out her notebook. 'Give me her name and I'll get in touch with the National Probation Service. They supervise prisoners with life sentences released on licence.'

'You can find out where she is?' There's surprise in Marcia Lennox's voice. And a hint of what? Fear?

'Probably,' says Boden. 'Let me ask you, Mrs Lennox, are

you scared of your sister? Do you think she may try to punish you through Phoebe? Maybe hurt her?'

There it is again. Boden can see it in her eyes. The evasion. The part of the story she's not telling.

But Mrs Lennox shakes her head, as if to erase a horrible thought.

'It's all such a mess,' she says. 'I told Phoebe I'd explain. I was going to tell her about Carol. But now she's disappeared again.'

'Wouldn't your father have told her?'

'Well, yes, he did. Not the entire story because he was using her.'

'Using her how?'

'To persuade Carol to come home. He believes Carol will forgive him. That's what he wants.'

'How do you know?'

'I took your advice and went to see him.'

'What was that like?'

'He's sober. He's doing the whole AA thing. Wants forgiveness all round.'

'You don't buy that?'

Mrs Lennox huffs. 'It's crap. He was always mired in self-pity. It's always been about him. Seems to me that hasn't changed.'

She shakes her head again. Although it's more of a shudder.

Boden is trying to read her. It's not easy. The woman's so tense; now her gaze is darting about. It's clear she's given Boden an edited version of what's going on. Perhaps she's confused too. If Phoebe Lennox is in danger from this aunt, it would justify checking her out with the probation service. But it's all a bit tenuous.

She knows what DCI Hepburn would say: where's the crime? The police are not social workers.

'Okay,' she says. 'You've been trying to call Phoebe, and she's not answering? Are you sure she's not just avoiding you again?'

'No. Definitely not.'

Boden shrugs. 'You said that before. What's changed?'

'We talked things through on the phone. We'd arranged to meet. And then I got this odd call where she was somewhere busy and noisy. She said she'd call me back right away, but she never did.'

'What sort of noise?'

'Traffic. Lorries? Next to a busy road?'

'Give me her new phone number and I'll request a cell siting. That might tell us more.'

'Thank you.'

'You want me to speak to your sister's probation officer?'

Mrs Lennox nods. 'Her name's Carol Cook.'

'You know her date of birth?'

'Tenth of June 1978.'

Boden writes down the details.

Mrs Lennox seems more collected, but still rigid with anxiety. She's only taken one sip of wine.

'Thank you for taking me seriously,' she says. This is more than politeness. She seems genuinely grateful.

'I'm only doing my job,' says Boden.

Not strictly true. And the DCI will have a fit if he finds out. But you could argue this is tidying up loose ends. That's what she'll tell him.

46

Wednesday, 6.15pm

Phoebe Lennox wakes with a thumping headache. Worse than the worst hangover. Her mouth is dry and everything hurts. It takes a moment for her eyes to adjust; it's dark, but there's a faint orange glow coming from somewhere. And then there's the smell. Damp earth and engine oil?

She's lying on her back on a hard, concrete floor. It's freezing, but she has a blanket over her. Thick and rough, it smells of animal.

With effort, she sits up.

The surrounding space isn't large. It could be a shed or a garage. Light is seeping in through a gap between the top of the door and the ceiling. Is it coming from street lighting? A nearby road? She can hear the faint rumble of traffic.

She throws back the blanket and tries to stand up. But her shoes are gone and there's something hard and metal round her left ankle. She explores it with her fingers. It's a ring attached to a chain. She's shackled!

Terror explodes inside her. She tugs at the chain. It's short and attached to something heavy.

The pain in her head is excruciating. She's nauseous too. But now she's remembering.

They'd left the petrol station and were listening to music. Dua Lipa. *Break My Heart.* And she was singing along. Steve said he needed to pull over and check something on the truck.

He drove off the main road and into a little clearing in the forest. He seemed to know where he was going. They stopped.

And that's when he said something weird. 'Sorry, babe. It's just business. Nothing personal.'

Then he got out of the truck.

'Steve!' she called after him. But he ignored her.

In the door mirror on the passenger side, she saw him walking behind the truck, hands slotted in his jeans. Was he waiting for something? She opened the door and jumped out.

'What the fuck!' she shouted.

They were about a hundred meters from the road in a small clearing, which had been used as a garbage dump. There was a mouldering sofa and a couple of fridges along with bin bags of refuse, torn open with rubbish strewn around.

She remembers being super-irritated when she saw the white transit van driving down the short track from the road towards them. It must've followed them.

Then she understood. Her instinct was right. She had to run. But the approaching van blocked the track back to the road. That left only one way to go. She set off into the woods.

She was fit and fast. Brambles tore her hands as she crashed through the bracken and undergrowth. But she knew she had to escape. She was rapidly calculating. She'd seen those two thugs beside the white van at the petrol station.

Solid muscle, but not as fast as her. She could outrun them. If she ran in a loop, she'd get back to the main road and could flag someone down. Plenty of traffic. She just needed to keep her nerve.

Focus, Ma would say. Focus and run.

Two, maybe three minutes, and she'd covered a lot of ground. She had her bearings; the road was to her left. She ran down a hill to a muddy brook and splashed through it. Fear and adrenaline drove her on.

As she powered up the other side of the hill, she heard them. Coming after her. Gaining on her fast. And barking.

Three large Rottweilers were in pursuit. Hunting her in a pack. Bounding up the hill after her.

She grabbed up a fallen branch to use as a weapon. But the dogs were canny. They formed a circle around her, barking. She swung the wood to ward them off. But they remained out of reach, snarling as they held her at bay.

Then she saw the two thugs running through the woods towards her. She had no choice; she had to make a break for it. But as she tried to run, one dog leapt forward and seized her ankle. Pain as its razor-sharp teeth broke the skin. The creature hung on until it brought her down. The dogs surrounded her, still barking.

It terrified her. Why was this happening?

Her heart was thumping in her chest. She screamed. 'Help! Help!' Her voice echoed through the tall, swaying trees. She was too far from the road. No one would hear.

The first thug approached. The one in the biker vest. Muscles, tattoos, a shaved head, a goatee beard.

He raised his index finger to his lips. 'Sssh! Don't be scared.' He seemed amused; he was enjoying this.

As he tried to grab her, she kicked out with all her might.

She got his shin, and he fell back. But the other one had caught up. He was slower but bigger, a huge monster. He threw his arm round her and held her in a choking neck lock. She continued to kick, but she couldn't escape and soon she couldn't breathe.

She felt a sharp sting in her arm. Her head spun. The monster released her and laid her down on the pine needles of the forest floor.

The last thing she remembered is the light through the trees and the two men bending over her.

They were grinning. The monster said something in a language she didn't understand.

She blacked out.

She reaches down to her unshackled right ankle. It's sore. This is where the dog bit her. It's wrapped in a crepe bandage.

Sssh. Don't be scared, he said. If they'd wanted to kill her, she'd be dead. The needle in her arm was to knock her out. These thugs must want her alive.

She checks her pocket. Her phone is gone. Also her credit cards.

They know who she is. They know her parents are well off.

Just business, that's what Steve said.

Now it's making sense. They've kidnapped her for ransom. And that bastard set her up!

Anger surges through her. But it brings energy and confidence.

Stuff like this happens abroad. Probably in the UK too. Even if you don't hear about it. They'll contact her dad and make their demands. They won't want to hurt her. That's why they've bandaged her ankle. They'll make a deal. It's all about money. Of course it is.

She'll be all right. Of course she will.

The floor is rough and cold as iron; her body shudders. Her head hurts. Her ankle hurts.

But she must sit tight and wait. And try not to panic.

47

Wednesday, 9.10pm

Marcia Lennox runs. Wherever she goes, she always takes her kit. Running is the one form of exercise you can do anywhere.

It's dark with an autumnal chill in the air. She has an app on her phone that plans a circular route wherever you are. She's on the outskirts of Cambridge. Housing estates, an industrial park, a stretch of dual carriageway; the pavements are lit but deserted.

When she runs, she's totally in the moment. All she thinks about is her breathing and her feet striking the ground. And when troublesome thoughts intrude, she ups the pace. If she pushes herself to the limit, it brings her focus back to the simple action of getting enough air into her lungs.

It blanks out the guilt and the self-hatred inside her. She stops remembering.

But not this evening.

She's knows she's beyond the pale. You reap what you

sow, Marcie. That's what her mother would say. No one can escape their moral responsibility.

She's failed in so many ways. Regret doesn't even come into it. The fortress she built to protect herself is collapsing like a house of cards. Serves her right, probably. Her marriage to Harry was the foundation. It gave her a secure place in the world and an identity. It made her Marcia Lennox, not the stupid girl from Essex with a mountain of debt and a baby.

What happens to her now? She'll still have money and a house, because Harry will pay up to get rid of her. She'll still have her job.

But it's all worthless, it's all for nothing, if she loses Phoebe.

She runs flat out until her legs burn, and the lactic acid forces her to slow down. Pain shoots up the back of her left leg; it feels like a pulled hamstring. The sudden agony is a relief. When she can no longer control and contain her emotions, when she's unmoored, physical pain grounds her. Gets her out of her head.

Forced to stop, she stretches the leg out in front of her, heel down, and pulls back on the toe. This eases it a little. With luck, it's a strain, not a tear. This is her body screaming a warning. Her heart is thumping.

Focus. Get things back under control. She can do it. She knows she can.

She limps along. After a couple of hundred meters, she can manage a slow trot, and she heads back to the hotel.

Now she's not sure why she went looking for DS Boden. Was it panic? With Harry gone, she reached out to the only potential source of help left to her? But it was foolish to involve the police again.

Speaking about the past, trying to explain it to another person, has made everything worse. She had to be careful what she said, skimming the surface. The sergeant listened. Was she smart enough to realise it's only part of the story?

Still, if she tracks Phoebe's phone, it will have been worth it. Finding Phoebe and ensuring her safety is the absolute priority.

Marcia tries not to think about the fallout; she'll just have to deal with that. She wonders if she should call Harry. But what would be the point? He can't do anything.

He'd just think she was being neurotic.

In the cascade of thoughts and recriminations inside her mind, she comes back to one thing. Why didn't Phoebe come back for her seminar? She knew how pissed off Grayson was.

Something happened after that last phone call. Something to stop her coming back.

And it's obvious there can only be one explanation.

Somehow she's found Carol. Or has Carol found her?

48

Thursday, 8.35am

Boden has wangled an extension of the authorisation for a cell siting of Phoebe Lennox's phone. She doesn't lie — she tells them the mother of a misper, who they'd previously located, has approached her — but she garnishes the truth. She mentions that the family has high-level connections. They hassled the Assistant Chief before and are likely to do so again. She expresses the opinion, and she emphasises it is just an opinion that the DCI would want them to cover themselves. They buy it. She gets the nod.

In fact, Marcia Lennox hadn't mentioned her husband at all, or any of their posh connections, which on reflection strikes Boden as strange. Her encounter with Mrs Lennox raises more questions than it answers.

Prisha Chakravorty is back in the office. Boden fills her in.

'What? She's missing again?' says the young DC. 'Do you believe that?'

'I'll be honest. I don't know what to think. But it just feels like there's something here we're not seeing.'

'Maybe she's still pissed with her mother?'

'Could be,' says Boden. 'But it's a messed up family. Murder, rape, drug dealing. There's quite some history. If I wasn't on this bloody course, I'd follow up myself.'

'Tell me what you want, I'll do it,' says Chakravorty. 'Good practice for me.'

'I've still got authorisation to track the girl's phone again. Different number.'

Prisha sighs. 'Most people get a new phone, they get their number transferred.'.

'When she got the second phone, perhaps she didn't want to be hassled. Particularly by her mother,' says Boden.

'I can relate to that,' says the DC with feeling.

Boden has a pang of conscience. Is it fair to drag Prisha into what Hepburn will probably regard as an off-piste inquiry?

She hesitates and sighs.

'I've always figured,' she says, 'there's two ways to be a copper. You err on the side of caution, make sure you tick only the right boxes, cross the Ts and dot the Is, and get promoted to DCI before your forty. That's obviously what we should aim for.'

Prisha nods.

'But, sometimes, I dunno…'

'You get a sixth sense?'

'I called Phoebe Lennox's number myself, last night and this morning. Straight to voicemail every time. She could've chucked this one away too, or left it somewhere and bought herself another new phone. In which case we look like plonkers. Again.'

'Or had it nicked?' says Chakravorty.

'Or had it nicked?'

'What if she saw that boyfriend, Jack whatsit, the one with the sportscar? It must've narked him that he got dragged in for questioning? Say they had a fight about it and he ended up hurting her?'

'I never thought of that.' says Boden.

'There are lots of possibilities.'

'I don't want to get you in bother with the DCI.'

'I don't see that we're doing anything wrong. We're just being thorough. Want me to find out more about the aunt who got done for murder?' says Chakravorty. 'Just background.'

'I got the number for her probation officer from the database last night. I left her a message. She's in Norwich. I'm waiting for a call back.'

'What's the second thing?'

Boden frowns. 'What second thing?'

'You said there are two ways to be a copper?'

'Oh, that's easy,' says Boden with a grin. 'Become a fuck-up like me, who can only get promoted by moving to another county. The rate I'm going, I'll end up in Scotland.'

49

Thursday, 8.40am

Marcia Lennox was up early; she left Cambridge before eight. In the long, wakeful hours, she formulated a plan. Relying on the police, or Harry, wasn't an option.

She's on her own. She's always been on her own, that's the reality. Knowing and accepting this gives her strength. It means she can do what's necessary.

As she drives into the yard of her childhood home, she sees Lacey outside the barn, tipping kibble into metal bowls for the hungry cats swarming round her feet.

The girl looks up and stares. Marcia gets out of the car.

The thought that she's related to this dumpy teenager is odd. Although, on closer inspection, the girl reminds her of Carol.

'Nice car,' says Lacey. 'What is it?'

'Mercedes CLS,' she says.

There's an awkward silence. She needs to connect with the kid.

'This must be weird for you,' she says, 'discovering you have a half-sister, who's old enough to be your mother?'

'And a niece who's older than me.'

'Phoebe told me you're the one who found her. That was clever.'

'I know.' Lacey cracks a smile.

'You met her? Did you like her?'

The girl gives her a sour look. 'I thought we'd be friends. Turns out she was only interested in Steve.'

'Steve's your brother?'

'Half-brother.'

Marcia nods. 'Of course, half-brother. Complicated things, families.'

Is this the boy Grayson was talking about? She said he spent the night in Phoebe's room, and she was seen leaving with him.

'I need to find Phoebe. Have you seen her?'

Lacey shakes her head. 'She went back to Cambridge with Steve, after the cops came.'

Sounds like he is the boy.

'On Tuesday?'

'Yeah.' Lacey tilts her chin and gives Marcia a defiant look. 'Y'know, you really upset my mum with the stuff you said before.'

'I'm sorry for that. But it was only the truth.'

'Uncle Brian says you always was a stuck-up bitch.'

Marcia frowns. 'I thought Uncle Brian couldn't speak since his stroke?'

'He doesn't say much.' Lacey pets the cats. She seems uncomfortable.

'What else does Uncle Brian say?'

'How should I know?' she huffs. 'Gotta go, I'll be late for school.'

She scurries off. Not towards the house. But into the old Dutch barn, which seems a peculiar route to school. In the distant past, Marcia also used the barn as a hiding place.

As she watches Lacey disappear, she wonders about Uncle Brian. That toxic piece of shit must be in his middle seventies. When she saw him before, he looked feeble and sick. Which is what he deserves. Why would her father even consider taking him in? The answer's simple; he could never say no to his older brother.

She walks up to the front door, lifts the brass knocker and raps.

After several moments, Celia answers. She's wiping her hands on a tea towel but stops and stares at Marcia. 'We didn't expect to see you again.'

'I didn't expect to be here. I'm looking for Phoebe.'

'She's not here?'

'What about your son?'

'You'd better come in. Derek isn't up yet.'

Marcia is tempted to say *he always was a lazy sod.* But there's no point being provocative.

She follows Celia into the house, and through to the kitchen.

This won't work if she's confrontational. Be nice.

'The place looks good,' she says, 'I'm sure it hasn't been this well-kept since my mother was alive.'

Celia dips her head to acknowledge the compliment. Then she fills the kettle and places it on the Rayburn.

'I am sorry for your mother's suffering,' she says. 'It must have been terrible for you, and for her. I have prayed for her soul.'

Marcia scans her. A small, stout black woman with kind eyes. Why the hell did she marry Derek Cook, a broken-down alcoholic? Perhaps for much the same reason Marcia married Harry?

'Thank you,' she says. 'I'm not a believer myself, but I respect your sincerity.'

Does she mean this? It sounds good. Too many years in the advertising business. It's made her cynical.

The irony is, it's the sort of thing her own mother would've said. Jill Cook was a woman of firm beliefs herself. An atheist and a socialist, a campaigner for noble causes and a better world. She and Celia would've got on. Both women of moral certainty. Unlike Marcia.

'Of course, I knew that Derek's first wife had died,' says Celia. 'But I didn't know how. He's never discussed it. He doesn't like to speak of the past. It's guilt. But we're all sinners. *Let he who is without sin, cast the first stone.* John, chapter eight.'

'He told you why Carol was in jail?'

'Oh yes. She killed your cousin. But none of the details. He blames himself.'

He should! Marcia bites her tongue. She needs to find Phoebe, that's the priority.

Celia continues. 'He's spoken about both you and your sister. Until Phoebe came into our lives, we thought you'd emigrated to Australia. He was proud of you. Obviously not so much of Carol.'

Marcia's realises she's forgotten about that particular lie. At one point she had a vague plan to emigrate. But then Harry came along.

'I'm worried about Phoebe,' she says. 'She worked hard to get to university, and now she's in danger of getting kicked out because of this wild goose chase after my sister. I need to find her urgently. Have you any idea where she is?'

Celia goes to the doorway and shouts up the stairs. 'Steven! Come down here now!'

She returns and stands beside the Rayburn, hands on hips. The kettle sings.

'Can I offer you tea or coffee?' she says. She's seems determined to be hospitable.

Marcia smiles. 'A black coffee would be nice.'

Celia surprises her by producing a cafetière, a grinder, and a bag of coffee beans.

'This is Jamaican Blue Mountain. I buy it for Derek.'

'My husband likes that,' says Marcia. Not that she'll be able to call him that for much longer. My ex-husband, making her the second ex-wife.

'A man of taste,' says Celia. 'I'd like to meet him.'

Why is she being polite? Perhaps it's just her nature. She seems a good person.

Marcia watches her prepare the coffee. She's meticulous.

She pours the water onto the freshly ground beans and, as the delicious aroma rises, a young man in boxers and a T-shirt walks into the room. He's much taller than his mother, with sculpted muscles from serious training.

'Wow!' he says. 'That's smells great. Can I get a mug of that?'

'Steven, we have a visitor,' says Celia. 'Where are your trousers?'

He looks at Marcia and smiles. It's clear why Phoebe was attracted. He's gorgeous with amazing dark eyes, which he turns on Marcia.

'Are you offended by my bare legs?' he says, with a cheeky grin.

'This is Marcia, Phoebe's mother,' says Celia. 'She wants to know where Phoebe is.'

His expression freezes, but only for a second. He shrugs and says, 'She's in Cambridge, I guess.'

'She isn't,' says Marcia. 'She left yesterday morning. With a young man. I'm guessing that was you.'

He sighs and then smiles. 'Okay, look, she swore me to secrecy.'

'I don't bloody care,' says Marcia. 'I just want the truth. Did you find Carol? Is that where she is?'

He seems in a quandary. He shakes his head. Folds his arms.

'You put me in a difficult position,' he says. 'A promise is a promise.'

'Oh, sod that!' says Marcia. 'I'm her mother. And she's in trouble with her college.'

'Steven,' says Celia. 'Last night you told your father and Brian that you'd found the place where Carol works. Somewhere near Diss?'

'In Norfolk?' says Marcia. 'Is that where Phoebe is? With Carol? In Norfolk?'

He shoots a glance at his mother. She wags her finger at him.

'Don't lie to me, boy,' she says. 'I've always taught you to speak the truth. The Lord sees you.'

He dips his gaze. 'I know that, Mum.'

'Is it true? You and Phoebe found her?' Marcia knows she must press him.

'Yeah, but...' he sighs. 'Yeah, we found Carol. And Phoebe insisted on staying there. Nothing I could do. I just came home. It's the last time I saw her.'

'What's the address?' says Marcia.

Steve smiles and tilts his head. 'Just promise me one thing,' he says. 'If you get there and find her, don't let on it was me. Okay?' He gives her a wink.

50

Thursday, 10.30am

Jo Boden sneaks out of the course during the morning coffee break. She has a pad full of doodles and a head full of questions. Mrs Lennox is an intriguing character, ultra-respectable, rich, but with a past that would mess up most people. It must've taken some grit to escape and make a success of her life.

The tracking of data in order to put together a chain of evidence is important to police work, Boden gets that. She's just not interested in doing it. She'd rather figure out what makes Marcia Lennox tick.

As she walks down the corridor towards the office, she meets DCI Hepburn coming the other way.

'Morning, Jo.' He has a peevish look on his face. 'How's the course?'

'Good sir, thank you,' she says.

'You've asked if you can track Phoebe Lennox's phone

again?' He raises his eyebrows, lets the question hang in the air.

'Yes. Mrs Lennox came to see me. She insists Phoebe's missing again. I didn't want any comeback if we did nothing.'

He exhales. 'Okay. Fair enough. However, Simon Lennox has made a formal complaint. He alleges we were aggressive in our questioning of him.'

'Come on, boss. That's nonsense. You saw the interview.'

'His grandfather is Sir Edwin Muirhead, used to be the Home Secretary. I suspect he's behind it. They're alleging we were sloppy, made assumptions and didn't check the facts. And he's got a point.'

Boden sighs. 'Harry Lennox behaved as if he was Phoebe's father. Saying to him, are you her biological father—'

'I accept it was an honest mistake. But you should always question the obvious.'

'We were running ourselves ragged trying to find the girl, sir.'

Hepburn sighs. 'You did the best you could. And we were short of a DI. But he's naming you specifically. And they're doing it through the IOPC.'

'Great.' Her heart sinks. If they've gone straight to the Independent Office for Police Conduct, they're out for blood.

The boss scans her. 'My advice would be, get the lid on this latest Lennox thing as fast as you can. Strikes me that, from the outset, this has been some fucked-up family nonsense. And we're not social workers.' The tone is brisk, bordering on unsympathetic.

Boden nods. 'Yes, sir.'

She watches the DCI walk away. *My advice would be...*

It's clear what that means. He's distancing himself. And it's a warning. If anything more goes wrong, she's carrying the can. Plus now she's facing a complaint which could turn into a lengthy investigation. This is the last thing she needs.

She walks into the office and heads for the coffee machine.

As she pours herself a mug, Chakravorty comes bouncing over. She's brimming with enthusiasm.

'I did the phone,' she says. 'Last call was from a petrol station on the A11 near Thetford. She called her mother. Fifteen seconds at 10.22 yesterday morning. Phone pinged off a mast about three miles down the road at 10.40, then it went dead.'

'Fits with what Mrs Lennox told me.'

'Yeah, but what was she doing there? It's thirty miles north-east of Cambridge. Whereas the farm is about twenty miles to the south.'

Boden shrugs. She's still stung by the DCI's attitude. It's doubtful she'll get his backing. 'I've no idea,' she says.

'I've looked on the map, if she disappeared where her phone went dead, it's in the middle of Thetford Forest.'

'Perhaps she took a walk and dropped it?'

'We could go to the garage and check their CCTV?'

Boden hesitates and sighs. The young DC's excitement is infectious. But she should resist it. If she's about to face an IOPC investigation, she could do with getting the DCI back onside. If they go rushing off after Phoebe Lennox, and it turns out to be another load of crap, Hepburn will not be pleased.

'I don't know, Prisha,' she says. 'I'm supposed to be on this course. I'll phone Mrs Lennox later and tell her about the phone. She may know why Phoebe was up there.'

Chakravorty looks crestfallen. She nods. 'Okay.'

'Sorry, I know I asked you to follow up. But I just think we're on a hiding to nothing.'

The young DC shrugs. 'It's fine. I volunteered.'

51

Thursday, 11.45am

The rain began at breakfast time; it's been pouring ever since. The field and the track to it have turned into a quagmire. Carol is humping the crates of cabbages onto the back of the trailer. Her boots are caked in mud, rain trickles down her face and neck. It's back-breaking work, but she welcomes the distraction.

Alina tried to cross-question her about her visitors; the poor woman ended up frustrated. Her lack of proficiency in English stymied her. Carol shrugged and pretended that she didn't understand.

But when Vasile returned in the evening, he insisted on an explanation.

It was after dinner. Carol was sitting alone. He brought a bottle of whiskey over, poured Carol a hefty slug and said, 'Now you tell me.'

Carol stared down at the amber liquid. Whiskey turns her stomach. Since childhood she'd smelt it on her father and then on Alan. When Alan got out the whiskey bottle, she knew she was in for a beating. But this was an important gesture from Vasile; he was giving her the benefit of the doubt, and it would be rude to refuse.

She took a mouthful. It burnt the back of her throat, but she swallowed it.

Then she said, 'I killed a man, and I went to jail. His family swore vengeance. His father has always wanted to kill me.'

It wasn't the whole story, but it was enough.

'What man?' said Vasile.

'A man who raped me when I was fifteen, fed me drugs, beat me when I talked back. Do I need to go on?'

She could feel Vasile's eyes on her, listening and judging. Would he keep her on, a convicted killer? Doubtful.

'This man,' said Vasile. 'He was bad.' A statement or a question?

Carol couldn't help smiling. 'Well, he certainly wasn't good,' she said.

'Your father, he should kill him,' said Vasile, 'protect your honour. Not you.'

'My father was a drunk,' said Carol. 'He didn't give a stuff about me.' She holds up her glass, smiles and takes another sip of whiskey.

'You go to jail, you serve your time,' said Vasile. 'Now is done. You work here now. We don't let no one come to kill you.'

He gave her a curt nod, picked up his whiskey and walked off. The matter was settled.

The next morning Carol left the smallholding at dawn with the rest of the gang.

. . .

As she works, Carol keeps thinking about the girl. She didn't recognise the name. But then the girl said she was Marcia's daughter; that was a shock. Carol tried to think when she last saw her. She was a tiny baby, only weeks old. Now she's this elegant and poised young woman, with a halo of golden hair. Carol can imagine how proud her own mother would've been to have a granddaughter like that. And how proud her sister must be.

The disturbing and puzzling thing is the old man sent her. That makes no sense. Carol can't imagine a situation in which Marcie would've allowed that.

She didn't want to frighten the girl, but it had to be done. How else could she hope to protect herself? But when she saw the effect her threatening behaviour had on that beautiful face, it tore her heart in two. Afterwards she cried. The first tears she's shed in years.

Now the rhythm of the work sustains her. The crates of cabbages are heavy, and placing them on the back of the trailer isn't easy. She wears thick work gloves, but her hands are sore. She doesn't mind. Physical hardship and discomfort are things she's been used to her entire life. Bruises, cuts, aches and pains are normal. If things get really bad, she'll take painkillers. But mostly she endures. It's the one thing she's good at.

The rain eases, and they stop for a hot bevvy. A Thermos of coffee gets passed around, and then a flask of something stronger to keep out the cold. Carol sits with the others, feet dangling, on the end of the trailer.

Vasile usually comes to check how they're doing during the morning; the rest of the time he's hustling up the next job. So it doesn't surprise Carol to see his pickup ploughing up the muddy track and into the gateway of the field.

She watches the vehicle approach. He has a woman with

him, but it's not Alina. The pickup stops. The woman gets out, picking her way through the mud in entirely unsuitable shoes. Then she tosses her head and pushes her hair out of her eyes.

A stab of recognition hits Carol. Her heart leaps. Is it even possible? She can't believe it.

She jumps down from the back of the trailer and strides towards the pickup.

The woman is standing there, one of her shoes has got stuck in the mud and she's in danger of toppling over.

Carol rushes forward to steady her.

'Marcie!' she gasps. 'Oh my god, it's really you!'

She flings her arms round her sister, enveloping her in a fierce hug.

Marcie loses her shoe. But she hugs her back.

They're both in tears. They hold each other, laughing and crying at the same time.

'Trust you to be up to your knees in mud on a bloody farm,' says Marcie.

'And trust you to wear the wrong shoes,' says Carol.

52

Thursday, 11.55am

The Mitsubishi truck belonging to the gangmaster has a comfortable back seat. He allows Marcia and Carol the use of it so they can talk.

Marcia can't take her eyes off her sister. The last eighteen years have left their mark on her. She was always much prettier than Marcia; the kind of busty, bubbly blonde that men liked. Her hair has faded to a wispy grey. Her cheeks are chubby and weather-beaten, and she's overweight. She looks tough, but Marcia can sense how fragile and damaged she is. This is her baby sister and seeing her like this is gut-wrenching.

She had the address that Celia's son provided, and it led her to an agricultural smallholding outside Diss in Norfolk. The fact she arrived in an expensive sports car seemed to impress the rough-looking Romanian who owned the place. He turned out to be a gangmaster providing agricultural workers to farms throughout East Anglia. He was also Carol's employer.

There was no sign of Phoebe, and he didn't recognise the video clip that Marcia showed him. But she persuaded him to take her to where Carol was working.

Marcia looks at her sister. Her eyes are still startlingly blue and full of tears. Her chin trembles.

Marcia seizes her hand; it feels rough and chapped, the nails dirty and ragged.

'Hey, c'mon,' she says. 'No need to cry.'

'I just… I thought I'd never see you again.'

'Well, here I am. Turning up like a bad penny. That's what Mum would say.'

'I met Phoebe,' says Carol. 'She came here. She's amazing. And it's a nice name. Very posh, very suitable.'

Marcia shrugs. She's consumed with guilt. She fears if she lets her emotions off the leash, the beast that emerges will destroy everything. Despite that, there's one question burning in her brain. She has to ask.

'I thought you might've told her,' she says.

Carol frowns. 'No,' she says. 'I never would. I swear to you.'

'But when you met her…'

'Marcie, we made a deal. When I realised who she was, it was quite a shock. I had a bit of a knee-jerk reaction. But I frightened her off. Sent her away.'

'You've had time to think about it. You might've changed your mind.'

'No, I haven't. I wouldn't do that to her. Or to you. She believes I'm her aunt. And that's how it should stay. I was an addict, a complete mess. What chance would she have had with me? I gave her to you because I knew you'd give her a much better life than I ever could. And it certainly looks as if you have.'

'I've tried my best.'

'And I knew you would. Being her biological mum is nothing, she's your daughter.'

Marcia can't help it; she tries to stop herself, but more tears come. In a flood of relief and guilt.

Carol cradles her and strokes her hair. They sit there together for several moments.

But then it hits her. If Phoebe's not here with Carol, where the hell is she?

A rising sense of panic grips her.

'When did she come here?' Marcia says.

'Yesterday morning,' says Carol. 'I was horrible. Waved a bread knife at her. It seemed the best way to get rid of her.'

'And she left straight away?'

'Yeah, she was with this boy. In a pickup truck, a bit like this one. They drove off.'

'You've not seen her since?'

'No,' says Carol. 'What's going on? She said some stuff about dad. What the fuck is he up to?'

'He's married again,' says Marcia. 'The boy is his step-son. Dad persuaded Phoebe to come looking for you. I knew nothing about it. He's as stupid and devious as he ever was. Now he's on some AA kick and wants your forgiveness.'

'He thought if I saw her, he could lure me back?'

'Yeah, something like that, I assume.'

'And he didn't tell her who I was?'

'No, apparently not. But Phoebe's missing. I don't know where the hell she is.'

'What do you mean missing?'

'She was supposed to meet me in Cambridge yesterday afternoon. She didn't turn up. Her phone's gone dead. Steven, he's the stepson, told me he'd left her with you. But he was obviously lying.'

Carol shakes her head. 'Oh no!'

'What? You know where she is?'

'No, but… that fucking bastard, is he still there at the farm?'

'Are you talking about Brian?'

Carol clenches her fists; she looks ready for a fight. Not quite the sister that Marcia remembers.

'He always wanted revenge,' she says. 'Alan was his precious bloody son. When he got out, he came and visited me inside. Told me in no uncertain terms he'd kill me. And every year, on the anniversary of Alan's death, I get this card.'

'From him?'

'Not signed. But printed. Like on a computer.'

'He is at the farm. But Carol, he's an old man. He's had a stroke. He can hardly speak. Walks with a frame. I don't see what he could do. You're being paranoid.'

'Am I? You think that would stop that evil bastard? As long as he's got breath in his body, he'll keep coming. He wants me dead. But what if he reckons he can get her too? Don't you see, that makes his revenge complete?'

Marcia feels a chill run through her. Uncle Brian? It seems impossible.

But where's Phoebe? And why did Celia's son lie to her?

53

Thursday, 12.05pm

Lacey is perched high up in her nest, looking down on the floor of the barn. She's eating a *Curly Wurly* and scrolling on her phone. It's unlikely the school will get its act together and phone her mum before Monday.

Her plan is to say that she's been bunking off because she's being bullied and it's affecting her mental health. As soon as you mention the B word, they all get twitchy. Instead of suspending her, she'll get sent for counselling. She likes the school counsellor. He's young and cool and listens to her. He's never once told her that the Lord sees her or that she'll go straight to hell if she doesn't do her homework.

Her real purpose in staying away from school is to think. And to spy on Steve. Her brother is up to something, no doubt about that. He lies to Mum about his drug dealing, but he's still laid back about it. This is different. She's never seen him this wound up. It's totally out of character. He's smoking much more than usual. Mum makes him go outside and freeze his arse off to do it. He's been lurking down below in the barn. The floor is littered with fag ends. The old man has warned him to be careful; one day he could burn the place down. That would be interesting.

Lacey has been online to check out her new sister. Marcia Lennox — she doesn't call herself Marcie anymore — pops up loads of times on a Google search. She works in advertising at a place in Notting Hill with a really cool website. Next summer Lacey must do a work placement. Her mum has a friend at church who's a florist. She wouldn't mind that, learning how to make bouquets and wreaths. But an advertising agency in London sounds way better.

She's fantasising and planning trips to London when her brother comes striding into the barn. He has his phone to his ear, and he doesn't sound happy.

'Hey, c'mon man, that's not right,' he says in a whining voice. 'I delivered the goods. That's what we agreed. That's your payment. What fucking difference does it make if she works for a bunch of Romanians? You saying you're scared of a few Romanians? You can still do the job. Yeah, I know circumstances can change. But I've shown you what I can do, surely that's enough. Oh, come on, Luca—'

Steve holds the phone away from his ear and curses. Lacey concludes that, whoever Luca is, he hung up.

Her brother slots the phone in his pocket, pulls out a packet of cigarettes and lights up. As he does so his gaze travels upwards; Lacey ducks down behind a bail of straw. But not in time.

'Lacey!' he shouts. 'Why aren't you at school?'

She tries to ignore him.

'Don't make me come up there and get you.'

She can just see him standing there, smoking his fag and waiting.

'I'll go and get Mum. I'm sure you don't want that.'

He's right. She doesn't. She's snookered.

She raises her head.

He laughs. 'You're such a sneaky little bitch, aren't you?'

'Who's Luca?' she says.

'Just someone I know.'

'What's he done to you?'

'Stiffed me on a drug deal. Or he's trying to.'

Lacey considers this. As lies go, it's passable. C plus to B minus.

'Why you smoking loads?' she says. 'You'll die of lung cancer.'

He chuckles. 'And you'll die of chocolate. We're both stuffed.'

'What did Phoebe's mum want?'

He huffs. 'If you want to talk to me, come down here. I'm getting a bloody crick in my neck looking up at you.'

She clambers down the tiered stack of bails and jumps onto the floor.

He grins at her. 'What's going on, Lace,' he says. 'Bunking off school? You like school. I don't think my little buddy's very happy.' He pulls out his cigarettes. 'Want one of these?'

'No,' she says. 'They're disgusting. You'll end up smelling like Uncle Brian.'

He tilts his head, puts his arm round her. 'You saying I piss my pants too?'

She giggles. 'No.'

'What's up? C'mon, you can tell me?'

She shrugs. 'I'm just a bit upset about Phoebe. I didn't find her just so you could go off and shag her.'

He sighs. 'Well, you're right. She was horrible to you, ignored you completely.'

'Treated me like a stupid kid. I'm fourteen.'

'You're right to be pissed off. And okay, I did shag her. But only the once. Truth is, she's a right stuck-up cow. Thinks she's better than the likes of us. You see these people on the net, and it's all a pack of lies. That's not who they really are. I'd forget her if I was you.'

Lacey looks at him. This is her brother. He loves her. He also uses her. And lies to her. But that's families, isn't it?

'Where is she now?' she says.

'I dunno. I left her in Cambridge, getting pissed in some posh bar.'

Lacey scans him. His eyes dart around. He's avoiding her gaze. And it's obvious he's lying.

54

Thursday, 12.10pm

Phoebe paces; three steps one way, three steps back. Like a caged animal or a criminal. It's as far as the chain allows her to go.

She spent the night on the concrete floor, hugging her own body, wrapped in the rough blanket, freezing and scared. She dozed fitfully. Strange sounds, the scrabbling and scurrying of rats, infiltrated her dreams. They went camping once when she was a kid and slept on the hard ground; her mum hated it. She should've listened to Ma and told that devious scumbag, Steve, to take a hike.

The pacing has helped prevent her bare feet from becoming numb. But, as the hours have passed, she's gone from optimism, giving herself little pep talks, to feeling abandoned and desolate. Harry would not refuse the kidnappers' demands; her mother wouldn't let him. They may be about to divorce, but he's still her father. Legally, morally. The last phone conversation she had with him, he made that clear.

'Hey, Pheebs,' he said. 'You're my daughter, you always will be. I'm always there for you.'

He won't let her down now.

She wonders what the time is. She relies on her phone. Rarely wears a watch.

The rhythm of walking up and down has calmed her. Other senses have come into play. Her eyes have adjusted to the gloom. She's being held in an old garage which stinks of engine oil and damp cardboard. The roof leaks.

There's a rough wooden workbench at the back, which she can skim with her fingertips, if she stretches out her hand. She's scanned it for any sort of tool to use as a weapon, or to break the chain. There's a screwdriver tantalisingly out of reach. It might help her prise open the shackle on her ankle. She's examined that in some detail. It's metal, but not that robust. It looks like something you might buy on the net from an S&M site. The inside of the ankle ring is lined with red velvet so it doesn't damage the flesh.

She's hungry and thirsty, and desperate to pee. If they keep her here much longer, she won't be able to hold it in. It offends her dignity more than anything, the thought that she might end up standing in a puddle of her own piss. Or worse.

For most of her life, Phoebe Lennox has been sheltered from hardship. She's only been exposed to adversity in managed chunks. Adventure courses, kayaking through the rapids, bungee jumping from a viaduct for charity. The fear involved was momentary and easy to master. Even skiing off-piste with her dad and brothers, she never felt that anything bad could happen to her. She realises now how cocooned she's been. How much Harry and Marcia have protected her. And how she's always taken it for granted. There are plenty of horror stories in the news, but they happen to other people, not to someone like her.

266

The door to the garage is secured with a heavy metal lock, and a bolt that goes down into the ground. It won't budge; she's tried it, booted it — even though that hurt — tugged at it. Outside, the traffic noise from the nearby road has grown. It can't be that far away. Perhaps a quarter of a mile? It means potential rescue is close. If she could just get out and make a run for it.

This is what she's thinking when she hears footsteps crunching on the gravel outside the door. A key rattles in the lock. The bolt is drawn. Her heart thumps in her chest. What now?

The door opens, and daylight floods in, blinding her for a moment. There are two of them. The thug in the biker vest with a goatee beard, the one she kicked in the shins, and a woman.

The woman is small and dark, about Marcia's age. She seems well-dressed, certainly a cut above the thug. She scans Phoebe and smiles. Then she says something in a foreign language. It sounds Eastern European, possibly Slavic. She seems in charge of proceedings, which is a relief. The thug takes a key from his pocket and unlocks the shackle around Phoebe's ankle. He grabs her arm; she tries to pull away, an instinctive reaction.

'Is okay,' he says. 'You come now.'

They must have been in touch with her parents. Soon this will be over. She lets him lead her out of the garage. The woman follows.

Stepping out into the fresh air is such a relief, escaping the stink of the freezing garage. There's a slight breeze. The day is overcast and cloudy with the scent of rain in the air. Phoebe tips back her head and inhales. Then she takes in her surroundings. She sees grass and trees, a rural location. The gravel path she's being led along crosses an area of rough turf, and up ahead there's a house. An old farmhouse? And there's the main road in the distance. She can see a stream of cars and lorries passing by.

They enter the house by the back door; it leads into the kitchen. It's homely and warm.

She turns to the woman. 'I need to pee. Toilet? Please.'

The woman looks at the thug; he translates. The woman raises her index finger and beckons. Phoebe follows her out into the hall. The place is neat, rather old-fashioned, with heavy wooden furniture and peculiar knick-knacks. The people who live here aren't poor.

The woman heads up a wide, carpeted staircase. She follows. The thug remains in the kitchen. Good. In a fight, Phoebe could overpower this little woman. But that won't be necessary. Soon they'll release her. It's all about money. She's sure of that.

The woman opens the door to a bedroom, and Phoebe follows her inside. It's spacious with a king-size bed, wardrobes along one wall and a twee vanity dressing table with a three-part mirror. The woman opens another door, which leads to an en suite bathroom. She points.

Phoebe hurries in. She tries to close the door behind her, but the woman places her foot in the way and shakes her head. 'Nu,' she says.

Waste of effort to argue; she just needs to go. She pulls down her jeans, sits on the toilet and pees with considerable relief.

As she does this, the woman goes over to the shower and turns it on. She points to it and then to a rack of towels. 'Te speli,' she says. 'A intelege?'

Phoebe nods. Take a shower. She gets it.

The woman walks out into the bedroom, leaving the door

open. It's clear she won't be allowed any privacy, but she's beyond caring.

She strips off her clothes and gets into the shower. The warm water soothes her aching body. It feels fantastic. There's shampoo and shower gel in a metal rack. She washes her hair, rinses it, washes her body. She luxuriates in the water. Her ordeal is almost over; they need to make her look presentable. Soon she'll be going home.

She gets out of the shower and wraps herself in a towel. The woman appears and hands her a bathrobe. It's pink and fluffy and soft. Phoebe puts it on. The woman scoops up Phoebe's clothes from the floor and puts them in a black bin bag.

'Hey,' she says, 'I'm going to need those.'

The woman ignores her. She carries the bin bag out into the bedroom and dumps it in a corner. Then she goes to the dressing table, opens a drawer and brings out a hairdryer. She plugs it in at the wall and holds it up, offering it to Phoebe.

'Usuca-ti parul,' she says.

Phoebe is wondering about the language. The police will want as much detail as possible later. Once the ransom has been paid, they'll be going after these fuckers.

'Albania? Or maybe Romania?' she says with a smile. 'Is that where you're from?'

The woman seems amused, but points to the hairdryer.

Once her hair is dry, the woman inspects her. She gives an approving nod and beckons for her to follow.

Now what?

Barefooted, and in the fluffy bathrobe, Phoebe follows her back down the stairs. The woman walks down the hallway to a door, knocks and opens it. She holds it open for Phoebe to enter.

It's an office. Bookshelves, filing cabinets, and a chunky wooden desk in the middle of the room.

A man sits behind the desk; he looks up from his laptop and smiles. Phoebe is useless at ages. He could be fifty or sixty. Grey hair, grey face, grey man. He wears rimless glasses and a brown cardigan and looks like the college librarian.

He nods to the woman. She disappears and closes the door.

The man steeples his fingers and scans her. His smile widens.

'Well, Phoebe,' he says. 'I hope you enjoyed your shower?'

At last, someone who speaks proper English.

'Have you been in touch with my father?' she says.

The man leans back in his chair, takes off his glasses and polishes them.

'Your father? Why would I be in touch with him?'

His manner is mild, and he has only a hint of a foreign accent. He looks puny, an unlikely gangster, but the eyes are small and bright, like a rodent.

'To get your money,' she says. 'Isn't that what you want? Money?'

He chuckles. 'Oh yes,' he says. 'You are worth a good deal of money. I love your YouTube channel. So many sexy videos. You have done all the marketing for us. Many people have seen you on social media. You're quite an influencer, PhoReal. Many followers.' He laughs. 'Yes, there's a lot of interest.'

'What are you talking about?' she says. 'Haven't you contacted my father? Isn't this why you've kidnapped me? For ransom?'

He considers this. 'Ah, I see,' he says. 'A misunderstanding.'

'What? What misunderstanding?'

He smiles. 'You are very beautiful, my dear. Young, white, English, well-educated. A premium product. It will be a lively auction.'

She stares at him. None of it makes sense. Bile rises in her throat.

'Let me explain,' he says. 'I'm an auctioneer, amongst other things. We run an auction site on the dark web, specialising in personnel, a very lucrative market.'

He makes it sound as if she's looking for a job. But it's more sinister than that.

'What are you saying? You plan to sell me? At an online auction?'

'Yes. Girls like you are a valuable commodity. Our client base is mainly in the Middle East. And other places, too. More traditional societies, shall we say? We have been circulating details and have a lot of interest already. Clients love your social media posts. You will fetch a very good price. There are many high-net-worth individuals seeking an English concubine. A billionaire, perhaps even a prince, if you're lucky. Some girls choose this work voluntarily. It can be a very comfortable life.'

Concubine? She's speechless. But she can't afford to panic.

'Listen,' she says. 'Contact my father. He's rich too. He will pay. Whatever you want. He will pay.'

The man shakes his head.

'No, no,' he says. 'Ransom is messy. Then the police get involved. Too much risk for us. I'm a businessman.'

'You can't sell me. I'm not an animal. I'm not someone's property.'

'That may be true in the UK. But I deal in the global marketplace. Different laws and norms apply.'

Phoebe stares at him. Her pulse is racing. It's pure fear. She takes a deep breath, turns on her heel and runs for the door. She wrenches it open, only to find that the thug in the biker vest is blocking her path. The woman is beside him with a syringe in her hand.

55

Thursday, 12.50pm

The Mercedes hits the A14 west of Bury St Edmunds. Traffic is heavy, streams of container lorries from the docks in Felixstowe. Marcia weaves in and out, and once she gets in the fast lane, she floors it. She has one thing in her mind and one absolute priority: find Phoebe.

Carol sits beside her as they speed along; she gives her a nervous glance.

'Bloody hell, Marcie,' she says. 'I remember when the old man offered to teach you to drive the Land Rover. And you refused. Said you hated driving and never wanted to learn.'

'He was drunk. That's probably why I said no.'

'This is some car. Must've cost a bomb.'

'Present from my husband.'

Marcia can feel her sister's gaze upon her. It's odd, but reassuring. This is the one person who knows who she is and where she's come from. There's no need to pretend.

'I'm glad you've found someone nice, who makes you happy,' Carol says.

'He's just left me. For a younger woman, who's pregnant.'

Carol laughs. 'You're joking, aren't you?'

'No. Harry's a bit of a cliché. He's fourteen years older than me. He was married with kids when I met him. Now he's trading me in for a younger model.'

'Does he hit you?'

'Oh no. Nothing like that.'

How can she explain to her sister that a man like Harry has such charm that he always gets his own way? He's one of the good guys, that's how he regards himself. He would never raise his hand to a woman. Such behaviour would disgust him.

They drive on for several miles in silence.

Finally, Marcia says, 'You don't mind that I changed her name?'

Carol shrugs. 'Jade wasn't my choice, it was Alan's. He wanted to put his stamp on her. Make her his baby.'

'But he realised she wasn't, didn't he?' says Marcia.

'Oh yeah,' says Carol. 'That's what drove him crazy. And I knew, eventually, he'd just lose it, kill me and kill her.'

'What happened to David?' says Marcia.

'They ran him off. Alan and Brian. That's what Dad said. I never saw him again.'

Marcia glances at her sister. Tears are brimming in Carol's eyes. Her hands are clutched in her lap. She's retreated to another place and another time. Marcia wants to reach out and comfort her, but it's been too long. The woman sitting by her side now is still her little sister, but she's also a stranger.

'I'm sorry I wasn't there for you more before she was born,' she says.

Carol smiles. 'When I was in the rehab place, it was fine. They got me off the drugs, helped me through the pregnancy. But it was just for addicts who were pregnant. Once she was born, and I was back at home, that's when the trouble started.'

'I should've got there sooner.' That desperate phone call. Her sister's cry for help; it still rings in her head.

Carol shrugs. 'I know you came as soon as you could.'

Marcia feels a pang of guilt; she didn't. She avoided returning to the farm for as long as she could. And Carol must know that.

She needs to move this on. 'I thought it was sensible to change her name.'

'Yeah, it was. Was it difficult to do?'

Now they're on safer ground. They're making conversation, like two casual acquaintances. But perhaps that's what they are now?

'No. She was three weeks old. You never registered her birth. When I got to London, I went to the register office, said she'd been born at home and gave her the name Phoebe. No one ever questioned it.'

'I like it,' says Carol. 'Mum would've liked it.'

'She's so smart,' says Marcia. 'It was tough at first, I was temping at various ad agencies, and taking her to the child-minder. But she adapted to every situation. She had such resilience and curiosity.'

'I think she looks like Mum, don't you?' says Carol.

'Yeah.'

Her sister seems sad and reflective. Is she imagining a different life and what might've been?

'I'm sorry about all this,' says Carol.

'How is it your fault?'

'When I got out of jail, he was always going to make his move?'

They're back to Brian. Marcia knows only too well what he was: a vicious bully and a criminal. But now? He's a doddery old man who didn't seem to recognise her.

'Well,' she says, 'I doubt he's behind this. But if he is, he's had help. No way he's acting on his own.'

'You're sure there's nowhere else she could be?' says Carol.

'Sure as I can be,' says Marcia. 'I texted Harry and the rest of the family last night. I was quite low-key. But no one's seen or heard from her. They all assume that she's in Cambridge. Back at uni. I've talked to the police too, but I don't think they're that interested.'

'He was always pure evil,' says Carol. 'Makes my skin crawl. This is him. I just know it.'

Marcia glances at her sister; she's stuck in a time warp. Perhaps that's what prison does to you?

The Mercedes pulls up in the yard of Elm Tree Farm.

'Are you ready for this?' says Marcia.

Carol is gritting her teeth; the tension is rippling through her jaw. She did this a lot as a child; Marcia remembers their mother chiding her for it.

'It doesn't seem much different,' Carol says. 'What's she like, the new wife?'

'Religious,' says Marcia. 'But she seems like a decent person.'

'Then why would she marry him?'

As they get out of the car, Marcia notices a figure watching them from an upstairs window. She looks up, and he retreats. But she recognises him. It's the stepson, Steven. This is who she wants to talk to. If anyone knows where Phoebe is, it's that lying little toad.

Before they can knock, the front door opens; someone else has seen their arrival: Celia.

She's smiling, but she seems apprehensive.

'Well,' she says, 'you'd better come in.'

Marcia doesn't care if this is awkward. Carol says nothing. They follow Celia into the house.

In the cosy farmhouse kitchen, Derek Cook is sprawled in the wooden rocking chair that once belonged to their grandfather; he's dozing.

Marcia watches her sister's reaction. She looks him over without emotion.

It's impossible to tell what she's thinking.

Celia goes to her husband's side and puts a hand on his shoulder.

'Derek,' she whispers.

Carol walks round the table, positioning herself with her back to the Rayburn. Marcia remembers, on cold winter mornings before school, this was always her sister's favourite spot, warming herself by the stove.

Derek's eyes open. He looks at Marcia first. It takes a moment for him to notice Carol. Their eyes meet; he stares at her in astonishment then he lets out a sob. A tear runs down his face. Does he see how broken she is? He should.

'You wanted to find her,' says Marcia. 'Well, here she is.'

He struggles to his feet, takes two steps towards Carol and then crumples to his knees. It's impossible to tell if this is deliberate or he's fallen over. But he clasps his hands together in prayer and whispers. 'Thank you, Lord.'

Carol doesn't move. Her blank expression turns to one of disdain.

'Oh, for fuck's sake,' she mumbles.

'I am sorry,' he whispers. 'I needed to tell you that.'

'What are you playing at, Dad?' says Carol. 'Is this the new game? Happy families? Bit late for that, don't you think?'

With Celia's help, and leaning on the table, he hauls himself to his feet.

'You have every right to be angry—'

'Let's cut the crap. I didn't come to see you. You and me, we were done years ago. Where is he? 'Cause I gather you've taken him in.'

'If you're talking about your uncle,' says Celia. 'It was the Christian thing to do.'

Carol glares at Celia. For a split second, it feels as if Carol might hit her.

But she says, 'You believe in God? What about the devil?'

Carol's face has a look of suppressed fury. She's morphed into a different person. Marcia wonders what she's let loose.

'Where is he?' Carol says. 'Upstairs? Or jacking off to porn in the sitting room? That's what he used to do.'

'He's an old man,' says Celia, 'He's had a stroke. You can't—'

'Oh, I'll find him. You forget I know this house, all its nooks and crannies. Where to hide, to avoid getting your head kicked in. You'd better look the other way, Dad. It's what you always used to do, isn't it?'

'Carol, please,' says Derek.

Marcia recognises that whine in his voice. She suspects Carol hates it as much as she does.

But Carol isn't listening. She takes a deep breath and hollers, 'Brian! You wanna kill me, now's your chance!'

Celia shoots an anxious glance at Marcia. What? She somehow expects her to intervene?

Marcia is transfixed. She wasn't expecting this. She's not sure what she was expecting. But this isn't the fragile drug addict, who stood in the dock and pleaded guilty in a whispery voice. This is another Carol. Carol, the ex-con. And she's scary.

A hunched figure appears in the doorway, leaning on his walking frame. But this time the eyes in his haggard face are alert. He moves quicker than when Marcia last saw him too.

Devious to the last, she thinks.

And he has a lopsided smile. 'Yes,' he says. 'I knew you'd come.' His delivery is slow, his speech slurred, but it's easy enough to understand.

Carol steps forward. 'Where is she? What have you done with her?'

'You'll never find her,' he says. 'She's gone.'

'Gone where?'

For a moment Marcia can't breathe. Her head spins.

Brian? This pathetic wreck. How?

She strides across the room and stops within inches of his face. 'Who's got her? Where is she? I'm calling the police.'

Brian's eyes glisten with hatred. His breathing is laboured.

'You think I care about the police,' he says. 'What can they do to me? Child of a whore. I've sent her where she belongs.'

Carol moves forward. But Marcia is closer and quicker.

She seizes him by the throat. 'What have you done? Had her killed?'

'Oh no,' he mutters. 'Worse than that. Far worse.'

56

Thursday, 1.30pm

DS Jo Boden is restless. She's been cooped up all morning, listening to a boring lecture on data analysis. The question of Phoebe Lennox continues to niggle her. But if she wants to keep the boss onside for the IOPC inquiry, she needs to let it go. She also needs exercise, so she walks into the town centre to get her lunch. She's at the counter of her favourite café, ordering a sandwich and coffee to go, when her phone rings.

Mrs Lennox.

She sighs. She's been putting this off. What can she say? *If I help you, my career's down the toilet?*

'Mrs Lennox,' says Boden. 'I've been meaning to call you, but it's been a busy morning.'

'Remember my uncle, I told you about my uncle.' She sounds breathless and agitated.

What did the DCI call it? *Some fucked-up family nonsense?*

'What about your uncle?' says Boden.

'He's done something terrible to Phoebe.'

Boden has a vague recollection of a doddery old man, sitting at the table next to Derek Cook. He didn't look capable of swatting a fly.

'How? Surely he's quite old?'

'Yeah, I know. But he instigated it. He's admitted it.'

'Okay,' says Boden. 'What d'you mean by instigated, Mrs Lennox?'

'I'm here at the farm with Carol,' she says. 'And you've got to listen to us.'

'Your sister?'

Who's just got out of jail and who she seemed scared of when they last spoke? This is getting confusing. But the posh, rather superior edge has disappeared from Mrs Lennox's voice. It's been stripped away by panic.

'Look,' she says. 'I'm reasonably convinced Steven's involved. He's been driving Phoebe backwards and forwards from the farm to Cambridge and also up to Norfolk, looking for my sister.'

'He's your father's stepson?' says Boden. He certainly has a record; though nothing recent.

'I think Phoebe was kidnapped when she was with him.'

Kidnapped? Boden considers this. The cell siting that they got on Phoebe Lennox's phone placed it on the edge of Thetford Forest, close to the A11.

Boden gets her coffee. She nods her thanks to the barista and walks out of the café.

'Hello? Are you still there?' says Mrs Lennox. She sounds desperate.

'I'm just getting my lunch,' says Boden. 'And I'm wondering, could your daughter's travels have taken her anywhere near the A11 to the west of Thetford?'

'Yes,' says Mrs Lennox. 'My sister's been working near

Diss in Norfolk. The route back to Cambridge would take them on A11. Why?'

'That's the last location of your daughter's phone.'

'Oh my God, it all makes sense! He has been using Steven, that's how he did it.'

Did what? None of it makes sense to Boden. But talking to Mrs Lennox is giving her an eerie sensation. Somewhere in this muddle, there's more than a grain of truth.

Kidnapping Phoebe? Why?

'What's this about, Mrs Lennox? Revenge?'

'Yes! He's been threatening to kill Carol for years. But Phoebe was easier to get to.'

'You think he's killed her?'

'He says it's something worse.'

'Worse than murder?'

This is crazy stuff. If she goes to the DCI with this, her career will be over.

'I know you think I'm mad,' says Mrs Lennox. 'And it probably doesn't help that I haven't told you the full story. But I promise you that this is real.'

Boden sighs. This is the woman who, a few days ago, was accusing her daughter's ex-boyfriend of abduction. Now the half-brother is suing the police and Boden's in the frame. The smart thing would be to fob her off and go back to data analysis. No one would blame her.

The problem is, she'd blame herself. There's a whisper of plausibility here that she can't ignore. And if Phoebe Lennox turns up dead, does she want that on her conscience?

Sod it!

'Okay,' she says. 'A colleague of mine has been looking into your daughter's case. I need to go back to the office and talk to her. Then I'll phone you back.'

'When?' says Mrs Lennox.

'Give me half an hour.'

'You're not just saying that to get rid of me?'

'Mrs Lennox, I believe you. Let me look into this.'

As Boden walks, she munches her sandwich. Does she believe her?

Why would an ageing thug take revenge for his son's murder on the killer's niece? Opportunism? She's easier to get to?

Because Carol Cook cares about Phoebe? But Carol Cook doesn't even know Phoebe Lennox.

Boden tosses her sandwich wrapping in the bin and calls DC Chakravorty.

'Prisha, that probation officer from Norwich, did she ever get back to us?' she says.

'Yes,' says the young DC. 'She called about an hour ago. We had quite a long conversation. She says that Carol Cook is petrified of her family, thinks they want revenge.'

'Okay,' says Boden. 'When we were looking for Phoebe before, we did an ANPR trace on a vehicle. That led us to Elm Tree Farm. The owner's name, was it Steven something?'

'Steven Jarman.'

'Same vehicle. We need to track it again. Can we place it on the A11 near the garage where Phoebe Lennox made her last call to her mother? I'll square it with the DCI later.'

After he suspends her.

'Yep, I'll get on it. I've got a confession to make, I know you said to leave it alone, but after I spoke to the probation officer, I was curious.'

Boden smiles to herself.

'You're a girl after my own heart, Chakravorty. Tell me what you've got.'

'I did some digging. Brian Cook, he's the uncle, and

father of the murdered cousin. Served time for drug dealing. But he's a nasty villain. The prime suspect in several murders. CPS could never make a case against him. But here's the interesting thing. He was suspected of killing a local man called David Harris. Essex police went to Elm Tree Farm and dug up a couple of fields, looking for a body. Found nothing.'

'When was this? Before or after Carol Cook went to jail?'

'Six months before Carol killed Alan Cook. Couldn't pin Harris' murder on him. They got Brian for drug dealing instead.'

'Mrs Lennox said he was in prison when the murder of Alan Cook took place.'

'Do you think there's a connection?' says Chakravorty.

'Get Mackie on the ANPR. We need to go to Elm Tree Farm and talk to Brian Cook.'

57

Thursday, 1.45pm

Phoebe is stretched out on the bed. She struggles to keep her eyes open. When the thug grabbed her, she kicked out with all her might. She knew they were going to knock her out again. And the injection was a strong sedative. Once it had taken effect, the fight went out of her. The thug picked her up and carried her upstairs to the bedroom.

The bed is soft; she sinks into it. Her hands and arms and feet and legs are all tingling, and a strange lethargy is seeping through her entire body. Her thoughts float and she has a sense of detachment and peace. There's an echoing some-where in the recesses of her brain. *You must get up,* it says. *You must run.* She hears it. But it's too far away. Her eyes close and she dozes a little.

Random thoughts slip through her mind, or perhaps she's dreaming. She's with her mother in Richmond Park. It's early morning and they've gone jogging together. But Phoebe stops to watch the deer. A fawn is grazing beside its mother. Phoebe tries to approach it; she wants to stroke its soft head. But the animals are skittish. As she moves towards them, they toss their heads and run. She tries to run after them, but they're too fast. She turns and sees her mother calling her, calling her name, and she sounds frantic. Phoebe feels a rush of panic. Should she run after the deer or return to her mother? She can't decide. There it is again: *you must run.*

There's a hand on her shoulder and she opens her eyes. The woman is standing over her. She smiles and pushes the hair back from Phoebe's brow. Her touch is gentle. This woman is taking care of her. She wants to believe that. But she knows the woman is a witch.

Now the man is standing across the room, but he has his back to her. She recognises the brown cardigan. A camera sits on a tripod with a chair placed in front of it. He's adjusting the camera.

The witch leans over her. She's smiling. She puts her hand under Phoebe's shoulder, encouraging her to sit up. Phoebe complies. She dangles her bare feet over the side of the bed. Little witch pulls open the front of her fluffy pink bathrobe and eases her arms out of it.

She's lightheaded. Everything is out of kilter. She's sitting on the side of the bed, and now she's naked.

The witch puts a hand under her elbow and helps her to stand up. She sways. Witchy is speaking soothing words that make no sense. She leads her over to the chair in front of the camera. Phoebe sits down. Witchy holds a hairbrush. She brushes Phoebe's hair. It falls loosely over her breasts. Witchy steps back.

Brown cardigan is behind the camera. Now he's speaking. His words drift towards her.

'Look at me, Phoebe,' he says. 'Hold your head up and look at me.'

Phoebe looks at him. The blood sings in her ears.

In her head, muffled this time: *you must run.* But it's fading away now. Easier to ignore it.

Brown cardigan is smiling at her; she smiles back.

'Very good,' he says. His voice sounds like a faraway echo. 'You have such beautiful blue eyes, Phoebe. Open your eyes wide and let me see your beautiful blue eyes.'

She has got beautiful blue eyes; she knows this. Her dad would joke with her. Where did you get those beautiful blue eyes? Her mother's eyes are grey. She can see her mother's face. She's calling her, but she's too far away. Her shoulders droop. She wants to sleep. Why don't they just let her sleep?

A hand on her shoulder rouses her. The witch is touching her, pushing her hair back across her shoulder to expose her naked breasts.

58

Thursday, 2.10pm

Marcia Lennox stares at her phone. Her hand shakes. It's been forty-three minutes since they spoke, and the sergeant has still not called her back. Without help from the police, how will they find Phoebe?

Brian is in his armchair, staring into space, defiantly silent. Marcia has a sense he's waiting. But waiting for what?

Her father sits in the rocking chair; he's pale and trembling. Celia stands beside him, keeping guard with a protective hand on his shoulder.

Carol walks back into the room. 'I've looked everywhere,' she says. 'I can't find him. But I found this one lurking in the barn.'

Lacey wanders into the room behind her, giving her mother a sheepish glance. The dog is at her heel.

'Why aren't you at school?' says Celia.

'I saw Steve sneak out,' says Lacey. 'Out of the back door and over the field to his truck. He parked it down the lane.'

'He will have gone to work,' says Celia.

'Where does he work?' says Marcia.

'He has clients all over,' says Celia. 'He sells Jacuzzis. My son has done nothing wrong except try to help his father.'

'He doesn't sell that many Jacuzzis,' says Lacey. 'Mostly he sells coke.'

'The Lord will strike you down, Lacey Cook!' says Celia. 'For telling such terrible lies about your brother.'

A wheezing and snuffling comes from Brian's direction. He appears to be laughing.

Lacey shoots a nervous glance at him. 'I know what I see,' she says.

'And the Lord sees you, Lacey,' says Celia, wagging her finger. 'The Lord sees us all. And we're all sinners.'

Derek takes his wife's hand. 'Celia,' he says. 'Don't be hard on the girl.'

Marcia's phone rings. DS Boden, finally!

She rushes out into the hall as she answers it.

'Sergeant,' she says. 'Thank you for getting back to me.' She must stay calm and rational. Ranting at the police won't help.

'Sorry for the delay, Mrs Lennox,' says the sergeant. It sounds as if she's in a car, in traffic. 'But we're on our way to you.'

Relief floods through Marcia. 'Thank you,' she says.

'A quick question for you. Who's David Harris?'

Marcia's heart skips a beat. David. Phoebe's real father? She can't say that. Not without a lengthy explanation. But why are the police asking about him?

'He was a friend of my sister,' says Marcia. 'They went to school together.'

'Are you aware,' says the sergeant, 'that the police questioned your uncle, Brian Cook, regarding the murder of David

Harris? Also, they searched your father's farm for his body. Did you know that?'

Marcia reels. 'My god,' she says. 'No, I didn't. When did this happen?'

'It was six months before the murder of Alan Cook,' says the sergeant.

Carol was pregnant and in the rehab place, so she wouldn't have known either. *They ran him off. Alan and Brian. That's what Dad said.*

'I was living in London then,' says Marcia. 'I rarely came back here.'

'We'll be with you soon,' says the sergeant. 'And we have some questions for your uncle.'

Marcia returns to the kitchen. She looks at Carol, and then she looks at her father. *They ran him off. That's what he said.*

She stares at him. 'You've known all along, haven't you?' she says. 'All this guilt, all this need for forgiveness. What's it really about, Dad?'

'I just want to make amends,' he whispers.

'Amends for what, though?' She points at Brian. 'Did you help him kill David?'

'What!' screams Carol.

'The police suspected that evil bastard; and they came here years ago looking for David's body. DS Boden just told me.' She turns to her father. 'He must've helped them cover it up.'

Carol takes a step towards her father; Celia moves between them.

Carol's chin trembles. Her face is red with fury. 'You said they ran him off. He disappeared. You said he wasn't man enough to stick up for me! He ran away. You convinced me of that.'

Brian shifts in his chair. He farts, chuckles to himself, and nods.

Marcia glances at him. Carol's right. He's half mad, but still dangerous.

Derek shakes his head; he looks sick and weary. Tears well and he says, 'They beat that poor boy to death and burnt his body. I couldn't stop them. They used the old pit in the bottom field where your grandad burnt all the carcasses of the cattle during the foot and mouth outbreak. I was trying to protect you, Carol.'

Carol stares at him, stunned.

'Telling the police,' says Marcia. 'That would've protected her.'

His voice is a whisper. 'I know. I was weak.'

And what if he had done that? For Marcia too, it would've meant a different life, a life without her daughter. Just a niece called Jade. She finds it impossible to imagine.

Celia is looking at her husband in horror. 'Is this true?'

He's avoiding her eye, but nods. 'It was the drink. I told you I was a sinner.'

Celia turns on Brian. 'If you have corrupted my son...'

Brian chuckles, a deep rumbling in his chest erupts into a fit of coughing.

For a moment, Carol seems frozen with horror. Now she steps forward; ready to tear him apart.

Marcia grabs her sister's arm. 'Carol, don't! He's not worth it. You don't want to go back inside.'

Carol meets her gaze. 'C'mon,' says Marcia. 'Leave it.'

As she clings on to her sister's arm, she can feel the rage pulsing through Carol's entire frame.

The doorbell rings, followed by a loud hammering on the front door. At last!

'The police are here now,' she says. She points at Celia. 'They'll track down her son, and they'll find Phoebe. Okay?'

Carol exhales and unclenches her fists. 'Okay,' she whispers.

Marcia walks down the hallway to the front door.

She opens it.

The blow to the chest is fast and brutal; it knocks her off her feet. It's from a mountain of a man with a shaved head; he comes barrelling through the door straight at her. She lands on her back, gasping for breath. He kicks her aside and continues down the hall. She gets a brief glimpse of a white transit van parked right outside the door.

A second man follows him in. He looks down at her and gives her a smug grin. It's Steve Jarman.

59

Thursday, 2.15pm

Carol is fighting to rein in her fury. The evil bastard killed David! Maybe in her heart she always knew it. But her father made her believe—

There's a commotion in the hall. What the hell? It doesn't sound good, and it doesn't sound like the police.

A massive thug erupts through the kitchen doorway. Bald head, fat neck, prison tats. Brian sits up in his chair and yelps with delight.

The thug has a piece of rope. Carol knows it's for her.

A young man comes into the room behind him.

'Steven!' exclaims Celia.

'Stay out of this, Mum,' he says. 'This is none of your business.' He looks at Carol and points. 'It's her!'

The thug lumbers forward. Not fast, but a solid, unstoppable mass. He has tiny piggy eyes, hands the size of meat plates. Carol seizes a knife from the block on the kitchen counter. She'll go down fighting. He smiles, muttering something in a foreign language. He's on one side of the pine table, she's the other. If he circles round it to get to her, she can make a break for the door. One chance is all she'll get. Her heart is thumping.

'Oh my God,' screams Celia. 'No! Stop this at once, Steven!'

'Shut up, Mum! An eye for an eye, that's what the Bible says? Word of God, according to you? She murdered Brian's son. Knifed him in his sleep.'

The thug is edging round the table; Carol moves to keep it between them. He's enjoying this game of cat and mouse. Brian watches with glee.

'No, no! This is wrong!' screams Celia. 'Stop this! I'm begging you!'

She rushes forward and grabs her boy's arm. He shoves her aside. Shoves too hard. She falls, hits the tiled floor, groaning as the wind's knocked out of her.

At the same moment, Marcie stumbles through the doorway. She's pale and shaking.

The boy is jittery. He's hurt his mother. Carol guesses this is not what he bargained for, and his nerve is cracking. He curses under his breath, reaches down and tries to help Celia to her feet.

Marcie slips behind him towards the Rayburn. On top of the stove, there's a red, enamelled steel kettle full of boiling water.

She grabs it, flings it at the back of the thug, and shouts, 'Run, Carol!'

The kettle glances off his shoulder, but the boiling water scalds him. He lets out a feral roar and turns towards her sister. Marcie faces him and she doesn't flinch.

An orange, cast iron frying pan hangs from a hook above the Rayburn. Marcie reaches up and grabs it. She grips its wooden handle with both hands and swings it backwards. The thug charges at her. Marcie clubs him with the frying pan, but he swats it aside. It clatters to the floor.

He seizes Marcie. His massive forearm goes round her neck, choking the breath out of her, and he drags her towards the door.

Celia screams.

The thug half hauls, half carries Marcie down the hall, and through the front door. She's gasping for air. He opens the back door of the transit van. Marcie's struggling. Kicking. But he holds her in a vice-like grip.

Carol rushes after them. She's outside. Should she just run? He'll be coming for her next. All she has is a kitchen knife. But that won't save either of them.

60

Thursday, 2.17pm

He throws her into the back of the van like a sack of rubbish. Her shoulder slams into the metal wheel arch. She hears the bone crack as she rolls away from it and across the hard floor. She ends up on her back. The pain is excruciating. Her lungs are still screaming for air after being held in his throttling grip. She's dizzy from lack of oxygen. Now she feels sick.

Her stomach clenches with fear. If she loses consciousness now, then it'll all be over. She must focus and fight back. But her head is swimming with random thoughts. She's spiralling downwards. The pain is fading. A bad sign. She remembers her mother's smile.

Is this how it ends? Slipping away. What do you think of in your last moments? Is it easier to let go, accept the inevitable?

A loud bang brings her to her senses. The van is moving, but stops with a jolt. Another bang. Some shouting. Words she can't decipher.

The back doors open. Bright light. Impossible to focus.

A hand reaches for her. Gently takes hold of her. A soothing voice.

'It's okay, Marcie. You're gonna be okay.' Carol.

She feels light-headed, close to fainting.

Her sister is beside her, helping her sit up.

The pain shoots through her shoulder. Agonising. She clutches her left arm. Another wave of nausea.

'I think I've broken something.'

Carol supports her. 'Just breathe,' she says. 'Concentrate on that.'

From the back of the van, she can see Celia slotting two new cartridges into the smoking chamber of a double-barrelled shotgun. Lacey is standing beside her, holding the box of cartridges.

'Celia shot out the back tyres of the van with the old man's twelve bore,' says Carol. 'She's not a bad shot.'

'Where's…'

'When the hired muscle saw the gun, that was it. He didn't want any of that.'

With Carol's help, she edges herself towards the back of the van and climbs out.

Across the yard Steve Jarman is backing his pickup round in a semi-circle. As he revs the engine, it throws up a spray of mud and water. The thug sits beside him with a sullen expression on his face. The truck roars towards the gate and disappears.

Celia breaks open the gun, removes the cartridges and sighs.

'That's it then,' she says. Tears welling up. She drops the gun on the ground, dips her head and walks back into the house.

Lacey looks at Marcia. 'You all right?'

She nods. 'Thank you,' she says. Her other sister. Another little sister. She gives her a smile.

Lacey smiles back and then follows Celia into the house.

Carol unfastens the leather belt on her jeans, re-buckles it and loops it around Marcia's neck to create a makeshift sling.

'What the fuck were you thinking, Marcie?' she says.

'I couldn't let them harm you.'

'He could've killed you. If I'd got to the door, I could've outrun them.'

'That's what I was hoping,' says Marcia. 'But you don't look like much of a runner to me.'

Carol grins. 'That's rude.'

As Carol adjusts the sling, the pain in her shoulder rips through her. She gasps. Her skin prickles with sweat.

'I'm sorry,' says Carol. 'Is that too tight?'

She winces. A broken, unkempt mess. Harry wouldn't recognise her.

The stabbing sharpness recedes and becomes a deep ache. 'No, it's okay,' she says.

'Oh, Marcie. I'm sorry for all of it.'

She looks at her sister. Carol's close to tears.

'What do you mean?'

'You know what I mean,' says Carol. 'We made a deal. She was safe with you. As soon as I'm back in her life, everything goes to shit. If anything happens to her now, I'll never forgive myself.'

'It's not your fault.'

'Isn't it? Don't you wish I'd stayed inside? Everything could go back to how it was? If she hadn't found out about me, she'd be safe.'

Marcia meets her gaze. 'You can't stop the clock.'

If only you could. But it's a foolish dream. To freeze time. To hold on to her precious little girl and live in that happy bubble forever. In her heart, hasn't she always wished for that?

Focus.

'We have to phone DS Boden,' she says.

'Yeah.'

Carol puts an arm round her waist and helps her into the house.

Brian sits hunched in his chair. He glares at them as they walk into the kitchen.

There's a heavy silence.

Celia is sitting on the old sofa with Lacey curled up beside her and the dog at their feet. Celia strokes her daughter's hair. She's ignoring their father.

He's staring into space. He's checked out, which is no surprise.

Carol eases her down into a chair. Her shoulder is throbbing. But she needs to find her phone and make the call.

Her sister walks over to Brian and bends over him.

Brian is rigid, jaw clenched. He closes his eyes.

'Your thugs are gone,' says Carol, 'and the cops are on their way. What you gonna do now, old man?'

Marcia watches him with a queasy foreboding. He knows he'll die in jail, but he doesn't care. That's what makes him so dangerous.

'Whore's child,' he mutters. 'You'll never find her.'

61

Thursday, 2.25pm

Boden and Chakravorty met up with the van load of uniformed officers, assigned to provide backup, on the outskirts of Saffron Walden. There was a certain amount of teasing. The Essex crew knew it was the second raid on Elm Tree Farm in less than a week, the first being a damp squib.

By the time Boden had got back to the office, Steven Jarman's Mitsubishi pickup had been tracked to the garage on the A11 where Phoebe Lennox made her last call. And DCI Hepburn was standing behind Mackie and Prisha, staring over their shoulders at the computer screen displaying Brian Cook's rap sheet.

He raised his eyebrows. 'All right, Jo,' he said. 'Don't look smug. Just get down there. I'll liaise with Essex Major Crimes.'

The backup van is first to turn into the lane leading to Elm Tree Farm. Boden and Chakravorty follow in their car. Progress is slow. Overnight rain has turned the narrow track into a quagmire. Boden leans out of the window and taps her fingertips on the car door.

They're only a few hundred meters down the mile long lane when Jarman's pickup comes heading towards them from the direction of the farm. The police van takes up the entire width of the track. Either side hedgerows and a barbed wire fence.

The pickup brakes as soon as it sees them and reverses. But Jarman is gunning it. The back wheels spin and skid in the mud, and within moments it's stuck fast.

The sergeant and officers from the backup team leap out of the van and charge towards it.

Boden gets out of her car and picks her way through the mud after them.

She sees Steven Jarman jump out of the driver's seat of the pickup and run back down the track towards the farm. Two of the Essex officers sprint after him. They bring him down and cuff him.

She notices the large, beefy individual sitting in the passenger seat of the pickup with his tattooed forearms folded and a glum expression on his face. He looks to Boden like some kind of enforcer.

Her phone buzzes in her pocket. Mrs Lennox.

'Where the hell are you?'

'We're nearly there, Mrs Lennox,' says Boden. 'Are you okay?'

It takes the convoy another ten minutes to move the pickup and get to the farm.

Marcia Lennox is outside frantically pacing. She looks dishevelled; her left arm is in a sling. There's a woman with her, shorter and tubbier, but the family resemblance is clear.

As the car pulls up, Mrs Lennox rushes forward. Boden hardly has time to open her door.

'This is my sister, Carol Cook,' she says. 'She's also Phoebe's real mother.'

'Okay,' says Boden, somewhat taken aback. She gets out of the car.

'But she doesn't know that,' says Carol.

'No, she doesn't,' says Mrs Lennox. 'And somehow our uncle has used Steven.'

'Yeah, he's targeted Phoebe to punish me,' says Carol.

Now it makes sense. The two women are staring at her expectantly.

'You have any idea where she is?' says Boden.

Mrs Lennox shakes her head. 'He won't tell us. He knows you're coming, and he just doesn't care. What the hell has he done to her, Sergeant?' There's a swelling desperation in her voice. 'Not death, but something worse? That's what he said.'

Boden takes a deep breath. She can see the sheer panic on both women's faces. This is no time for niceties.

She turns and calls out, 'Prisha! Get them to bring Jarman into the house.'

62

Thursday, 2.50pm

Marcia leads the sergeant through to the kitchen. She hopes the large, uniformed officers that follow them will intimidate Brian. But he continues to stare into the middle distance. Face blank. No emotion.

DS Boden confronts him. 'Mr Cook,' she says, showing him her warrant card. 'I believe you may be involved in the disappearance of Phoebe Lennox. I'm going to caution you. You do not have to say anything. But, it may harm your defence if you do not mention when questioned something which you later rely on in court. Anything you do say may be given in evidence. Where is she, Mr Cook?'

His eyes come into focus on the police officer's face, and then he whispers, 'No comment.'

A sudden crash, as a chair is flung back and hits the floor on the other side of the room. It's the old man struggling to his feet. He's angry and shaking.

'For crying out loud, Brian,' he shouts. 'Stop this now! She's a kid. Tell them where she is.'

Brian focuses on his brother for a moment. 'Fuck off, you stupid tosser,' he spits.

Celia grasps Derek's arm to steady him.

Marcia watches Brian; this is his swan song, and the evil old bastard is enjoying it. He thinks he's won.

She exchanges glances with her sister. The fear in Carol's eyes mirrors her own. But the fear is for Phoebe.

The sergeant's young sidekick, the Asian DC, comes in and behind her two officers with Steve between them. He's handcuffed and covered in mud. He glances at Celia.

She shakes her head and presses her hand to her mouth to suppress the tears. 'Oh my God,' she says. 'Dear Lord, deliver us!'

'Right,' says the sergeant, turning to face Steve. 'You've already been cautioned, and you're under arrest for conspiracy to kidnap Phoebe Lennox. But what you decide to say and do now, Steven, will determine how long you go to jail. Accessory to murder carries a life sentence. Think about that.'

He shoots a look at Brian, then dips his head. 'I don't know what you're talking about.'

The sergeant points at Brian. 'Get him out of here,' she says.

It takes several moments for Brian to be helped up from his chair and escorted out of the room.

As the police officers are doing this, Celia steps forward to confront her son.

'Steven,' she says. 'For pity's sake, tell them what they want to know. Who are you protecting?'

'Myself!' he replies savagely. 'You don't get it, Mum, do you? You never have? You bring me here. You marry that

304

fool. What am I supposed to do? I get beaten up in school 'cause I'm black. What's here for me? Nothing. A job shovelling shit on a stinking farm? You gave me no choice.'

'There's always a choice,' says Celia. 'You have the choice now to save that poor girl's life.'

'Look, she's not gonna die,' he says.

'How can you be sure of that?' says DS Boden.

'You got nothing on me,' he says. 'I dropped her off on the A11. You can't prove nothing.'

Lacey has been sitting in the corner. She gets up.

'He made a deal with someone called Luca,' she says. 'I heard him talking on the phone.'

'Shut the fuck up, Lacey!'

'He told me Luca was trying to stiff him on a drug deal. But I don't think it was that. He said: I delivered the goods. That's what we agreed.'

Steve is glaring at his sister.

'You delivered the goods to Luca?' says DS Boden. 'Luca who?'

Steve shrugs. 'She's a lying little bitch. You can't believe a word she says. Always bunking off school.'

'I believe her,' says Marcia. 'Do you hate my daughter so much that you would give her to this Luca? What did he pay you? I'll double it. For his name.'

Steve laughs. 'Money, money, money! 'Cause you're rich, you think you and your precious daughter are special. There she is on the net, prancing around, flaunting herself and all her posh clothes. Boasting about her fine life and all the cool places she goes. Fuck the both of you!'

Marcia turns to the sergeant. But she's getting out her phone and walking away. Marcia follows her.

'What are you doing?' she says. 'You've got to get him to tell us more!'

DS Boden raises her index finger. 'He might've told us enough. Give me a moment.'

'Who are you calling?'

'A friend of mine at the National Crime Agency.'

Marcia follows DS Boden out into the yard.

The call is answered.

'Mike, hi,' says the sergeant. 'It's Jo Boden. I've got an emergency here. Girl's been kidnapped; eighteen, attractive, white. Possibly by an East Anglian based OCG. We could be talking people traffickers. I've arrested an enforcer who speaks no English. I'm guessing illegal. Could be Albanian or Romanian? I've got a first name: Luca. He could be the boss. Yeah, I'll hold.'

Marcia is watching her. Tough, efficient, professional, all the things she never would have expected.

'What's an OCG?' she says.

'Organised crime group,' says the sergeant. 'I used to work with Mike. He's with the NCA's Anti-kidnap and Extortion Unit. Your uncle was a career criminal. He's likely to still have connections. He could've used Steven as a go-between.'

'To do what?'

The sergeant hesitates and frowns. Whatever she's thinking, she's reluctant to share it.

'Just tell me,' says Marcia. 'Please. I'd rather know. Not knowing is torture.'

'Okay,' the sergeant sighs. 'Something worse, you said. What's worse than dying? How about slavery?'

'Oh my god!'

'Modern slavery is big business. But we have an extensive database of suspects and subjects of ongoing inquiries. We might get a match.'

Bile rises in Marcia's throat; her shoulder throbs. Slavery? Phoebe is in the hands of gangsters who would sell her?

She throws up. She can't stop herself. She spatters her own feet with vomit.

DS Boden reaches out and takes her good arm to support her.

'You okay?'

'I'm sorry,' she mutters.

The sergeant hands her a tissue. 'In a way it's good news, Mrs Lennox. If this sort of gang has got her, it's in their financial interests to keep her alive.'

That's good news!

DS Boden turns back to her phone. 'Mike, yeah. Okay. Luca Florescu. Yeah, I see. Okay. Email me the file. Thanks.'

She hangs up, looks at Marcia. 'Sure you're okay?'

Marcia nods. 'I'll be fine.'

The sergeant strides back into the house. Marcia hurries after her.

DS Boden walks up to Steve. 'Luca Florescu, that's who we're talking about, isn't it?'

He shrugs and folds his arms. 'Never heard of him.' But it's clear he's nervous.

'Here's my theory,' says the sergeant. 'You're a small-time drug dealer, but you'd like to move up. You got drawn into this thing by your uncle. But then you saw an opportunity to impress Florescu. Human trafficking is a highly organised business. The big time. Serious money. You've sourced one girl for him, and he's pleased with you. You fancy your chances.'

'Don't know what you're talking about.'

'Did you use a burner when you talked to him?' She's scanning his face. Noting every reaction. 'Gets expensive, doesn't it? Trashing a phone after every call. Maybe you only recycle your phones every week or two?'

His eyes flicker; she's touched a nerve.

'Ah,' says the sergeant with a smile. 'I'm guessing you didn't use a burner. And we'll find the calls to him on your current phone. That's sloppy. You reckon you're hard, Steven. But you're not. I'm going to go and knock on Florescu's door. What do you think'll happen when I tell him you led us to him?'

'But I didn't.'

Marcia watches anxiously. The sergeant is getting under his skin.

'You're right to be scared,' she says. 'He'll want you dead. The thug we arrested with you, I expect he's got a few more of them, hasn't he?'

'You can't threaten me like this.'

'I'm not threatening you. I'm just explaining to you what's likely to happen. And I'm giving you an opportunity to tell me the truth. What does Luca Florescu plan to do with Phoebe Lennox? Who's he planning to sell her to?'

'I don't know.'

Derek steps forward. 'Tell the truth, Steven. You're not a gangster. You want to end up like Brian, in and out of jail, a bitter old man, full of hate?'

Steve dips his head. He's struggling. 'I am telling the truth. I don't know.'

'Tell us what you do know,' says the sergeant.

He sighs, 'He runs an auction on the dark web. Sells girls to the highest bidder. Mega rich clients, they'll pay up to a million dollars for the right sort of girl. Sends them all over the world.'

'Sends them how?' says the sergeant.

'It's a big operation. He hires private jets to deliver them.'

'Where from?'

'I dunno. Stansted, I guess.'

He gives his mother a sullen glance. She's staring at him with tears in her eyes. Her lip trembles.

'What kind of man have you become?' Celia says. 'I don't know you.'

63

Thursday, 4.25pm

Phoebe gazes out of the window at the setting sun. A warm peachy glow behind fluffy grey clouds which are so soft and billowing she wants to stroke them. She's giddy; it's not unpleasant. Her limbs are loose, hard to control, and her vision swims in and out of focus. But sinking into the amazing colours steadies her. She's never seen such a beautiful sunset. Unbelievable. Also sad because it's just out of reach.

She's riding in the back of a luxury people carrier. And he, the man in the brown cardigan, is sitting beside her, checking his phone. The witch is in front. She's wearing this long black thing, like a cloak. Phoebe knows the name of it; it has a special name. But her brain can't for the moment retrieve it. All her thought processes are incredibly slow. She can't concentrate. Thoughts come, but she can't grasp them. They float away.

She was sitting on the bed naked when witchy gave her another injection. They dressed her in leggings and a T-shirt. But then over it this cloak, this thing. What's it called? What happened again? They dressed her? Now she can't remember. It's gone.

'Well, Phoebe,' he says. His voice is echoey and far away. 'I don't want you to be scared. There's no need. Your new master is a man of taste and discernment. He's paid a lot of money for you. Obey him, satisfy his needs and you'll be well treated.'

'I want…' she says. The words are hard to form. 'To go…' Go where? Now she can't remember. The word has slithered away.

He pats her hand. 'During the flight, the drugs will wear off,' he says. 'You'll begin to feel more yourself.'

Home? Is that the word?

The people carrier stops. The back door slides open and he gets out. It closes behind him.

Witchy turns round in her seat to face Phoebe. She says something. Then she reaches over and picks up one corner of this thing and draws it across Phoebe's face. The silk is soft on her nose and cheeks. She tucks the end in.

How did she get here? Witchy dressed her in this? Is that what happened?

The door slides open again. He reaches in and takes Phoebe's arm.

'Come along, my dear.'

She steps out. The light is fading fast. The colour is gone. She stares at the sky.

They're outside. An open space. A chilly breeze. It ripples over the tiny part of her face that's exposed.

There's a sudden roar of engines. It makes her jump. An

aircraft taking off? Up into the sky like a bird. She wishes she could fly. Fly away.

In front of her is a steep set of metal stairs. It is an aircraft. No birds. She's on the tarmac at the airport. And she's about to board an aircraft.

Her body is ahead of her brain. It stops. It knows something she doesn't. It knows she must run.

But her legs are wobbly. They won't do it. She can't make them.

Witchy has her by the hand, pulling her towards the stairs.

Brown cardigan stands beside the stairs, and he's talking to another man. In some kind of uniform. Epaulettes? An official wearing epaulettes?

Brown cardigan is speaking. 'She has such a terror of flying,' he says.

Their voices are peculiar, bubbly, as if they're underwater.

Epaulettes says, 'Some people find hypnotherapy works. You could try that.'

'That's an excellent suggestion,' says brown cardigan. He's nodding his head.

Phoebe tries to turn. She must speak to epaulettes. An official. She must tell him.

Tell him what? Now she can't remember.

Epaulettes gives brown cardigan something. Documents? He waves his hand and says, 'Have a good flight.' Is he talking to her?

He's walking away.

Phoebe takes a breath. She wants to call him back. But why? She can't recall. The impulse is gone.

Witchy tugs at her arm. Now cardigan is behind her. He pushes her up the metal staircase.

In the cabin of the aircraft there are four big plush

armchairs with tables in between. Witchy shepherds Phoebe to a chair and sits down next to her. Cardigan reaches over, pulls the seatbelt across her lap and straps her in.

He pats her knee. 'There,' he says, 'try to relax. Get some sleep. Goodbye, Phoebe.'

He disappears.

Next to her, there's a window. She turns and looks out. Dark now, but lots of lights. They sparkle. Like at Christmas. Some are red and blinking.

A rumble as the engines start. They're moving now, rolling backwards.

She has a flash of memory: her first time in an airplane. She was quite young, sitting next to her mother, and clutching her hand. Mum! She wants her mum.

Her eyes fill with tears. She blinks them away.

Witchy glances at her.

Now they're moving forward, taxiing towards the runway.

Where are they again? On a plane?

It's speeding up.

Suddenly the plane lurches and stops dead.

She pitches forward in her seat.

Witchy unclasps her seatbelt and gets up. She goes towards the cockpit. She bangs on the cockpit door.

Phoebe looks out of the window. Now the lights are blue. Vehicles with blue flashing lights circling the plane.

The door at the back of the plane opens. She can feel the cold air rushing in.

Then there are men. Men in uniforms with guns. They fill the cabin.

Then there's a woman. Does she know her? It's the cop! The cop who came to the farm.

The cop pulls the hijab off her face. She unfastens her seat belt.

She's smiling. A smiling cop.

'Remember me, Phoebe,' she says. 'DS Boden. You're safe now. Everything's going to be all right.'

64

Thursday, 5.35pm

Marcia walks beside DS Boden, Carol follows behind. The sergeant leads them through the A&E department, and into the treatment area. She stops outside a curtained cubicle.

A nurse comes out and smiles at them. Another concerned, detached professional looking at her as if she's a madwoman.

'Is she all right?' says Marcia.

She is a madwoman. Unkempt, an out-of-control mess. Her pulse is thrumming. Too much adrenaline. Too much cortisol. An hour ago she was praying, that was the measure of her desperation. Since she heard the police had rescued Phoebe, her thoughts have been in a spin. Elation and then dread. What now? How to put this right? Can she put this right?

Her anxiety is in overdrive. And she's run out of Xanax.

Once Phoebe knows the truth, she'll hate her. And rightly so.

'She's coming out of it quite well,' says the nurse. 'We think it's just heavy sedation, could be ketamine, but we're running some blood tests. We'll keep her in overnight under observation, just to be sure.'

Marcia turns to the sergeant. She wants to hug her. But that would be awkward. 'I don't know what to say,' she says. 'I mean, thank you, obviously. But that hardly seems—'

DS Boden cuts her short. 'Go in and see your daughter. We'll need to take a statement from her. But that can wait until tomorrow. How's your arm?'

Her arm is strapped to her chest. 'I've broken my collarbone,' she says. 'Nothing too drastic.'

Battered and bruised. Rung out until she's emotionally numb. Her shoulder is the least of it. A dull ache, nothing compared to the torment and the fear of what might happen next.

'We'll need a statement from both of you too,' says the sergeant. 'About what happened at the farm.'

Marcia nods. The farm. She always knew going back there would be a disaster. And she was right.

Carol is staring at her feet.

The sergeant smiles and walks away.

Marcia looks at her sister. Carol is jittery. She hangs back.

'Listen,' she says. 'You should go in on your own.'

Marcia hesitates. 'But—'

'It's you she needs,' says Carol. 'I'm the crazy aunt who waved a knife at her.'

Marcia touches her sister's arm, then slips behind the curtain.

Phoebe is lying on the hospital trolley. Her eyes are closed and she's pale. She looks young and fragile; Marcia swallows hard. The nightmare of what's happened to her child is bad enough. But the horror of what could've happened, that she tries to expel from her mind.

As she steps into the cubicle, Phoebe opens her eyes. The same cornflower blue as Carol and the old man; family traits passed down the generations. The relief on her child's face as she sees her makes Marcia's heart soar. Losing her was a torment. What she faces now is worse. She must tell her the truth. She knows that. But not yet. Not yet!

Phoebe has tears in her eyes; she reaches out for her hand and grasps it. 'Oh, Mummy! I'm sorry. I'm completely stupid.' She hasn't called her mummy for years.

Marcia leans over and kisses her forehead. Hugs her as fiercely as her shoulder allows.

Phoebe clings to her. 'I'm a total idiot,' she whispers through her tears.

Marcia doesn't want to let go, ever, but she forces herself.

'No, my darling,' she says. 'I'm the stupid one. Stupid for not telling the truth, for not explaining about my father.'

'I really thought Steve liked me.'

She smiles. 'I can see the attraction. But he used you, Phi. It was a set up. He's a drug dealer with a police record.'

Phoebe shudders. 'It was horrible. Those people! I thought I'd never see you again.'

The tears trickle down her daughter's face. Marcia wipes them away with her fingertips.

'I just want to go home. Please take me home.' Phoebe's sobbing now. She holds fast to Marcia's hand.

Marcia perches on the side of the trolley and cradles her daughter with her free arm.

Phoebe needs her. That's the only thing that matters now.

'Sssh! You are going home. As soon as the doctor says it's okay. You're in shock.'

'They said I need to stay overnight. I don't want to be on

my own.' Her voice is tremulous like a child afraid of the dark.

'I know, darling. But I'll be right here with you.'

Marcia rocks her. Kisses her forehead.

'Will you?' says Phoebe. 'All night?'

'All night, I promise.'

'I keep thinking they'll come back.'

'They won't come back. The police have got them.'

She doesn't know this for sure. The police have given her no details. But she's seen how DS Boden operates.

'What's happened to your arm?' says Phoebe.

'I've broken my collarbone.'

Phoebe winces. 'How?'

'One of the gang that got hold of you attacked me. They came to my father's farm.'

She can see the confusion and panic in her daughter's eyes. This is all too much. Too overwhelming.

'I don't understand,' says Phoebe.

'And that's my fault. I should've told you about my family. And about my sister, Carol.'

Phoebe grimaces. 'I met her. She's really nasty. She threatened me with a knife. I can see why you wanted nothing to do with her.'

Marcia takes a breath. There's so much to explain. But it's too soon.

'Listen, my darling,' she says. 'Carol wanted to frighten you, to make you go away. She was trying to protect you. She would never harm you.'

'You sure about that?'

'Absolutely. But let's not talk about that now.' Too much. Too soon.

Will Phoebe ever trust her again once she knows the truth? Phoebe is frowning and scanning Marcia's face. She looks young and frightened, still a child in many ways. Still her child. She must protect her.

'Don't worry,' she says. 'They'll be lots of time to talk, and we will. You just need to rest and recover. And I'll be right here.'

'Promise?'

'I promise.' She strokes her forehead. 'Lie back and relax. Everything's going to be okay.'

More lies.

65

Thursday, 6.55pm

DS Boden and DC Chakravorty enter the office to be greeted with whoops and fist pumps from DC Mackie.

'Way to go, girls!' he shouts. He and the several analysts sitting alongside him clap.

Boden smiles, but she says, 'Girls? Are you being sexist, Mackie?'

'Would I dare, Sarge?' he says. 'Boss said to tell you he wants a word. And we're all going down the Feathers for a drink.'

She smiles and glances at Prisha. They're both dog-tired. As the adrenaline rush has faded, all she can think of is something easy in the microwave, a large glass of wine and an early night. Her shoes are still caked in dried mud from the track leading to Elm Tree Farm.

She walks down the corridor to the DCI's office. He's on the phone but waves her in and indicates that she should sit.

'Yeah,' he says. 'Excellent result all round. Cheers, mate.'

He hangs up the phone. 'That was Mike Bullivant at the NCA. He's happy. Once they get Phoebe Lennox's testimony, it should be enough to send Florescu down and dismantle his network. Essex have got him and his crew in custody. He's been on the NCA's radar for a while, but they could never get the evidence to make a case. The cyber guys have found the auction site. The list of buyers who use it is eye-opening. Whitehall will be interested in that.'

Boden lets the words wash over her. He seems pleased with her, and that's a relief. Tracking back through the shell companies that Florescu used, and linking one to a specific jet charter firm, had taken over an hour. It was touch and go whether they'd get there before she was gone.

Once they got to the airport, it had been a mad dash across the tarmac to reach the private Gulfstream jet before it could take off. A call from Mike to air traffic control had stopped it in the nick of time.

'We were lucky, boss,' she says. 'I didn't think we were going to make it.'

'Not just luck, Jo. Data analysis.' He smiles. She realises he's teasing her. She smiles back.

'How's the girl?' he says.

'In hospital, but okay.'

'And I understand Essex have got a cold case murder that they're following up on.'

'Yes.'

'Well, a bit of good news for you. The complaint against you to the IOPC has been withdrawn. I gather Harry Lennox persuaded his son to drop it.'

Boden just nods. She knows she'll feel relieved later. But right now?

She walks back down the corridor to the office. Everyone's gone. She picks up her bag and heads out.

Her phones buzzes. Mike Bullivant.

'Hey, Mike,' she says.

'Boden, I despair of you,' says her old DI. 'Why did you leave the Met? What the hell are you doing in Cambridge?'

'I pissed a few people off in London. Had to get a transfer.'

'From what I hear, it wasn't your fault. Come and work for me. I need a proper detective. I'm surrounded by geeks who are glued to their computer screens all day.'

'Data analysis, Mike. It's an essential tool.'

'Doesn't replace what you've got, Jo. I'm serious.'

'I'll think about it.'

66

Saturday, 10.15am

Marcia pretends not to listen. She arranges segments of nectarine on a plate. It's not as neat as she'd like, but she is working one-handed. Her left arm remains strapped to her body, supporting her broken collarbone.

Phoebe is still in pyjamas; an old snuggly pair she hasn't worn for years. The sliding doors from the kitchen to the garden are open, and pale rays of autumn sunshine are flooding in. Phoebe wanders in and out as she talks to Harry on the phone.

'Yeah, and the detectives are really pleased. Jo said it's a major bust for them. I'll have to give evidence. There'll be a big court case.'

She sounds breezy, making light of her ordeal. Telling the story as if it's a bizarre adventure.

But Marcia knows it's a front. In the night, Phoebe had cried out and woken up sobbing. Did her daughter learn it from her, this ability to dismiss her own suffering? To always appear to be in control and cope? The thought is chastening.

Phoebe had spent Friday morning sitting up in her hospital bed and giving a statement to the police. Calm and matter-of-fact. But hearing the details had made Marcia blind with fury. If she'd met Luca Florescu in person, she would've torn his heart out.

They'd driven back to London on Friday afternoon. Phoebe listened to music through headphones and kept dozing off. Just having her daughter there in the car beside her was enough for Marcia. After the nightmare Phoebe had been through, she needed time to recover. The last thing she needed was more trauma. But Marcia also knew the longer she held off telling her about Carol, the worse it would be.

Phoebe hangs up the phone and dumps it on the counter. She's frowning.

'How was that?' says Marcia.

'Says he'll try to pop over tomorrow.'

Marcia notes the disappointment in her voice. What a selfish bastard he is! She could wring his neck. Why didn't he rush to Cambridge to their daughter's hospital bedside? But she knows the answer. Harry's moved on.

She bites her tongue.

Phoebe meets her gaze. 'Apparently Marie-Claire isn't feeling well. Morning sickness.'

'Poor Marie-Claire,' says Marcia drily.

A flicker of shared understanding passes between them; years of the daily routine of living in this house, in this family.

Phoebe cracks a smile. 'I shouldn't be surprised, should I?'

'Probably not.'

'He's such a knob. How did you stay married to him for this long?'

'Perseverance.'

What she doesn't mention is the money and the fact Harry was never violent. The basics for Marcia. And because of those things, Phoebe has had a different upbringing.

'Don't write him off, Phi. He loves you. In his way.'

'He loves himself more.'

'Harry's been spoilt for a lot of his life. It's not his fault.'

Phoebe glances at her, eyes brimming with pain and confusion.

'Am I spoilt?' she says. 'Is that why this happened? Because I'm a brat and it's what I deserve?'

'Oh, my god, no,' says Marcia, reaching out for her daughter's hand. 'Don't ever think that? None of this is your fault.'

'But I was stupid. And I was angry with you for never telling me about granddad.'

'You were right to be.'

The terrible death of her mother. Her father's denial. Another topic to add to the daunting list yet to be discussed.

Marcia sighs. Adjusts the sling supporting her busted collarbone. It's become a dull ache. She needs more painkillers. For a second, the terror of being thrown in the back of the van by that thug flits into her mind. She pushes it away.

'Why don't you make us some coffee, darling? I'm finding it a bit difficult one-handed.'

'Yeah, sorry,' says Phoebe. 'You're struggling. I should be making breakfast.'

Phoebe's flustered. It's hard to watch. This is not the girl she was. This is what those bastards have done to her. But not just them. Marcia must face her own culpability. The web of lies she created.

'Let's do it together,' she says gently.

The distraction works, and Phoebe busies herself with the coffee maker.

They work side by side in silence. The coffee is made.

They're sitting at the counter eating Marcia's homemade granola with fruit and yogurt when the doorbell rings.

Phoebe shoots her mother a nervous glance. 'She's early.'

'I just want you to forget what happened before. Imagine you're meeting her for the first time. Because really you are.'

'Yeah, I get it,' says Phoebe. 'I know she's your sister, and this is important to you.'

Marcia tries to ignore that, goes to the front door and opens it.

She can see Carol has made an effort to smarten herself up. Not successfully. She has a cheap polyester holdall hanging from one shoulder. It looks half empty. All her sister's possessions don't even fill a bag. That brings a lump to her throat.

Carol gives her an anxious smile. 'This is pretty fancy,' she says.

'You took a taxi from the station, like I said?'

Carol nods.

Marcia reaches out her one good arm and pulls her sister into a hug. 'Hey, come here!'

The embrace is stiff and fumbled. Two strangers trying to pretend they're close. Marcia lets her go.

'How's she doing?' says Carol.

'Okay. I think.'

'Y'know, Marcie, we don't have to do this. I can just be the crazy aunt who went to jail.'

Marcia has spent two sleepless nights hoping her sister would say that, and knowing it was wrong.

It's tempting. Sweep it all back under the carpet. Move on.

'No,' she says. 'She deserves the truth. And so do you.'

'The truth about what?' Phoebe is standing in the kitchen doorway watching them.

67

Saturday, 10.30am

Carol follows her sister into the kitchen. She's never been in a house like this before. It's the sort of place you only see on television or in glossy magazines. And it's enormous. It smells clean and fresh, as if its inhabitants never sweat or come indoors with shitty shoes.

She looks down at her trainers.

'Shall I take my shoes off?' she says.

Marcie turns and smiles. 'No, it's fine. Relax. I want you to feel at home.'

How is that ever going to happen in a mansion like this? Carol feels awkward and out of place. She just wants to escape.

Phoebe is smiling at her. She's pretending their previous encounter never happened.

'Have you had breakfast?' she says. 'Can I get you some granola?' All very polite. Which makes it worse.

Carol had treated herself to an Egg McMuffin at the

station, using some of the cash Marcie had forced her to take to cover her journey. She'd returned to the picking gang on Thursday evening, worked on Friday, then asked Vasile for a few days off.

'I'm okay,' she says. 'Got something at the station.'

'Coffee, then?' says Phoebe. 'How do you take it?'

'Milk and two sugars.'

'I can do you a cappuccino?'

'Yeah, great.'

Phoebe gets on with the coffee. Carol and her sister exchange covert looks.

'Put your bag down,' says Marcie gently. 'You can take it upstairs later.'

Carol tucks the bag under the breakfast bar. The top is black marble. She can see her reflection.

Marcie pulls out a stool for her and smiles. 'Sit down. How was your journey?'

'Yeah, not bad.'

'You got the train from Diss?'

'Yeah. I like watching the countryside go by. Colours of the trees this time of year.'

'We'll have to show you Richmond Park.'

Phoebe places a mug in front of her. It has froth and sprinkles on the top, like you'd get in a coffee shop. The mug is white bone china. Carol stares at it. They're both staring at her. She picks it up. But her hand shakes. Her knuckles are red and chapped. She wishes she'd cleaned her nails.

'I think I'm nervous,' she says.

'I think we're all nervous,' says Marcie.

Phoebe is watching her. The look appears to be neutral, but it's hard to tell.

Carol realises she's avoiding her gaze. Nothing has been said yet, but already she feels judged and rejected.

'Well,' says Marcie. 'There is no easy way to talk about this. I'm just going to do it.' She turns to Phoebe and takes her hand. 'But I want you to understand, my darling, that it's always been about keeping you safe.'

Phoebe nods; a tension in her face, a rigidity in her shoulders. A sudden intuition strikes Carol. She knows. Or she's guessed.

Marcie is standing between them. She rests the hand of her uninjured arm on the beautiful marble. Her nails are manicured. Perfect and clean.

'I wasn't always your mother,' says Marcie. 'I became your mother when you were three weeks old. Carol asked me to take care of you. Because she couldn't.'

Phoebe shoots a glance at Carol, then turns away. Shock. Disbelief? Disgust? She says nothing.

Carol stares at her coffee.

Finally, Phoebe says, 'What are you saying? She's my biological mother? Not you, Ma?'

'Yes,' says Marcie.

'I'm sorry,' says Carol.

Phoebe glares at her, chin quivering. 'Sorry for what?' she says. Is she angry or confused? Or both? It's hard to tell.

There's no going back. She's longed for this conversation, but she's also dreaded it.

'When you were born,' she says, 'I was a complete mess. I was in rehab. I was with this man called Alan. He was my cousin. I thought he was going to kill me and kill you. And he would've done.'

'That's why you killed him?' says Phoebe.

Carol glances at her sister. 'It was the only thing to do. But when Marcie arrived, I begged her to take you. Because I knew she would give you the life that I couldn't. I was in a state. I would've been a crap mother. A liability. I didn't want you growing up with that.'

Carol watches Phoebe's face as she processes all this. She's stunned. Of course she is.

Marcie has her head dipped, staring downwards. Carol can't imagine what her sister is feeling. Have they done the right thing? Truth can come at a terrible price. She wonders if it's worth it.

Phoebe frowns and says, 'The man you were with, that you killed, is he my father?'

Carol shakes her head. 'No, absolutely not. He knew you weren't his baby. And he was mad as hell about it. Your father was called David.'

'Where is he now?'

'He's dead,' says Marcie. 'We didn't know back then, but it was Brian and Alan who murdered him. Brian is Alan's father.'

'They killed him because of me?'

'When I became pregnant,' says Carol, 'the timing was all wrong. Alan knew it couldn't be his. I went to school with David. We'd known each other since we were kids. We were going to run away together. But he disappeared. I thought he'd got cold feet and left me. That's what my father told me.'

'But he was dead?' says Phoebe. 'They'd murdered him?'

Carol dips her head and nods.

Phoebe folds her arms and turns away.

Carol looks at her sister. She's pale, her face pinched. It looks as if her world has ended. Carol's stomach is a tight knot of guilt and regret.

No one speaks for a full minute.

Then Marcie says, 'It was an impossible situation, Phi.'

Phoebe turns to face them.

'How did you kill him?' she says. 'With a knife?'

'Yes,' says Carol.

'When I was chained up in that garage, I could see a screwdriver on the bench. It was out of reach. But, if I could've got hold of it, I would've tried to stab them. If someone is threatening you, you defend yourself. Instinct. You have to.'

'It's my fault you ended up there,' says Carol. 'Brian wanted revenge for his son's killing. He wanted to harm you, because of me.'

'And Steve helped him do that?' Phoebe has tears in her eyes.

'Brian has always been a criminal,' says Marcie. 'They both are. My father was too scared to challenge him.'

Phoebe heaves a sigh. She smiles at Marcie. 'I can see why you didn't want me to meet him.'

'If I thought about him at all, I assumed he was dead. That the drink would've killed him. I never imagined he'd get sober.'

Phoebe looks at Carol directly. 'This is weird,' she says. 'But when I first heard about you, I had an odd feeling. Maybe that's why I agreed to try to find you.'

'What sort of feeling?' says Marcie.

'Something about my upbringing never made sense. You always wanted to make everything perfect for me, Ma. You were always worried about getting it wrong. Like I was a project, or a test? You were scared you'd fail. And be judged. Not just by people like the Muirheads. It was as if someone else was always watching. I realised most parents aren't like you. They don't try so hard. They muddle along.'

'I wasn't aware I was trying. I just love you.'

Phoebe takes her hand. 'And I love you too. But it's like

you always thought one day I'd be gone. I didn't understand why you were endlessly anxious about me.'

'I've only ever wanted you to have your own life.'

'I know. But you're part of my life. And always will be.' She turns to Carol. 'But you're the missing piece in the puzzle. And now it makes sense. I have two of you. Two mothers.' She grins. 'I'm far more interesting than I ever imagined.'

Carol watches her. Her tiny baby. All grown up. The smile, the confidence. She's such a smart kid. Mum would be proud.

68

Saturday, 7.30 pm

Marcia Lennox sits across the room from her sister. A bottle of Sancerre is in the wine cooler on the coffee table between them. They'd ordered an Indian takeaway and eaten it, all three of them, in the kitchen. Carol seemed comfortable with that. Phoebe had found the online menu for a local place, which she and her friends used. The vegetable curry was better than Marcia expected.

Carol and Phoebe had chatted throughout the meal. It wasn't easy to watch.

Phoebe had asked questions. About jail. About being released on licence. About getting clean.

As Marcia listened to how tough her sister's life had been, a queasy guilt flowed through her. She'd abandoned Carol. Left her to her fate. Walked away. It was wrong!

'I've always wondered about my real father,' Phoebe said. 'Tell me about David.'

'His family were farmers too,' said Carol. 'They lived a

few miles away. But David wanted to be a photographer. He was forever taking pictures. No one taught him, he just had the eye for it.'

'He was visual?' said Phoebe. 'Like me.'

Marcia let it play out. She owed it to Carol. She owed her this. And much more.

After dinner, Phoebe retreated to her room.

The two sisters settled on opposite sofas in the sitting room. The alcohol had helped Carol relax. She took off her shoes and tucked her feet under her, as she used to when she was a child.

Marcia scans her.

'That was a fantastic curry,' says Carol. 'But you didn't eat most of yours. I'm guessing it's not what you'd normally choose.'

'I'm a vegan.'

'Okay. Is that hard?'

'No. I became one ages ago. But not for the usual reasons.'

'Why then?'

'I worked in a burger bar for three years when I was a student. I ended up hating the smell of meat cooking. Turned me veggie then vegan.'

'I don't remember that,' says Carol.

'I probably never mentioned it.'

So many things she never mentions. For years, secrets have driven the deep current of her life. In its hidden depths, the lies, omissions and guilt mingle. Keeping it all concealed has sapped her spirit. The designer labels and the perfect home form the carapace she created to protect herself.

And Harry's right of course, she is inaccessible. She's had to be. When she picked up her baby niece and walked away from Elm Tree Farm, she entered a jail of her own. A prison built on deception.

She looks at her sister. They've lapsed into silence. There remains a tension between them. Perhaps it's inevitable after all these years. They're like strangers, but with a shared history.

Carol is gazing at the large abstract oil painting above the fireplace.

'I like that,' she says.

'Harry bought it as an investment. He's offered me the house and contents to settle the divorce. But when he realises how much that's worth now, he'll want it back.'

Carol nods. The life Marcia has ended up with must seem surreal to her.

'It's ridiculous, isn't it?' says Marcia.

'What is?'

'All of this.'

Carol shrugs.

'And I've been thinking,' says Marcia, 'of going to the police and telling them what really happened to Alan.'

'Why?'

'Because it's the right thing to do. That's what Mum would say.'

Carol scowls at her. 'No, she wouldn't.'

'She'd expect me to tell the truth. Then you'll be exonerated.'

'Well, what is the truth? Where do you start?' says Carol.

'I killed him, not you.'

Carol shakes her head. 'No, that was how it ended. You go to court, you're supposed to tell the whole truth. Not that anyone does. You held the knife, but it's far from the whole truth.'

Marcia sighs. 'Okay, it starts when I broke my promise to Mum. She told me to look after you.'

'And you did. You tried. After you graduated, you had that flat. I can't remember where?'

'Shepherd's Bush.'

'Yeah. I came there once. And you begged me to stay and live with you. But I went back. And you know why? Finding a job in London was too frightening. I preferred hanging out at the farm and getting wasted. It was easier. That was my choice, Marcie. I couldn't do what you've done, I didn't have the guts.'

Is that how it was? Marcia's unsure. Her own memories are flimsy.

Carol smiles wistfully. 'Remember what Mum used to say to us. *Do it again and do it properly!* She was always on at us. Everything had to be perfect. You managed it. I couldn't. I was useless, always in trouble. Perhaps she thought she was preparing us for a tough world. She succeeded with you, but not with me. I gave up. Bit like Dad.'

Marcia considers this. The struggle each day to get through her lists. The discipline of focusing on each task and getting it right. Feeling guilty when she didn't. Yes, her mother had trained her to be a perfectionist. The flip side was the anxiety as she lost control. Sleepless nights, and the guilt that never went away, that lurked in the darkness. Waking up every morning and popping pills. Is this what Carol means by guts?

She realises her sister is staring at her.

'Don't do it,' says Carol. 'For my sake. For Phoebe's sake. Don't. We made a deal. You take the baby and leave, I take the rap. I stand by that. It's the best decision I've ever made. The one thing I got right. And Mum would see that.'

Would she?

Marcia sighs. 'I just want some kind of peace. To be able to stop.'

'Do you remember what happened?' Carol says. 'When you turned up, I'd already got the knife from the kitchen, I was crying and desperate and I was gonna to use it. I wanted to kill him before he killed me. And I would have. But I had two broken fingers from where he'd stamped on my hand. My right hand was so swollen I couldn't grip the knife. Remember? And you took the knife and did it for me. But it's my crime, Marcie, always has been. You just helped me do it.'

'That doesn't make it right.'

'What's right? It was self-defence. You defending me, when I couldn't defend myself, which is what you promised Mum you'd do. And defending Phoebe. Do you regret any of that?'

'No.'

And that's the truth; she never has. Not regret. But is it possible to have guilt without regret?

The details of that terrible night, she's kept packed away in her head for too long. Only fragments remain, and she's not even sure if her memory is trustworthy.

The baby was crying. The place stank of booze and weed and piss. Carol was on the floor, bleeding. And she did already have a knife in her hand.

Marcia should've called the police straight away, but she didn't. She froze. Then he woke up. Swore at them. He was a big bloke, dangerous even when drunk. It petrified Carol. And Marcia realised they'd been there too many times before. Even if he got arrested, he'd be back. She couldn't let him win again. She made a snap decision.

'Do you think it was wrong?' says Carol.

Marcia sighs. She took a life; that will always weigh upon

her. She made a choice. A choice fuelled by rage. Rage at what he'd done to her and to her sister. But was it wrong? Much harder question.

'I just wanted to stop him. Permanently.'

'And you did.'

Marcia is holding her wine glass. Her hand shakes. She takes a sip to steady it.

'In jail,' says Carol, 'I learned how to survive. For ages, I was pretty crap at it. But there's a choice. Survive or go under? I only had myself to look after, you had Phoebe. We both did what we had to.'

'Don't I deserve to be punished?'

'What for? For Alan?'

'For taking a life.'

'And saving two.'

Marcia considers this. Can you trade one against the other?

'I'm begging you, Marcie, don't do it. What would be the point? I've done the time, paid the debt. Who does it help? Not me. Certainly not Phoebe.'

'Then I'm no better than Brian.'

Carol gets up and comes to sit down beside her. She grasps Marcia's hand. Her grip is firm, her skin rough.

She squeezes Marcia's hand. 'Let yourself off the hook, kiddo. We did what we did. I think it was the right choice. And I can live with that. If you think it was the right choice, you have to do the same. Live with it.'

'Aren't you resentful of the years you've wasted inside?'

'No. I learned to be more like you. More focused and determined.'

Marcia smiles. 'It has its downside.'

'I needed determination to get off the drugs. Inside, I saw loads of women who'd wrecked themselves with drugs, just trying to escape from horrible lives. While you were bringing up Phoebe, I had a chance to sort my head out. I could never live up to Mum's expectations, but in the end I realised it didn't matter. I am who I am.'

'What do you want to do now?'

'Nothing complicated. Maybe live in the country. I used to fantasise about setting myself up as a dog walker. Looking after people's pets for them. I think I'd like that.'

'Okay,' says Marcia. 'I can help you do that. And I've got a cottage in Cornwall. It's yours.'

'What d'you mean? I can live there? Pay you rent?'

'No. It'll be yours. I'll give it to you.'

Carol shakes her head. 'I can't let you do that.'

'Why not?'

'I dunno. Because…'

'Because of what? Don't be silly. I need to make amends. Let me. Please.'

A glint of excitement creeps into Carol's eyes. 'It would be a dream come true. Thank you!'

Marcia watches her. Such joy might become infectious if she allowed it. And perhaps Carol's right. She should let herself off the hook.

The past is irredeemable. And would she do anything different if she could? Murderer is an ugly word. It'll be there, nagging away until the day she dies. She is her mother's daughter. But absolution from the guilt? Like her sister, she's served her time. Maybe one day that will be possible.

FREE AND EXCLUSIVE TO READERS OF SHE'S GONE

Want to know what happens to Marcia and the other characters in *She's Gone?* Get your free, exclusive copy of *He's Gone at:*

susanwilkins.co.uk/hes-gone/

*Please be sure to read *She's Gone* first before moving on to *He's Gone*.*

Scan the QR Code to sign up for He's Gone

NEXT IN THE SERIES

HER PERFECT HUSBAND

Sophie Latham is a tough businesswoman used to getting what she wants. At thirty-nine, with her biological clock ticking, she wants a baby and marriage to her gorgeous personal trainer, Ollie Harmon.

But Ollie has a younger half-sister he's desperate to protect. Kristin Kelly is a supermodel, the trophy wife of a controlling billionaire. When he's accused of murder, Sophie finds herself drawn into a web of lies and obsession.

As her fairytale marriage spirals into a waking nightmare, she discovers she's neither as smart nor as good as she thinks.

Order your copy now from Amazon.

Scan QR code to buy Her Perfect Husband

LEAVE A REVIEW

If you feel like writing a review, I'd be most grateful. The choice of books out there is vast. Reviews do help readers discover one of my books for the first time.

Scan QR code to review She's Gone.

A MESSAGE FROM SUSAN

Thank you for choosing to read *She's Gone*. If you enjoyed spending time with Marcia and the other characters and want to find out what they do next, you can. I'm offering readers a short story *He's Gone*. Go to:

susanwilkins.co.uk/hes-gone/

*This offer is only available in digital format and requires a digital device in order to enjoy the content.

Do get in touch and let me know what you thought of *She's Gone*. I love hearing from readers. You can message me at:

susanwilkins.co.uk/contact/

BOOKS BY SUSAN

The Informant

The Mourner

The Killer

It Should Have Been Me

Buried Deep

Close To The Bone

The Shout + The Right Side Of The Line (Free when you sign up to Susan's newsletter)

A Killer's Heart

She's Gone

Her Perfect Husband

Lie Deny Repeat

BOOKS CONT.

facebook.com/susanwilkinsauthor

twitter.com/SusanWilkins32

instagram.com/susan_wilkins32

ACKNOWLEDGEMENTS

Huge thanks to Colin James for his expert advice on how the police would proceed, and for understanding when I've twisted his advice for the purposes of drama.

Thanks to the independent publishing community, the Alliance of Independent Authors, and the many indie authors out there, who are so generous with their time and advice. The publishing landscape is rapidly changing and we're all playing catch up. Thanks also to my fellow crime writers, and the Crime Writers' Association, who continue to provide advice and support.

Big thanks and hugs to the Brighton-based co-coaching gang, who've welcomed me back into their midst, even though I now live in Devon. Your Zoom calls have really helped me through these Covid times.

Last, but never least, my enormous gratitude to Jenny Kenyon for her sharp eye on the manuscript and all her marketing advice.

However, this stage in my writing journey, moving from traditional publishing to becoming a hybrid author, would be impossible without Sue Kenyon. I just write the books. She does everything else.

Published by Herkimer Limited in 2021
Summit House
170 Finchley Road
London NW3 6BP

Scan QR code to go to susanwilkins.co.uk

ISBN 978-1-9169012-1-6

Made in United States
North Haven, CT
30 October 2022

26124926R00212